I0600592

The Guardian of Cahokia

Douglas L. Gifford

Copyright © 2026 by Douglas L. Gifford

Published by Historynutt Books

Winfield, Missouri

ISBN: 979-8-9946234-0-4

To order additional copies of this book or contact the author directly, please use the email address below.

historynutt@hotmail.com

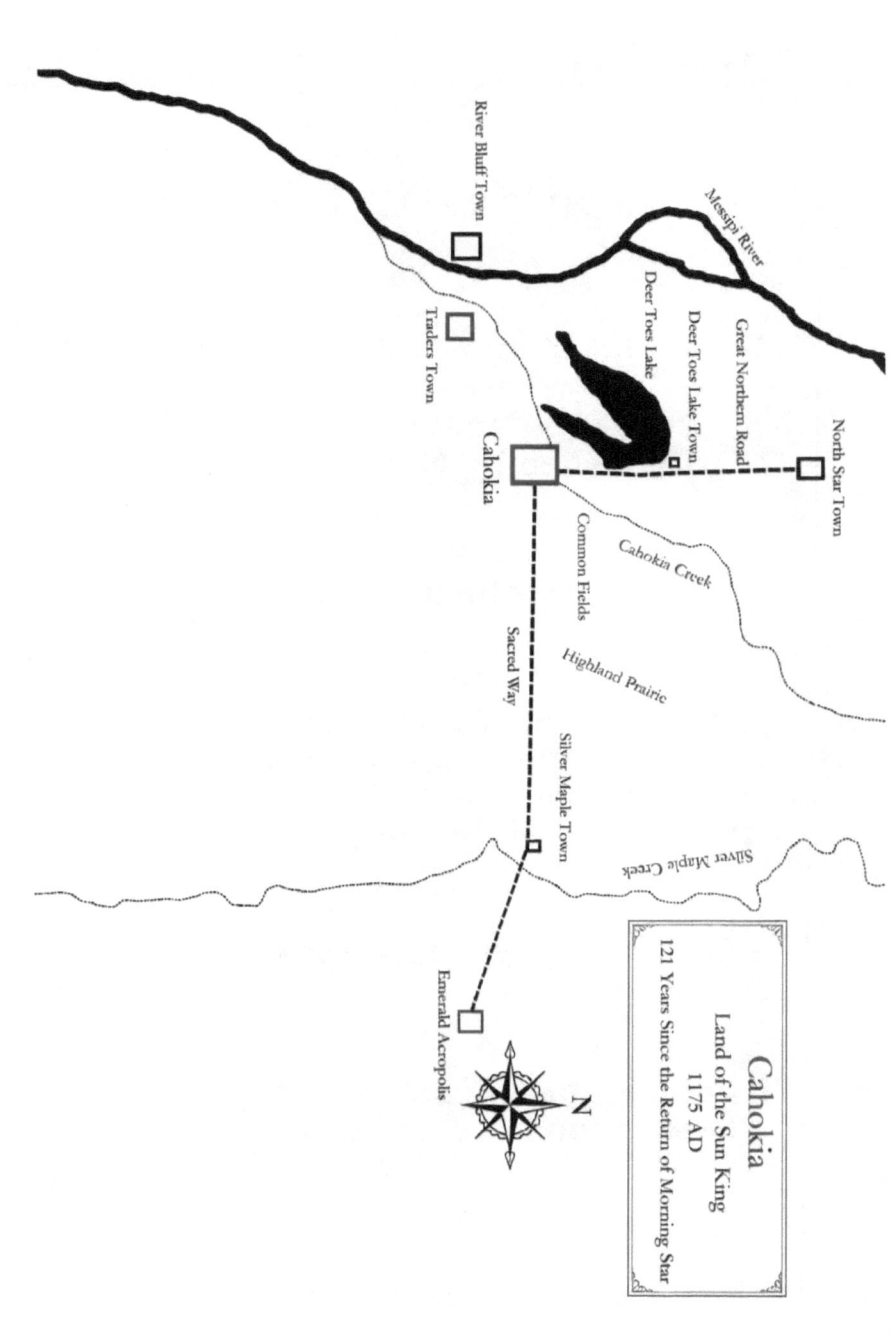

Cahokia
Land of the Sun King
1175 AD
121 Years Since the Return of Morning Star

N

River Bluff Town

Messipi River

Great Northern Road

Deer Toes Lake

Deer Toes Lake Town

North Star Town

Traders Town

Cahokia

Common Fields

Cahokia Creek

Sacred Way

Highland Prairie

Silver Maple Town

Silver Maple Creek

Emerald Acropolis

Chapter 1

The day that would become the first in the most exciting and yet terrifying period of my life began no differently than the thousands that came before it. At that time, I had lived thirty-eight cycles of the seasons in the lands of the Sun King. That morning, like most in the heat of summer, the workers in my family's copper workshop labored under the ramada—a roofed shelter with no walls—attached to our building. The inside of the workshop became unbearable during the warm moon cycles, so we did most of our hammering and cutting beneath the shade where breezes moved freely through the Valley of Cahokia.

As the men worked at their craft, I checked the small piles of raw copper, examined completed sheets cooling on deer hide, and looked over the apprentices' work, correcting shapes with small gestures or quiet instruction. Our workshop transformed rough copper nuggets into ear spools, pendants, gorgets, headdresses, armbands, ritual blades, and plates used by Warriors, Priests and Nobles throughout the kingdom. It was work requiring fire, muscle, patience, and precision. Every man, from my eldest son to the newest assistant, understood that the most minor error could reflect poorly on our reputation as master copper workers.

As I oversaw the fire in which one of my workers heated a rough copper nodule, I felt the routine comfort of a life balanced, predictable, and—so I believed—secure. I was familiar with every sound: the crackling fire, the tapping of stone hammers on copper, the rhythmic scraping of files, and distant city noise echoing across the new East Plaza. I lifted my head only because I sensed movement that did not belong in my workshop—three Cahokian Warriors stood in the street, watching me.

It was uncommon to see Warriors in the city outside the Sacred Precinct unless they were escorting a criminal, enforcing orders from the Sun King, or conveying messages too serious to entrust to ordinary couriers. They were clearly not lost or wandering; their eyes were fixed entirely on me. My workers noticed them too and slowed their hammering. When the tallest of the trio gestured toward me, the other two Warriors followed him without hesitation.

My eldest son, Red Hawk, stood quickly, his hand instinctively moving toward a carving tool as if it were a weapon. The Warriors stopped beneath the ramada.

"Sit," I said quietly, though firmly. Red Hawk obeyed, but his jaw remained tight. My workers stared at the intruders, apprehensive and fearful.

The tallest Warrior spoke. "You are the coppersmith, Walking Stick." He did not ask—he was merely confirming what he already knew.

Up close, it was clear he was no ordinary soldier. His frame was tall and powerful, yet lean, built with the strength of a man skilled in combat rather than brute labor. His eyes were sharp and calculating, the expression of one trained to notice danger before it appeared. Fine muscle rippled beneath his bare arms and across his chest. A lightning-bolt tattoo on his chest, symbol of Cahokia's Warriors, marked him as one who had proven himself in combat many times before. Strikingly, his face bore no Clan tattoo, indicating either that he was a member of no Clan or that his Clan forbade facial markings. His breechcloth and cape were dyed a deep red, the color reserved for the nobility, Priests, or War Captains, and trimmed in gold. He wore well-made sandals of wood and woven rattlesnake master fiber. The war club on his belt and long spear in his hand told me he was prepared to use force if necessary—though he wore no armor, likely because an old coppersmith with five children posed no danger to him.

"I am Walking Stick," I replied evenly.

"Good," he said. "Come with me."

He did not explain why, and I did not ask. Warriors summoned men for many reasons, and questioning them seldom led to clarity. If something bad awaited me, I would know soon enough.

Turning to Red Hawk, I instructed, "Stay here. Continue working. Wait for me." Though worry flashed across his face, he nodded.

I followed the Warrior out from under the ramada and into the glare of the sun. We passed the Deer Clan lodge adjacent to our workshop and moved along the edge of the new East Plaza. Children played chunkey there and chased one another, laughing without care. Their joy stood in sharp contrast to the uncertainty rising in my chest.

Soon we reached the Sacred Way—the great road stretching from the Emerald Acropolis in the far east, across highland prairies, through the Sacred Precinct, and onward to Traders Town beside the Messipi River. We turned west. In the distance, the newly built stockade surrounding the Sacred Precinct rose against the skyline. Massive logs formed its tall palisade, with rounded bastions set at regular intervals for archers. It was so large that men whispered the builders consumed as many trees as would heat the city for many moon cycles. To erect that wall, entire neighborhoods and the once-bustling East Plaza were destroyed. Such a fortification had never existed in my lifetime nor in my father's. Cahokia had always lived with the confidence that no army could approach the city of Morning Star. Yet the wall stood, and though no one spoke openly of fear, it was present, like smoke that lingers even when the fire is out.

Passing through the guarded gate, we stepped into the enormous Grand Plaza. Ahead stood the Great Pyramid, the heart of Cahokia and the seat of the Sun King. Its terraces, buildings, and high platforms dominated the landscape, demonstrating both the engineering power and spiritual certainty of our civilization. Even though I was often near the Great Pyramid, I seldom approached it closely.

Halfway across the vast plaza, the Warriors stopped before the base of the Great Pyramid. I froze—not from fear, but disbelief. I had never expected to be brought before anyone residing upon that mound.

A guard demanded proof of our authorization to ascend the ramp on the south side of the Great Pyramid. The young Warrior drew out a parchment marked with seals I could not identify, but the guard recognized them immediately and stepped aside. We climbed the ramp to the first terrace. There, my excitement died abruptly, for instead of continuing upward, the Warriors turned and walked toward a structure built at the terrace's southwestern corner. The view from that height, however, struck me—Cahokia stretched outward in every direction: plazas, Temples, mounds, farm fields, neighborhoods, workshops, and countless homes—an entire world built from earth, sweat, and unshakable belief in the goodness of Morning Star and the power of the Sun King, his representative here in the Middle World.

A second guard checked the Warrior's authorization before letting only the two of us pass; the other soldiers remained behind. Ahead, a man emerged from beneath the ramada of the building and sat on a stool. His deliberate movements suggested authority, not weariness.

He was much older than I, perhaps fifty cycles of the seasons. His face bore the tattoo of the Beaver Clan—one of the most powerful Noble Clans in Cahokia. His clothing was well-made: boots of rattlesnake master fiber and a long tunic reaching nearly to his knees, despite the summer heat. His hair was tied into a topknot, and his teeth, notably intact, testified to status and access to good healers. Then I noticed something that struck me personally—human head earrings, shaped in the style produced in our workshop.

The man introduced himself. "I am Muskrat Waits."

I had never heard of Muskrat Waits. I stared without knowing how to respond, until he added, "Minister of Security to His Highness, the Sun King."

The title hit me like a spear-thrust to the heart. What offense could I have committed requiring my presence before the Minister of Security? I lowered my eyes instinctively.

He studied me with a sly expression, then said, "And you are Walking Stick." His tone made clear this was not the beginning of his knowledge, merely confirmation.

He continued speaking, listing details that only someone investigating my family would know. "You were born into the Deer Clan. You currently serve on the Deer Clan Council. Your wife, Whispering Doe, is a Matriarch of the Black Bear Clan. You have five children. You are a respected citizen of Cahokia. A member of a well-known family, though not of the Noble Clans."

He paused as if expecting an objection from me. I had no objections—he was correct.

"Yes, Minister," I replied. "My family and I have always served Cahokia faithfully for many cycles of the seasons."

"And your family runs the copper concession in Cahokia," he stated.

I nodded, wondering where the conversation was headed. "Yes, we own the copper concession.

Muskrat Waits smiled wickedly. "You may *run* the copper concession, but you do not *own* the copper concession. Although your family has operated the copper works well for many cycles of the seasons, ultimately it is the Sun King who allowed it." His remark was calm, but the meaning was unmistakable—my family's prosperity could be taken as quickly as it was granted.

Then, once he had established my vulnerability, he nimbly changed the subject.

4

"Did you once know Prince Ranging Fox, brother of the Sun King?"

Surprised, I answered truthfully: "Yes. Many cycles of the seasons ago, when we were boys, we studied under the tutor Bowed Willow. I have not seen the Prince in many cycles of the seasons, since we were boys."

"The Prince remembers you, as well," Muskrat Waits said. "And holds a high opinion of your abilities."

His words unsettled me more than they reassured me. Few men are summoned to the first terrace of the Great Pyramid because of fond childhood memories. I was, however, flattered that the Prince remembered me fondly after so many cycles of the seasons.

Muskrat Waits then asked directly, "Tell me, Walking Stick—are you a clever man?"

I tried humor to lessen my tension. "Sometimes my wife calls me a genius, though I am not sure what she truly means by it."

He did not smile.

Trying to recover, I said, "Our old tutor, Bowed Willow, taught us how to think critically and logically, and how to think through problems. I have a reputation in our Clan and the East Precinct area where we live, so sometimes people come to me with their problems and ask me for help."

"That is why you are here," he replied. "The Sun King requires your service."

I was stunned. "Minister, I help people with small problems, but you have trained agents, experienced soldiers, officials, and Priests. Why would you need a coppersmith?"

Muskrat Waits's tone hardened. "Because my agents cannot be used. They are visible, feared, and easily noticed. If they begin questioning farmers and immigrants, rumors will spread faster than the truth. Panic will follow. Many in the immigrant community won't talk to the Warriors or my agents. However, you are different. You are ordinary in appearance, respected, intelligent, and safe to speak with."

Only then did he reveal the actual reason for my summons. "Several immigrant farmers north of Cahokia have been murdered during the last moon cycle—killed violently, dismembered, and left purposely along public roads where they would undoubtedly be found." He described the horrible mutilation of the bodies in great detail, to shock me, I speculated, so that he could gauge my reaction.

I was stunned. "I have heard no rumor of this."

"You were not meant to," he replied conspiratorially. "The victims were immigrants—strangers, without alliances, Clan protections, or strong voices. Their deaths could be concealed. But fear is growing in the immigrant communities to the north of Cahokia, and soon it will reach the city. Fear spreads faster than disease."

"It is the fear that worries you, not the deaths of the immigrants," I observed.

"Of course it is!" Muskrat Waits snapped at me. Then, more calmly, he explained what mattered most to him: the threat not to lives, but to Cahokia's stability. "Everything we have built here, from trade networks to pilgrimage traffic to agricultural labor, depends on the belief that Cahokia is safe, blessed, powerful, and protected. If immigrants flee, if traders choose other ports, or if pilgrims turn to rival cities, Cahokia will weaken, perhaps collapse. And if trade collapsed, the copper industry would collapse with it."

My family could lose everything.

Understanding struck me like a blow. Our wealth did not belong to us—not truly. It rested on invisible agreements, fragile confidence, and the Sun King's will. Our business rested on a delicate balance. If pilgrims stopped coming to Cahokia, if the carefully structured trade networks collapsed, and the elite could no longer afford to buy our products, we would lose everything.

"I will do as you ask, of course, Minister," I said. "But I need more information to begin."

Muskrat Waits looked pleased for the first time. He knew that if I wanted to keep the copper works, I had no choice except to help him.

He told me that the remains of the murder victims had been transported to the charnel house.

Instinctively, my eyes wandered to the south, across the Grand Plaza to the charnel house and its adjacent burial mound on the opposite side of the Sacred Precinct. I imagined that I could smell rotting flesh.

"Not that charnel house," Muskrat Waits corrected in an exasperated tone. "The victims were peasant farmers. They were not brought inside the Sacred Precinct to be processed in the Sun King's holy charnel house. I ordered the bodies taken to the charnel house at the Emerald Acropolis, far from Cahokia. You will travel there, question the Priests, learn what you can about the deaths, identify the victims, and find a murderer before fear tears the city apart."

Muskrat Waits paused for a moment and then issued an order to the War Captain standing behind me—I learned his name was Spotted Lynx—who had escorted me: "You will accompany Walking Stick as a bodyguard and observer."

Although he said nothing and I could not see his face, I am sure that I heard Spotted Lynx's jaw drop at what was obviously an odious mission. Guarding an old coppersmith was not a glorious assignment.

Our audience was concluded. Before departing, I foolishly asked if I would have the honor of seeing the Sun King to thank Him for the honor of serving Him during my new assignment. The Minister gave me a withering stare. I thought that he must practice that look.

"No, I suppose not," I answered for myself, bowing slightly and swallowing my pride. Clearly, the Minister and I were not going to become friends.

* * *

After Spotted Lynx and Walking Stick left the Great Pyramid, another man emerged from behind the building—a man wearing a golden breechcloth, copper ear spools, armbands, and a tall eagle-feather headdress. A Sun Family tattoo adorned his right cheek. His bearing was unmistakable. Prince Ranging Fox.

He asked Muskrat Waits, "So, what do you think of him?"

Muskrat Waits sighed. "Are you certain, Your Highness? He did not seem very bright, and I could do without the humor."

The Prince laughed softly. "Walking Stick has always used humor to hide his intelligence. It is not foolishness. It is armor. I can assure you that he is very clever."

Muskrat Waits shook his head. "For his sake, and for ours, I hope you are correct."

Chapter 2

After my interview with Muskrat Waits, I went straight to the copper works. Everyone was relieved to see me. I led my son outside so I could talk to him without the others hearing.

"I thought we would never see you again," Red Hawk said once we were out of earshot. "What did they want?"

I hesitated momentarily and then touched my son's broad shoulder. "I cannot tell you." He frowned. I chuckled at his consternation. "Right now, it is safer if I do not tell anyone what I am doing. I need you to trust me, and I need you to run the shop for a while."

"Are you going somewhere, Father?" He asked.

"Yes, and I am not sure for how long. I will be very busy, so even when I am home, I will not be able to come to the shop. But I want to tell you something important. I do not want you to tell anyone, not even a family member. What I am doing right now is important and could determine whether we can keep the copper works. It could even determine the future of the copper concession. You have been working here since you were a child, and you know the place inside and out. You can run this shop as well as I can. So, please do this for our family and me. I trust you to run the copper works more than anyone else."

Red Hawk looked appalled at the situation, but proud of the trust I placed in him. "Of course, Father, I will do as you ask, even if I do not understand."

"I know you will, or I would not trust you with this responsibility. Now, I need to go speak with your mother." I quickly left the copper works and went to find my wife.

Our home was situated just a few hundred steps away from the copper workshop, located between the East Plaza and Cahokia Creek. It was one of eight homes belonging to my wife's Black Bear Clan, arranged around an oval plaza or common area. All family members utilized a raised storage area at one end of the common. Our family's World Tree Pole, stained bright red with white stripes, stood in the center of the common area. It was a smaller version of the Sun King's World Tree Pole, which was located at the summit of the Great Pyramid. The World Tree pole represents the Great Oak Tree, which connects the Above World and the Below World with the Middle World, where we humans reside.

I found my wife, Whispering Doe, working in her garden beside our home. Although the Black Bear Clan women farmed a common field just north of Cahokia, Whispering Doe insisted on growing a small garden of maize, sunflowers, squash, and tobacco next to our home for security against hard times. Beads of sweat ran down her bronze body and over her naked, sagging breasts. She stood up and brushed her shiny black hair, now streaked with gray, from her eyes as she straightened and stretched the muscles in her aging body. The Black Bear Clan tattoo on her face had faded to the point that it was now unrecognizable. She looked from her work to find me leaning against the side of our home, ten steps away, staring at her. Red Horn be praised; she was beautiful.

She smiled and stared at me with her large, soft, brown eyes. "What are you doing at home in the middle of the day, husband?" I walked to where she was standing and embraced her. After a moment, she slipped out of my embrace to look me in the eyes and asked, "What is the matter?"

I sighed and said. "Maybe nothing, maybe much," she sucked in a breath. "I was summoned to the Great Pyramid today for an interview with the Sun King's Minister of Security."

At first, I believe she thought I was joking—why she would think that I was joking, I had no idea. However, once she realized I was serious, her large, soft eyes grew even wider as I told her about my conversation with Muskrat Waits and the implications for our family. She put her arms around my neck and held me tightly. After a few moments, she released me, straightened her skirt, and said, "Well, we will have to trust in the goodness of Morning Star. If anyone can solve this mystery, it is you, husband. Have you told anyone else?"

"No, it is too dangerous for anyone else to know. I left Red Hawk in charge of the copper works, but I did not tell him why, only that I must be away from the shop for a while."

"That is good. I am glad you put him in charge. He can do the job, and it will make him feel good knowing that the father he admires trusts him. Now, the food will not cook itself. I have a meal to prepare." She left me standing in the garden while she started the evening meal.

I watched her go, with a love and respect I held for no other person. I had known Whispering Doe since we were children. She grew up in the Black Bear Clan compound where we now live, while my family ran the copper works a short distance away. We played together almost daily as children on the now-destroyed East Plaza and nearby Cahokia Creek. There was never any doubt that she would become my wife. We had been together now for 22 cycles of the seasons. She had survived eight childbirths and raised five of our children through infancy. She was intelligent, sensible, and hardworking. She was the rock of our family and the Black Bear Clan.

* * *

After speaking with Whispering Doe, I needed to consult with one other person. I retraced my steps past the copper workshop to a mound overlooking the new East Plaza. Atop the mound stood one of our two Deer Clan family shrine houses. I climbed the ramp to the top of the mound—about seven steps of a man high—and found an old man sitting in a wooden chair under a ramada beside the shrine house.

Rattlesnake was my mother's oldest brother and Patriarch of the Deer Clan. He had once held my position as master of the copper works, but he turned over that responsibility to me more than ten cycles of the seasons ago. Although he was not a Priest, Rattlesnake spent most of his time in the shrine house, advising Clan members and working for the Clan's benefit. He was also a respected member of the Cahokian East Precinct community, a part of the city built around the new East Plaza, east of the stockade wall and the Sacred Precinct. Rattlesnake was old, even older than my parents, who had already departed our Middle World several cycles of the season past and traveled the Path of Souls through the stars to reach the Land of the Dead. Although I have observed that some people lose their faculties as they age, Rattlesnake seemed to grow wiser. I needed his advice now.

"Uncle, I need your advice."

"So I have heard."

I wondered how he could sit here under this ramada all day and still know everything happening in Deer Clan. "Today, I was summoned to the Great Pyramid to speak with the Sun King's Minister of Security."

That information got his attention. "I heard you left the copper workshop with some Warriors today, but I had no idea you went to the Great Pyramid. What did the Minister want from you?"

I told him about my conversation with Muskrat Waits.

"I remember Muskrat Waits."

"You know him?" I asked, surprised.

Rattlesnake smiled conspiratorially. "Many cycles of the seasons ago, when I ran the copperworks and Muskrat Waits was a young man, he worked for the Sun King, collecting the King's share of trade from the merchants. Every summer, I took what we owed the Sun King to the Trade Master's Guild in the Grand Plaza, where Muskrat Waits checked our account and ensured the Sun King received his due. Of course, I never quarreled with Muskrat Waits or tried to trick him. He was fair but very, very strict. He ensured the merchants paid everything they owed, and woe to the merchant who attempted to cheat the Sun King of his rightful share. More than one merchant departed this world after being garroted, flayed, or burned alive by the Sun King's executioners on the word of Muskrat Waits."

"What am I going to do, Uncle?"

He paused for several heartbeats, thinking. Finally, he said, "I do not believe you have a choice. For the sake of the Clan's future, you need to solve this mystery. Muskrat Waits is correct that our business relies on the wealthy and a reliable trade network. We lose everything if no one can afford to buy our copper. Muskrat Waits is using the copper concession to force you to do this task. He has the power and authority to take the copper concession from us if you refuse. And he is vindictive enough to do so."

"I have already told him that I will investigate the murders."

"Good. As I have said, you have no choice if you want to keep the copper concession. And even if you do your best but cannot find the murderer, Muskrat Waits might still punish you out of spite. I do not envy you this task, nephew. Muskrat Waits has pulled you into a dangerous game. He probably has motives he is not revealing to you, as well. Your life is of no consequence to him. Be careful, and do not trust Muskrat Waits."

* * *

As the sun passed beyond the hills west of the Messipi, the family gathered for the evening meal under the ramada beside our home. Whispering Doe had prepared a stew made with hominy and two squirrels she had purchased from a pair of neighborhood boys. She seasoned the stew with wild garlic and thickened it with cattail root flour. While the stew bubbled in a large ceramic pot, Whispering Doe pulled a loaf of acorn bread from the ashes, where it had been baking beneath a layer of dampened cattail leaves.

During the evening meal, I made an effort not to let the day's events disrupt the family. However, my middle son, Dancing Copperhead, had been at the workshop during the day and had seen me leave with Spotted

Lynx and his men. He knew his brother, Red Hawk, was now running the copper works. He held his tongue like a respectful son during the meal, but he questioned me as soon as everyone finished eating, and the women began cleaning up.

"Father, where did you go this afternoon when you left the shop with those Warriors? Red Hawk will not tell me."

"I cannot tell you either," I replied tersely.

"Why not?" He asked, more insistent than before.

I studied my son for a moment, deciding how much to tell him. I looked at the faces of the people sitting and working around me. The people who lived in my home. The people who would be most affected if my mission failed or something happened to me.

Dancing Copperhead was 14 cycles of the seasons and would soon marry a girl from the Coyote Clan and move in with her family. My youngest daughter, Walks in Water, was 16, an advanced age for a woman to be unmarried and still looking for a husband. Then there was my youngest son, Willow Tree, who was only five cycles of the seasons old. Willow Tree—whom I named after my old teacher, Bowed Willow—was born when Whispering Doe was 31 cycles of the seasons old, an advanced age to survive childbirth and bring forth a healthy baby. My daughters were appalled that their mother had become pregnant, but her pregnancy resulted in a healthy, curious boy.

In addition to the children who lived with me, I had two other children. My oldest son, Red Hawk—whom I entrusted to run the copper works— was 20 cycles of the seasons old. He, his two boys, and his wife, Morning Dove, lived with her Sky Clan on the opposite side of the Grand Plaza near the Sun Calendar. Passing Doe, my oldest daughter, was 18 and lived with her husband, Bear Claws, and my wife's widowed sister and her two remaining children in the home next to ours. Passing Doe already had a daughter and was expecting another child.

"Listen," I told Dancing Copperhead, "I have to be away from the shop for a while. I cannot tell you what I am doing. Just know that it is for the family's good. I will tell you everything when I can, but I do not want you to mention my absence from the copper works to anyone. I do not want you to discuss it with anyone, even if they ask. Your brother is in charge of the shop now, and I want everything to continue, both at the copper works and at home, as if nothing had changed. Until I finish what I am doing, there will be no more discussion. Is that clear?"

Dancing Copperhead looked crestfallen but said, "Yes, Father, I will do as you ask." Although he was not happy about the situation, he went about his business for the rest of the evening without mentioning my coming absence again.

When the women finished cleaning up, I put more wood on the fire, and the family gathered for story time. From the house next to us, Whispering Doe's sister, Soft Elk, our daughter Passing Doe, and her daughter joined us around the fire. Our granddaughter was only three cycles of the seasons old and not yet old enough to have her naming ceremony. Although the family called her "Daughter" or "Granddaughter," like all unnamed girls, I thought of her as Red Bud because of her perpetually red cheeks. When the time came for her naming ceremony in another cycle of the seasons, I intended to insist on naming her Red Bud.

In Cahokia, storytelling is deeply ingrained in our society. Our families spend many evenings listening to epic tales recounted by our elders or a *woorak horak*—a professional storyteller. Epic sagas of Cahokian heroes and culture, chronicled by Cahokian *woorak horak* for people abroad, draw pilgrims and immigrants to Cahokia from around the world. Instead of sending armies across vast distances of the Messipi Valley, the Sun King and His Priests use heroic storytelling to spread Cahokian influence and religion worldwide.

As we sat around the fire, Red Bud asked, "Grandfather, can you tell me the story of Red Horn's wife?" Red Bud liked romances.

"Of course, I love that story," I said.

"After Red Horn transformed himself into an arrow to win a great race," I began, settling into the familiar rhythm of storytelling, "his fame spread far and wide. Every young woman in the village wanted him as her husband. Among them lived an orphan girl, raised by her grandmother because she had no parents. They were desperately poor, and though the girl's clothing was shabby and plainly stitched, she always wore a white beaver-skin cape that set her apart from all the others. Despite her poverty, she was gentle, clever, and beautiful—everyone knew this except, perhaps, herself."

I shifted slightly to face Red Bud as I continued.

14

"The grandmother, however, was not so kind. She bullied the orphan girl to use her beauty and wit to win Red Horn's attention and become his wife. But the girl refused. She truly admired Red Horn and wanted no deceit in her heart when she approached him. Still, her grandmother continued to scold and pressure her until, worn down, the girl finally agreed to seek him out.

"When she did find Red Horn," I said, "she quickly learned that she was not the only one chasing him. All the young women from the village crowded around him, trying to impress him with flattery, gifts, or charms. The orphan girl could not compete with fine clothes or sweet talk, so she took another approach—she teased him. Her playful words made Red Horn laugh, and when he smiled back at her, the other girls grew furious. They scratched and shoved her away, shouting, 'You are too poor and too foolish to speak to him! Leave him alone!'"

Red Bud leaned forward, wide-eyed.

"Well," I resumed, "soon afterward, Red Horn and his companions planned a journey to battle the *Wage-rucge*—the man-eating giants. They camped outside the orphan girl's village before setting off. As was tradition, the young women brought new shoes to the Warriors so they would walk swiftly and return safely. The orphan girl arrived with the pair she had made for Red Horn. Though her stitching was plain compared to the others, he accepted her gift with gratitude.

"When Red Horn and his Warriors returned victorious, the jealous girls decided to drive the orphan girl away for good. They bribed the village sentries to announce that Red Horn and one of his closest companions had been killed in the fighting. At this terrible news, the grandmother began cutting her granddaughter's hair, as if she were already Red Horn's wife in mourning. But then the Warriors marched into the village alive and unharmed. Realizing her mistake, the grandmother cried out, 'What have I done? I have ruined my granddaughter's hair!'

"The village held four days of celebration for the victory," I said. "During the feasts, many Warriors tried to persuade Red Horn to marry their sisters, boasting of their beauty or their skill in weaving or cooking. But Red Horn's heart was already decided. He asked the elder women, 'Where does the girl in the white beaver-skin cape live?' They told him, and that night he went to her house. He asked the orphan girl if he might lie

15

beside her. She agreed, and when he did, her grandmother dropped a blanket over the two of them and declared the marriage sealed."

Red Bud laughed aloud at this part.

"Not long after," I continued, "Red Horn and his closest friends—Turtle, the Thunderbird Storms-as-He-Walks, and others—again faced the *Wage-rucge*. This time, the giants challenged them to a high-stakes stickball game. The losers would die. Red Horn accepted the challenge.

"The giants' greatest player was a young woman with long, bright red hair—just like Red Horn's. During the game, Red Horn used the tiny faces that grew on his ears to distract her. They joked and chattered until she laughed so hard that she could not focus on the play. The giants lost the match, and Red Horn and his friends killed every male *Wage-rucge*. But Red Horn spared the red-haired woman. He married her as his second wife so the race of giants would not vanish entirely.

"Red Horn brought the red-haired woman home. She and the orphan girl became like sisters, living peacefully under one roof. Both soon bore sons, and the boys called each woman 'mother,' for no difference was made between them."

I paused dramatically.

"Perhaps," I said to Red Bud with a grin, "I should go kill a few giants myself and bring home a second wife. Then Grandmother would have help with her work, and you would have two grandmothers to spoil you."

Red Bud giggled, but as I glanced at my first wife, I caught her expression in the corner of my eye. It told me plainly that—giants or no giants—I would not be bringing home a second wife anytime soon.

* * *

Whispering Doe and I lay awake on our pallet of furs under the ramada that night, talking as our children slept near us. A low, smoky fire burned near the ramada to keep the mosquitoes at bay. As was common practice among most families, we generally slept outside under the ramada, except during rainy or cold weather. "What are you going to do tomorrow?" She asked.

"My bodyguard will be here after sunrise."

"Bodyguard!" She exclaimed. "You never said this task was going to be dangerous."

"Maybe bodyguard is not the right word. More likely, Muskrat Waits ordered him to go with me to keep an eye on me rather than out of any fear for my safety."

"Who is this bodyguard that's supposed to be keeping an eye on you?"

"His name is Spotted Lynx," I replied. "He is a War Captain of Cahokia, young, with no Clan affiliation, but from what I can gather, he's intelligent, responsible, and trusted by the Minister of Security. He is also not happy about the assignment." I chuckled as I thought about Spotted Lynx's reaction to his assignment as my bodyguard.

"Well, when he shows up tomorrow morning, I am going to have a word with that young man and make sure he understands that, whether he likes his assignment or not, I expect him to bring my husband back to me unharmed. Or he will answer to me." She said insolently. I could not wait for Spotted Lynx to arrive at our house in the morning and get an earful from Whispering Doe.

"Once Spotted Lynx arrives in the morning, I want to go to the Emerald Acropolis. The murdered immigrants were taken there and given to the Priests to have their bodies prepared for burial. The Priests might be able to tell me something about how they died. I also hope they can tell me the names of the men who were killed and where they live. Right now, I do not know if the victims were men or women, where they lived, or anything else about them.

"If the Priests can tell me anything about the families, I will try to find them and see if they know anything useful. But I do not know if I will be able to get any helpful information from them. From what I have been told, they are new to Cahokia. These immigrant families are not part of a Cahokian Clan or have much of an extended family. They are entirely on their own. Many of them do not even speak Cahokian."

"It sounds like the Minister has given you an impossible task," Whispering Doe commented. That thought had also occurred to me. "The Emerald Acropolis is so far away. You will not be able to walk there in the morning and make it home by tomorrow night."

"No, after I speak with the Priests at the charnel house, I will probably spend the night at the Deer Clan Shrine House at the Emerald Acropolis. I will try to find the families of the victims the day after tomorrow. After that, I do not know."

"What about your bodyguard?" She asked. "He will not be able to stay at your family's Deer Clan Shrine House."

"No. Maybe he can stay with the Priests," I suggested. Even a strong young man like Spotted Lynx would surely be appalled at the thought of spending the night with Priests from a charnel house. "Anyway, he is not my problem."

"Well, you had better pretend to be nice to him," Whispering Doe advised as she snuggled close to me. "If you expect him to protect you when you get yourself in trouble."

"I very seriously doubt that I will get myself in trouble," I replied, somewhat offended.

As a reply, Whispering Doe only grunted sarcastically as she drifted off to sleep.

Chapter 3

I awoke the next morning later than usual, well after the first sunlight had begun filtering through the ramada's roof. The air beneath the roof held the comfortable smell of wood smoke and maize, warm and familiar like the embrace of a good cloak. Whispering Doe and Walks in Water were already awake and working, their quiet movements steady and practiced. A small fire glowed in the hearth, burning cleanly. They were kneeling near the flat hearth stones, scooping handfuls of maize mixed with ashes, water, and a little animal fat, shaping the dough into thin round cakes with the ease of long habit, then setting them carefully onto the hot rocks beside the flames to cook.

I lay still for a moment, watching them and feeling the pleasant heaviness in my bones. At last, I rose, stretched my back, and stepped outside to relieve myself in the usual place. Several other men were returning from doing the same, and I exchanged a few idle words with them — the kind of short morning greetings that speak more of shared routine than of anything meaningful.

When I returned to our home, I stopped short. Walks in Water was nowhere to be seen, but Whispering Doe and Spotted Lynx were standing near the hearth in close, comfortable conversation. She was laughing — not merely smiling politely, but laughing openly, her hand resting lightly on his arm as though they had known one another for many cycles of the seasons. Spotted Lynx was smiling as well, relaxed, clearly enjoying her company. I felt a jolt of surprise, followed swiftly by a sting of irritation and something very much like jealousy — though I would not have admitted that aloud.

This was not at all how I had imagined their first meeting. In my mind, she would confront him indignantly, accusing him of carelessness before he even had the chance to prove himself, demanding that he swear to protect my life with his own. Instead, the two of them looked as though they were siblings reunited after a long absence — perfectly at ease and seemingly fond of one another already. I had a sudden, unpleasant feeling that the day ahead would not unfold entirely in my favor.

I approached them with my irritation still simmering beneath the surface. "What are you doing here so early, Spotted Lynx?" I asked, my tone sharper than I intended.

19

Before he could answer, Whispering Doe jumped to his defense. "He came in case you wished to make an early start," she said, defending him as though he were already a cherished son-in-law. "Warriors always rise early. He did not know you would sleep so late."

Her statement sounded suspiciously like a reprimand. I had earned the right to sleep a little late after over ten cycles of the seasons running the copper concession — work that demanded both skill and constant responsibility.

"One of the privileges of being older. And wealthy," I responded dryly.

Spotted Lynx only smiled at me, unfazed. He seemed to be in an annoyingly good mood.

"Stop behaving like an old grouch," Whispering Doe said firmly, though not unkindly. "Sit down and eat. I invited Spotted Lynx to join us this morning."

Of course, she had invited him. I suspected Spotted Lynx had arrived early, hoping to get a good meal and pleasant company from a kind woman like Whispering Doe. Who could blame him? The food served in the Warrior barracks was probably terrible, and Whispering Doe was a wonderful cook. She hovered around us like a mother eagle arranging her nest, drizzling honey over the cakes, refilling plates before we could ask.

As we ate, Willow Tree arrived and slipped into the empty place beside me. Without a word, Whispering Doe handed him a plate as well, as naturally as if she had expected him all along.

"Where are your brother and sister?" I asked.

"They already ate," he replied. "Dancing Copperhead went to the shop early to help Red Hawk. Walks in Water went with her friends to pick blackberries."

"And what are you doing?" I asked.

"I was still hungry, so I came back for more maize cakes. Then I am going with you."

"You are?" I asked, raising my eyebrows. "Do you know where I am going?"

He shook his head, unconcerned. "I do not need to know."

"Well, this time you cannot go with me," I said gently.

He looked appalled. "Why not?"

"Because I might be gone for several days," I explained. "Someone needs to stay here and help care for your mother and sister. Dancing

Copperhead will be at the copper works, and Red Hawk will have heavy responsibilities. I need someone dependable at home. Can you do that?"

Willow Tree looked down, thinking with surprising seriousness for his age. Finally, he nodded. "Yes, Father, I can do that. But if I stay here, who will take care of you?"

I gestured toward Spotted Lynx. "This is Spotted Lynx, a War Captain of Cahokia. He will keep watch over me."

Willow Tree stood, moved directly in front of Spotted Lynx, and examined him with bold curiosity. He pressed his fingers against the young Warrior's upper arm, testing the muscle. Spotted Lynx flexed for him, making Willow Tree grin.

"He seems strong," my son declared. "He should be able to protect you."

Spotted Lynx leaned forward slightly. "Do not worry. I will bring your father home safely if you stay here and take care of your family."

"That sounds fair," Willow Tree said with great dignity, and he resumed eating.

When we finished eating, I prepared for the journey. I dressed simply: a doe-hide breechcloth, leather shoes, and my knife at my waist. I tied my hair in a topknot secured by a strip of bright red cloth. Whispering Doe had prepared a travel bag, filling it with a spare breechcloth, a light cloak for night temperatures, and a bison robe sleeping fur in case we slept outdoors. She also packed my ceramic water bottle, my buffalo-horn spoon, my pipe, and a small packet of her tobacco — the best in Cahokia, though I am biased. Then she handed me food for the journey: sunflower-seed bread, dried squash, deer jerky, and a bark container filled with dried fish.

She walked with us to the edge of the city. Before we parted, she kissed my cheek and said, "Take care of yourself, you old fool." Then she pointed at Spotted Lynx. "And you — take good care of him. I expect him to return in one piece."

Spotted Lynx grinned and promised her he would.

We left the noisy, smoke-filled city behind and followed the Sacred Way eastward. The Sacred Way stretched fifty steps of a man in width and ran straight as a spear shaft across the flat, fertile floodplain of the Messipi River. Fields of maize, goosefoot, squash, and sunflowers lay on either side, tended by families who lived in scattered farmsteads. Most of the farmers along this stretch of road were Cahokians — people whose ancestors had lived and worked in the lands of the Sun Family for many generations.

The further we walked, the quieter it became. The clamor of the marketplace faded, replaced by the soft sounds of morning birds and the far-off thuds of chert hoes striking soil. Farm dogs barked from time to time, but little else disturbed the peace. After some time, the fields thinned and the Sacred Way began to rise. The Great Valley narrowed, and the wooded bluffs loomed ahead — dark, rugged, and bearing the look of ancient endurance.

The climb out of the valley was steep, and even with my experience traveling to Traders Town and River Bluff Town, I felt the strain in my legs. Spotted Lynx, of course, walked easily, hardly looking winded. Warriors spent their lives building strong, reliable bodies; merchants trained mostly in patience and numbers. When we reached the top of the bluff, I was breathless, so we paused in the shade of a wide-limbed oak whose trunk was broader than three men standing shoulder to shoulder.

The upland forest around us was dense with oak, hickory, and maple — tall old giants rising from a broad, open understory. Few saplings or tangled bushes grew beneath them because the Sun King's foresters burned away unwanted growth every few cycles of the seasons. These woods were sacred, valuable, and fiercely protected. Cutting down one of the Sun King's trees without permission meant death. Every citizen knew it, and no one was foolish enough to test the law.

The forest provided much more than wood. At the fall equinox, the hickories and oaks dropped enormous harvests of nuts and acorns, an essential winter food. In late winter and early spring, when dried meat and grain grew dull in the stomach, and sickness stalked the settlements like a prowling cat, the women drilled holes in maple trees and collected the clear, faintly sweet sap into large jars. The sap restored strength, cleansed the body, and eased the fatigue left by long moon cycles without greens.

While standing on top of the ridge, I asked Spotted Lynx, "Have you ever been to the Emerald Acropolis?"

He nodded. "Many times over the cycles of the seasons. Since becoming a Warrior, I have traveled to every corner of the Sun King's domain."

I took a moment to look at him with fresh curiosity. Now that he was no longer wearing his scarlet Warriors breechcloth and war cape, he looked different — younger and less imposing but still unmistakably strong. His simple breechcloth, sandals, and tied-back hair made him blend in with ordinary working men, though the knife and war club at his belt reminded me that he was no laborer. Scars crossed his arms, ribs, and shoulders in patterns that suggested hardship and danger.

"How did you become a soldier?" I asked.

"My parents were immigrants from the lands along the Waapaahshiiki River, many days' travel to the east. They came here before I was born, when Cahokia's blessings were spoken of far and wide. They came to be close to the Sun King and bask in Morning Star's blessings. But the prime farmland near Cahokia was already claimed by established families, so my parents traveled across the Messipi to the valley of the Wide Muddy. That is where my brother, sister, and I were raised —on new land, with good soil in a new settlement. My parents worked hard, but we were never wealthy. Still, my parents were content living so close to Cahokia."

He looked ahead, his lips turning slightly in a smile at the memory.

"When I turned twelve cycles of the seasons, I realized my body would grow strong, but my heart would not survive a life tied to a hoe. I had seen the great city of Cahokia only during its great festivals, but even in those brief visits, it felt alive. I wanted to be among the noise, the chants, the games, the traders, the colors — even the smoke. So, with my parents' blessing, I left and walked to Cahokia. Becoming a Warrior was my path out of the fields. I trained hard and never left. Ten cycles of the seasons later, I am a War Captain."

"You truly chose the opposite direction from your birth," I said. "My destiny, however, was chosen for me many generations ago when my family received the copper concession from the Sun King."

After we left the bluffs, the Sacred Way carried us across the highland prairie — a vast, rolling land of tall grass, scattered trees, and distant smoke trails rising from farm households. Here, settlements grew fewer. We passed some villages, most no larger than a handful of houses, though a few boasted single mounds that held a Temple or chief's residence. Men and women on the road nodded politely at us, then hurried on. No one questioned our purpose. Two men traveling together was nothing remarkable — though if anyone recognized Spotted Lynx as a Warrior, they wisely pretended not to notice.

The sun climbed high, and the heat increased until our breechcloths stuck unpleasantly to our skin. It had been only one moon cycle since the summer solstice; we were in the middle of the hottest days in the cycle of the seasons, and many hot days still lay ahead. We walked for a long time without words, saving our strength. Hunger eventually gnawed at my stomach, and thirst scratched like sand across my throat.

By the time we reached Silver Maple Creek — a wide stream whose waters ran clear and cold — we were grateful for shade. The settlement near the creek, known as Silver Maple Town, held four mounds. We knelt at the bank, cupped our hands, and drank. I washed my face and neck, savoring the relief. Then we refilled our water bottles.

The sun had begun to shift toward the west. "A good place to eat," I said, and Spotted Lynx agreed.

We found a large flat rock beneath a cottonwood tree and sat down. I opened the pack Whispering Doe had prepared.

"Did you bring food?" I asked.

"Yes," he said. "Maize cakes and deer jerky from the barracks. But I doubt they are as good as what your wife makes."

I chuckled. "I am sure you are correct. Whispering Doe is a wonderful cook." I tore the sunflower seed bread in half and gave a portion to Spotted Lynx.

We traded food, each trying the other's with politeness. The dried fish and bread from Whispering Doe tasted rich and satisfying. The jerky from the barracks was tough and nearly flavorless, but I ate it anyway — men who share travel must share meals without complaint.

The breeze cooled our sweat, and neither of us spoke for several minutes. The silence felt companionable rather than awkward.

Eventually, Spotted Lynx said, "You and Muskrat Waits both spoke yesterday as if a few murders could destroy Cahokia. I do not see how that is possible. It sounds like fear talking."

I paused, choosing my words with care.

"Cahokia looks powerful — unshakable. But its greatness is balanced on four pillars: food, trade, faith, and unity. If even one weakens, cracks appear."

He turned to listen more closely.

"After the return of Morning Star, immigrants poured into Cahokia. They became farmers because the growing city needed food. They spread

24

across the valley and uplands, working the soil. Farmers are the base of our wealth, even though the Nobles never admit it. If the farmers become frightened or believe the land has become cursed, they could leave. Without food, craftsmen stop producing goods, traders take their goods elsewhere, and the Sun King loses legitimacy."

"So if we lose farmers, Cahokia collapses?" he said slowly.

"Yes," I replied. "Every other danger flows from that."

He leaned back against the tree, considering this. "Then we must find whoever is doing this."

"Yes," I said. "We must."

Spotted Lynx was quiet for a time after that, gazing across the prairie grass as if he were trying to imagine the world collapsing from a threat he could not yet see. Finally, he asked, "Muskrat Waits also said that you once knew Prince Ranging Fox. Is that true?"

"Yes," I answered. "I knew him many cycles of the seasons ago, when our greatest concern was whether we could throw a spear farther than the boys from the neighboring Clans. We studied under the same tutor — Bowed Willow — the most brilliant man I have ever met."

"Why did the Prince study with a boy from one of the common Clans?" Spotted Lynx asked.

"It was unusual," I admitted. "The Sun Family hired Bowed Willow to teach their youngest son, but Bowed Willow refused to teach only Nobles. He believed that learning belonged to those who sought it, not just to those who could pay for it. He allowed a few other students into his circle if he believed they possessed the ability and the discipline. The Prince and I both met that standard."

Spotted Lynx absorbed this in silence. His expression softened, no longer purely curious but quietly respectful.

"Ranging Fox was a fine student," I continued. "Bright, thoughtful, quick with numbers, and blessed with a steady hand in martial games. He would have made a great merchant, or scholar, or even a Priest if he had not been born into royalty. We were never equals in standing, but at that age, we did not think about those things so much."

"And the current Sun King — did he also study with you?" Spotted Lynx asked.

"No," I said. "The future Sun King, even when he was a boy, was kept close to his father. He learned the rituals, blessings, diplomatic ceremonies, sacred calendar, and the art of ruling. The people needed him to embody divine guidance, while Ranging Fox was trained to understand how the world actually worked—food, resources, trade, military tactics, and the temperament of ordinary people. The two were being prepared like two halves of a bow and string."

Spotted Lynx nodded. "That makes sense. A leader who understands only ceremony is no leader at all."

We rested for a few more heartbeats, then repacked our food and rose to continue our journey. The sun was tilting toward the west, but there was still plenty of daylight remaining on that clear summer day. After refilling our bottles from the stream again, we crossed the shallow place where stones made a natural bridge and returned to the Sacred Way. The road curved gently upward into higher prairie land. The walking was difficult until our muscles warmed again, but step by step, the aches eased.

To distract my mind from fatigue, I told Spotted Lynx the full story of Cahokia's transformation — one that every Cahokian knew, though each family told it with different emphases.

"When my grandfather's grandfather was a young man," I began, "Cahokia was already a large town. Clans built mounds for their Temples, and traders passed through often enough that the elders believed the town might eventually become an important center. But the Sun Family had even greater ambitions."

"Before they were the Sun Family, what were they?" Spotted Lynx asked.

"A Noble Clan with a leadership gift," I replied. "But no more divine than any other, or so it seemed."

I explained how the Sun Family had begun reorganizing the growing town, constructing larger public spaces and Temples, and improving trade routes. They were ambitious, determined, and organized — but they were still mortal.

"That changed," I said, "on the day Morning Star returned."

I slowed my pace slightly, remembering how the elders always lowered their voices when they reached this part of the tale.

"He appeared in the sky as a flash of light, brighter than any other star, visible day and night with no fading for half a moon cycle. People feared it meant that we had offended the Creator and he had returned to punish our people. Priests sought omens, mothers wept for their children, and Warriors sharpened their weapons, expecting disaster."

Spotted Lynx walked silently, listening patiently. Like all Cahokian children, he had heard the stories of Morning Star's return many times before.

"The Priests at the Emerald Acropolis prepared themselves for guidance. They fasted, prayed, consumed black drink to purge both body and spirit, and entered trance journeys through the sacred datura plant. When they finally emerged, they declared that the Creator had not sent Morning Star to curse us, but to bless the work of the Sun Family— that he had come to confirm that Cahokia was chosen.

"The Sun King then ordered a ritual cleansing — the burning of every structure in the city. Some families resisted; most surrendered their homes to the sacred fire. When the ashes cooled, the engineers redesigned everything: new plazas, wide sacred roads, mounds aligned to sacred orientations, and fresh Temples. The Great Pyramid—which had already been under construction—rose faster than ever, fueled by devotion, momentum, and a shared conviction that Cahokia now aligned with the will of the Creator. Morning Star remained in the night sky for two more cycles of the seasons, watching the rebirth of Cahokia, until he was assured that the Sun Family was carrying out the will of the creator. Then, he went away.

"After that," I said, "people came from every direction. Thousands. Traders, pilgrims, dreamers, farmers, artisans, mystics, Warriors — all wanting to be part of the new center of the world."

"And immigrants like my parents," Spotted Lynx added quietly.

"Yes," I said. "And like your parents, they were not wealthy, but saw opportunity in the shadow of divine favor."

I explained the founding of Traders Town, which became the hub of commerce near the Messipi, filled with warehouses, foreign lodges, and river landings. River Bluff Town was rebuilt on the western bank of the Messipi, controlling movement beyond the river. And dozens of satellite towns joined them, forming a new political alliance made stronger by a shared vision and the power of the Sun King.

Through it all, the copper works became crucial. Cahokia needed valuable gifts to send to allies and rivals — not as bribes, but as symbols of prestige, legitimacy, and divine wealth. Copper, rare and striking, spoke louder than speeches. Those who received it could display it in rituals, burials, and negotiations. And because the Sun King trusted my family's honesty and management skills, the monopoly came to us."

"That is why you worry about the murders," Spotted Lynx said. "Your family stands close enough to power to benefit, yet also close enough to be swept away."

"Exactly," I responded. "And not only for selfish reasons. If Cahokia falls, thousands will suffer."

The sun drifted lower as we spoke, tinting the horizon with yellow and pale orange. The prairie grasses waved as though stirred by gentle spirits moving just beyond sight. The path sloped upward again, and as we reached the crest, we paused. Ahead, in the far but unmistakable distance, stood the Emerald Acropolis — raised above the land like an island rising from a grass sea.

The Emerald Acropolis. The holy city. Built long before Cahokia, it is the birthplace of our civilization. Even from where we stood, the place emanated a quiet power. It rested upon an escarpment, shaped not by accident but by intelligent hands long ago, leveled and sculpted until it aligned with the sacred lunar maximum moonrise. Every eighteen and a half cycles of the seasons, the moon revealed itself along that perfect line — a sign, according to ancient teachings, that knowledge flows not only from above but also from careful observation of the natural world.

"That is a place where men speak carefully," Spotted Lynx murmured.

"And where spirits may answer," I agreed.

We continued walking. The prairie dipped into another shallow stream valley, then climbed once more toward the base of the sacred rise. The sun no longer burned fiercely, but exhaustion weighed on my legs. The last stretch felt longer than any that came before, though it could not have been more than a short walk.

At the northern foot of the escarpment, the sacred spring flowed. Its water emerged not from the valley floor as ordinary springs do, but high up from within the earth beneath the Holy Mound, as though the spirits pushed it upward from the Below World. Priests said that the spring carried messages, and that ancestors sometimes came near its edge in dreams.

We knelt and drank deeply. The water was cool and clean, tasting faintly of stone and sweetness. I filled my bottle once more and let the liquid run over my wrists and neck until my body felt renewed.

From the spring, the Sacred Way rose in one final ramp up toward the plateau. Our Deer Clan Shrine House lay behind the plaza, fifty steps or more from the Noble Clan shrines. Because Spotted Lynx bore no Deer Clan mark, he could not lodge in our family shrine house and instead turned toward the residence of the High Priest, who also acted as the civil administrator.

"Tomorrow morning, I will prepare myself in our Deer Clan sweat lodge and then seek a vision in the Clan Shrine House. I will come find you when I am finished, and then our true task begins."

He nodded once, firmly, then walked away.

I watched him go, then turned toward the ramp and breathed the sacred air of the Emerald Acropolis.

Chapter 4

From the gate of the Emerald Acropolis, I walked across the flattened summit of the sacred hill, where the grass lay scorched by countless fires of devotion. The mid-summer air shimmered above the pale earth, and the cries of a lone crow circled down from the sky, echoing off the terraces. The plaza stretched before me—broad, sun-washed, almost deserted. Long lines of shrine houses stood sentinel around the plaza like weary pilgrims. Wind hissed through gaps in their wattle and daub walls, carrying the resinous scent of cedar ash and the faint tang of burnt fat, remnants of past sacrifices.

The Acropolis village was vast—hundreds of small houses and sweat lodges crowded the hilltop around the Sacred Plaza—but few souls stirred among them. Most families came here only when ceremonies called them; between festivals, the shrines slept. The silence was heavy, sacred, and strangely expectant, as though the ancestors were holding their breath.

Our Deer Clan Shrine House stood near the plaza's eastern edge, just behind the houses of the Noble Clans. It was newer and cleaner than most; the plaster had been recently renewed, and its doorway was framed with bundles of dried sweetgrass. We were not of the Noble Clans, yet the Deer Clan had long been known for our piety and careful keeping of ritual obligations. The shrine walls gleamed in the sun as if newly anointed with clay slip.

I found the caretaker, Cougar Walks, sitting cross-legged in the shade beside the entrance. His hair was thin and silver, his body knotted with age. He had once been a Deer Clan council elder, but time and misfortune had reduced him to service here. The council had granted him the role because his children were dead and his wife was frail. The Deer Clan still honored its own: in exchange for tending the shrine, they fed him, lodged him, and gave him purpose.

As I approached, he raised his head, blinking as if to be sure I was no spirit. Then recognition softened his face. He rose with effort and spread his arms.

"Ah, young Walking Stick, master of copper and honored cousin! The Deer Clan is blessed. Morning Star himself must smile to see you climb this hill. Welcome home to your ancestors' fire."

He bowed formally, his voice still proud though his hands trembled.

I smiled. "It is good to see you, Cougar Walks. I have come far from Cahokia, and I am weary. I will need food, a place to rest, and the sweat lodge tomorrow for cleansing before seeking a vision,"

He nodded, eyes brightening with the old dignity that age had not extinguished. "Yes, yes. Of course. My wife will be honored to prepare the meal. We are between observances—no other guests have come since the summer solstice. You will have peace here, cousin."

He brought me a bowl of cool water drawn from the sacred spring. I splashed it over my face and neck, letting the chill bite my skin. My hair, loosed from its topknot, fell damp to my shoulders. The heat and dust of the road lifted from me with the water, replaced by a faint exhilaration, as though the Acropolis itself were cleansing me.

Cougar Walks went to tell his wife to expect a guest for the evening meal. Alone, I stepped into the shrine.

Inside, the air was cool and dim. The scent of cedar smoke clung to the beams. Offerings—shell beads, polished river stones, and a little bowl of copper flakes—rested before the wooden effigy of Morning Star in the guise of Red Horn. Above it hung a bundle of feathers tied with a red cord, the symbol of life returned after death. I set down my pack beside the inner wall and unrolled a fur pallet near the doorway. The quiet pressed against my ears; outside, even the wind had fallen still.

I lay down and closed my eyes to rest for a few moments before the evening meal, when I heard a low moaning, not of wind or beast but of people, coming from the plaza.

I stepped outside and walked toward the noise.

The Sacred Plaza lay bathed in amber light. Figures moved there—men, women, and children—arrayed along the edges as if drawn by an unseen force. Their clothes were torn, their faces streaked with mud. Peasant farmers, I thought, from the Valley of Cahokia. Their voices wove together in a wordless chant that crawled beneath my skin.

At the top of the Temple Pyramid, shadows stirred. A procession of men began to descend the ramp—thin, ragged, their eyes hollow. They moved with the slowness of sleepwalkers. The crowd's murmur turned to cries, then to shrieks. I could not understand the words.

I pushed forward and seized a woman by the arm. "What is it? Why are you shouting?"

32

She turned to me, her mouth open in a soundless scream. Terror flared in her eyes—terror so raw it struck me like heat. She tore free, pointing toward the pyramid's base.

Something waited there.

Underwater Panther.

The demon rose from the earth itself, vast and glistening, scales gleaming like wet copper. His body was feline but longer, heavier; a serpent's tail coiled and lashed behind him. Antlers arched from his skull, sharp as winter branches. His mouth yawned open to reveal teeth the size of spear points, and within the sockets of his eyes burned a red light that seared the air.

Underwater Panther crouched, muscles rippling beneath the scales, and then sprang. His claws caught the first of the descending men. The body split apart as though made of reeds. The next was torn in half before his scream escaped his throat.

Blood drenched the steps.

The farmers did not flee. They walked forward as though commanded, their faces calm, accepting. One by one, they entered the reach of the monster, and one by one, they were shredded, strewn across the plaza in pieces. Their entrails steamed in the evening light.

Then the ground itself heaved. From the blood-soaked clay of the plaza rose four giants—the *Wage-rucge*, the man-eating giants of ancient legend. Their skin was the color of raw clay, their teeth jagged as chert blades. Each bore a club bound with sherds of chert. They bellowed once, and the air trembled.

The *Wage-rucge* waded into the crowd. Heads flew. Limbs fell like snapped branches. The people screamed and ran, and the giants pursued, smashing bodies into pulp.

In the center of the plaza, I noticed a field of maize that I had not seen before. The plaza's parched soil drank the blood until the plants themselves caught fire—flames leaping up the blood-stained stalks. The red-and-white-striped sacred World Tree Pole in the center of the plaza blazed beside them, the sky blackening with smoke.

I stood frozen in place, unable to move. The heat pressed against my skin. The screams grew to a single continuous roar. And then I screamed.

A hand clamped my shoulder. I whirled, shouting, striking blindly.

The scene vanished.

Cougar Walks stood before me, his thin arms raised to shield his face. The interior of the shrine house surrounded us once more, quiet and dim. My own breath came in ragged gasps.

"Easy, easy, master Walking Stick," he said softly. "It is me, Cougar Walks. You must have had a powerful vision."

I wiped sweat from my forehead and tears from my eyes, trying to steady my hands. "A vision," I muttered. "If it was a vision, it was a terrible one."

Cougar Walks looked at me knowingly. "Yes, it was a vision. This holy place grants visions to those who are meant to receive them. You have been touched by the spirits, cousin. Whatever you seek here, Morning Star wishes you to see it clearly."

"I was not seeking anything yet," I protested. "I planned to purify myself tomorrow—to fast, to drink the black drink, to enter the sweat lodge. I was not ready."

"The Divine Ones choose their moment, not we," he said. "Visions come when they will. Some gentle, some fierce. Yours... was fierce."

He studied my trembling hands, then nodded toward the door. "Come, wash away the fear. The vision has spoken; now you must interpret it. But not tonight. Eat first. Rest. Morning Star will reveal what it means."

I could still taste the smoke of burning maize in my throat. My legs felt hollow, my body drained. Yet beneath the fear pulsed something colder, more rational—the sense that what I had seen was not only a message from the gods but a clue, a warning bound to the murders I had been sent to investigate.

I followed Cougar Walks into the cooling dusk. He led me down the slope toward the cluster of houses at the Acropolis's edge. The air smelled of damp earth and the faint sweetness of late-blooming milkweed. Twilight thickened the color of the world into copper and smoke.

His home was a modest structure—a wattle and daub house joined to a small ramada of poles and cane matting. A thin thread of smoke rose from a hearth just outside, where his wife, Pleasant Dove, sat tending the fire. Her back was straight despite her years, her gray hair bound in a bun. At our approach, she looked up and smiled, her eyes the pale gray of weathered shell beads.

"You did not tell me our guest was the master coppersmiths," she said. "Morning Star must be generous indeed tonight."

34

Cougar Walks chuckled. "He is tired and hungry, woman. He needs some of your cooking to revive his strength."

Pleasant Dove ladled a steaming liquid into a clay cup and handed it to me. "Sassafras tea with honey. It will cool your throat."

I drank deeply. The tea tasted of forest roots and sunlight. After the raw terror of the vision, the brew brought a calming sensation.

She turned the rack above the coals where ribs of whitetail deer sizzled, their fat dripping into the embers. Beside the fire, a pot of stew burbled—a blend of new maize kernels, squash blossoms, dried morel mushrooms, and wild onions thickened with powdered sassafras leaves. The scent was intoxicating.

Cougar Walks motioned for me to sit on a log beneath the ramada. Pleasant Dove placed a plate before me—ribs browned to perfection beside a roasted arrow leaf tuber split open and gleaming with melted bear fat.

"Eat, cousin," said Cougar Walks. "The spirits take no pleasure in a man who starves while pondering their messages."

"What about you two?" I asked.

Pleasant Dove laughed softly. "We will have stew later. The ribs are for honored visitors. Besides," she added, tapping her gums with a grin, "we have few teeth left for such luxuries."

I tried to protest, but Cougar Walks waved me off. "To serve is our joy. Accept it, Walking Stick."

I obeyed. The first bite of meat filled my mouth with smoke and salt and sweetness. The tuber's soft flesh melted in my mouth. I ate hungrily until the ribs were stripped of all their meat. Then Pleasant Dove handed me a bowl of stew and a round of goosefoot bread. The taste was rich and earthy; its warmth steadied me.

While she and her husband finally served themselves, I leaned back, savoring the fire's glow. The night had cooled sharply. Beyond the ramada, fireflies glimmered like sparks rising from unseen fires.

When the meal was finished, and Pleasant Dove quietly gathered the bowls, Cougar Walks reached for his small clay pipe. With the same care he might offer a prayer, he packed the bowl with dark, pungent tobacco. I drew out my own—a treasured piece crafted long ago with the image of Red Horn, carved by a master craftsman. The pipe's red flint clay had been dug from the hill country south of River Bluff Town, on the far bank of the Messipi River.

I filled the bowl with the tobacco Whispering Doe cultivated in the garden behind our house, each leaf cured and dried beneath her watchful eye. Touching a burning twig to the bowl, I inhaled deeply. The smoke rose smooth and sweet, carrying the faint scent of river mud and summer rain. Whispering Doe's tobacco had a soul of its own—richer and more fragrant than any leaf sold in the markets of Cahokia—and for a few quiet breaths, it carried me home.

The air beneath the ramada thickened into a blue haze. Mosquitoes avoided the cloud, and the evening settled around us like a soft blanket.

For a long while, none of us spoke. The crackle of the fire and the rhythmic chirp of katydids were the only sounds. Finally, I said quietly, "I had forgotten how good it feels to sit among kin and hear nothing but the night."

Pleasant Dove smiled. "The city steals silence. The hills give it back."

After a time, she retired to her chores. Cougar Walks and I remained by the fire. His profile glowed bronze in the flickering light.

"Tell me, cousin," I asked, "how long have you served here?"

He drew on his pipe, then exhaled slowly. Four cycles of the seasons. After our son, Caterpillar Wool, died of the coughing sickness. He had married a woman of the Bobcat Clan, but they bore no children. After his death, she returned to her Clan. Our daughter was taken long before that—less than one cycle of the seasons old. There was no one left to care for us. The council allowed us to take this post. We tend the Deer Clan Shrine House and offer shelter to travelers."

His voice did not falter, though sorrow rippled beneath the calm. "It is good work. The shrine needs hands, and Pleasant Dove and I need purpose. The Clan provides grain and firewood. In return, we keep the sacred house alive."

I nodded. "The Deer Clan cares for its own. That is as it should be."

He puffed again on the pipe and looked into the fire. "Yet even in service, there is mystery. Sometimes at night, when the wind turns and" the owls call from the mounds, I hear voices in the plaza. Chanting. Drums that aren't there. This place is full of old breath. It remembers."

His words sent a shiver through me. I stared into the embers, seeing the blood-red eyes of Underwater Panther and the towering forms of the *Wage-rucge* again. Was it possible that the earth truly remembered? That what

I had seen was not a vision but residue—a spiritual echo of ancient sacrifice, rising again to warn the living?

Cougar Walks turned toward me. "You will ponder your vision, yes?"

"I will," I said. "But it frightens me. I have never seen such horror in a dream. I can still smell the smoke, still hear the screaming."

He nodded, untroubled. "Fear is part of revelation. The Divine Ones speak through awe. Remember, cousin: The gods were both the giver of life and the bringer of war. When you stand between light and darkness, both will try to claim you."

The statement struck me with unexpected force. If the gods mirrored both creation and destruction, then perhaps the murders I was sent to investigate were not mere crimes but signs—an echo of imbalance between the worlds. If that was so, I wondered whether the killer understood the myths he reenacted.

After a time, Pleasant Dove returned, her hands folded in her lap. She accepted a pinch of tobacco from me and packed it carefully into her pipe. The three of us smoked together, old and not quite so old, united in ritual stillness.

Looking at their simple clay pipes beside my polished red one, I felt a pang of guilt for the difference between us. Age and loss had stripped them of worldly wealth, yet their dignity outshone any ornament. I thought of the copper trinkets I made for nobles, gleaming things that would one day tarnish. Here, by the small fire, was what endured: kindness, duty, and memory.

"I still want to try for another vision tomorrow," I stated. "I do not know if the Divine Ones will grant me a second vision, but I want to learn more about today's vision. If they will let me."

Cougar Walks nodded, "As you wish. But the Divine Ones do not make their will easy to understand. They give hints, and then they expect us to figure out the meaning for ourselves."

When the last of the embers turned gray, Cougar Walks gestured toward the darkness beyond the ramada. "Will you sleep in the shrine house?"

I hesitated. The image of flaming maize still flickered behind my eyes. "I think… I will stay here tonight, if you do not mind."

He smiled faintly. "The spirits will not begrudge you that. Rest where you feel safe."

They unrolled their own sleeping mats of woven cane and deer hide. I fetched my bison robe sleeping fur from the shrine house, spread it on the packed earth under the ramada, and lay down. The couple had already drifted into quiet breathing. Pleasant Dove curled beside her husband like a bird beside its mate.

The night wind carried the scent of river mud and drying maize from the valley below. Somewhere far off, a drum sounded—one slow beat, then silence. Was it real? Or was the drum beat the echo of a memory from the past?

I lay awake for a while, tracing the stars through the gaps in the ramada roof. Exhaustion pressed me toward sleep. I feared the return of the vision, yet when sleep finally came, mercifully it left only fragmented dreams—shadows without faces, whispers without words.

That night, I slept more deeply than I had in many moon cycles. No waking to the aches of age, no dreams sharp enough to pierce the dark—only the steady pulse of my heart and the whisper of the spirits around me.

Whatever lay ahead, I sensed that my path had shifted. The gods had shown me something, though I did not yet understand what. The murders, the vision, the silence of the Sacred Plaza—all were connected by threads unseen. My investigation into the immigrant murders had begun.

Chapter 5

As was my habit, I slept late the following day, and it was not until well after sunrise that I opened my eyes and stared into the summer sunlight filtering through gaps in the ramada's roof. Pleasant Dove had long since rekindled the fire near the ramada and began to prepare the morning meal. She worked so silently, and I slept so soundly that she had not disturbed my sleep.

"Well, I thought you were going to sleep all day," she said teasingly when she noticed I was awake and watching her work.

I sat up, stretched, and replied. "You sound like my wife. She is always commenting on how I like to sleep late. Back home, I seldom wake up before sunrise."

"Humf," she snorted. "Men can afford to sleep late. But women have work to do."

I did not have a witty comeback to that statement that would not get me in trouble, so I got up without commenting and walked to the edge of the village to relieve myself. I am not a young man anymore, and I wasn't used to doing as much walking as I had the day before, so I was stiff and sore when I got out of my sleeping robe and began moving around. The walk to the edge of the village and back helped loosen my stiff muscles, and I felt better when I got back to Pleasant Dove's ramada.

While washing my face with water from a large bowl, I noticed a pot containing a dark liquid steaming next to the fire when I returned from relieving myself. "Is that the black drink?" I asked.

"Yes," said Pleasant Dove. "It is ready now. Cougar Walks is already at the sweat lodge. He kindled a fire earlier this morning, and the rocks are heated. He sent a boy to fetch water from the spring. By the time you have taken the black drink, everything at the sweat lodge will be ready for you."

Pleasant Dove inserted a stick into holes in the rim of the cooking pot, raised it from the fire, and poured the steaming black drink into a bowl. She handed me a ceramic ceremonial beaker, and I carried the beaker and the pot filled with the black drink to the family sweat lodge next to the Clan Shrine House. Cougar Walks had everything ready when I arrived. I stripped off my breechcloth and sat on a deer skin before the sweat lodge. I poured the black drink from the bowl into the beaker and took my first swallow.

My throat burned, and I almost gagged at the bitter taste of the black drink as the liquid went down my throat. Although necessary for proper cleansing, I dreaded it every time it was required. In addition to being unpleasant, the black drink was also expensive. Made from the dried leaves of the yaupon holly bush, the plant grew only in the South near the Great Southern Sea and was imported from the South to Cahokia by traders. When brewed into a strong tea and consumed in large quantities from a ceremonial beaker, the black drink served as a purgative, causing ritual vomiting, which was necessary before entering the sweat lodge and seeking a vision in the shrine house.

Despite the dreadful taste, I downed the first ceremonial beaker of black drink. I hoped that by drinking rapidly, I could force vomiting swiftly without having to drink so much of the noxious brew. After three beakers of the foul drink, I fell over, retching violently. I rose to my feet and splashed water on my face to wash away the sweat and vomit. Cougar Walks was standing close by in case I needed help. He smiled and nodded his approval—it was a good purging.

Next, it was time to enter the sweat lodge. The sweat lodge was a small, circular building about three steps in diameter and not tall enough to stand inside. It was constructed by bending saplings into a dome shape and covering the frame with thatch, much like a home.

To prepare for the purification ceremony, Cougar Walks started a fire inside a hearth made of stones in the center of the sweat lodge. The stones used in the sweat lodge were round or oblong-shaped and about the size of a man's fist. Rocks of that shape and composition came from creek beds near the Emerald Acropolis. The rounded-shaped rocks cracked less frequently and repelled water more evenly, producing more steam. When the inside of the sweat lodge and the stones in the hearth were scorching hot, Cougar Walks extinguished most of the fire, leaving only a few twigs to provide light and serve as a receptacle for burnt offerings.

Cougar Walks helped me into the sweat lodge and handed me a water-filled pot. As I stepped into the sweat lodge and Cougar Walks closed the entrance with a bison robe, a wave of blisteringly hot air immediately assaulted my lungs, nearly taking my breath away. I made my way to the middle of the sweat lodge and poured water from the bowl over the hot rocks. As the cool water hit the hot stones, it produced a wave of steam that instantly engulfed the sweat lodge and rolled over my naked body.

I prostrated myself in front of the hearth and breathed in the steam. The steam entered my nostrils and worked its way through my sinuses. I held the steam for several heartbeats, then blew it out of my mouth. I repeated the process several times, then blew mucus out of my nose onto the floor of the sweat lodge. I sat cross-legged next to the hearth and poured more water onto the rocks, refilling the room with steam. Sitting in the darkness, I tried to clear my mind of all thoughts and worries, blocking out all sounds. After a time, Cougar Walks began beating a drum and chanting outside the sweat lodge to assist my purification, and I adjusted my thoughts to align with the drum's rhythm.

I began to pray. I shifted my body to face south, toward the powers of the Below World. I reached out to First Woman, also known as Old-Woman-Who-Never-Dies, and then to Underwater Panther, offering my respect and imploring them to help me in my quest to find the murderer of the immigrant farmers. I asked for the protection of Cahokia's people, the grandchildren of First Woman. To show my respect to the Below World, I tossed a handful of tobacco onto the fire as an offering. The pungent smell quickly filled the room. I used the best tobacco grown by Whispering Doe, so there was no doubt the offering was strong enough to reach the Below World.

I then turned to the North, toward the powers of the Above World. I stretched my mind to reach the consciousness of the Creator and Morning Star, also known as Red Horn and Thunder Bird, protector of the people and nemesis of Underwater Panther. I implored these spirit beings to protect my family and business and to bring prosperity. I sprinkled dried and crushed sassafras leaves over the fire as an offering. The leaves popped and sizzled as they were consumed by the flames, revealing that the Above World had received my offering.

Next, I turned to the east, the direction of rebirth and First Man, who separated the Below World from the Above World to create the Middle World, the Axis Mundi—the center of the world—home to the Great Oak World Tree, connecting the three worlds, and the people of Cahokia. If it was his will, I asked First Man to grant me another vision to assist me in my quest. To honor First Man and gain his support, I pricked my finger with a bone awl. The heat of the sweat lodge caused the blood to run freely from my finger onto the hearth, creating a satisfying sizzle as the dark red liquid hit the hot rocks.

41

Taking no chances, I turned west, in the direction of the setting sun. I said a prayer to Evening Star, daughter of First Woman and First Man, and mother of Lodge Boy and Throw-Away Boy, imploring her to control her mischievous twins so that they would not cause trouble for the people of Cahokia, and the Middle World could stay in balance.

Once I completed my supplications and offerings to the Divine Ones, I crawled to the sweat lodge's entrance and stepped out into the cooler late morning air. Cougar Walks was waiting for me, two bowls of water in hand. I bent down, and he poured the first bowl of water over my head and shoulders and the second bowl over my back and chest. I stood up and let the water run down my body. The water, fresh from the spring, felt cold against my heated skin, sending a tingling sensation through my entire body. The heat from the sweat lodge had driven all the soreness of the previous days' trek from my body, and in fact, I felt better than I had in many moon cycles. I should probably use our Deer Clan sweat lodge in Cahokia more often. I dried myself with a doeskin from Cougar Walks, then put on my breechcloth.

Reaching the Clan Shrine House from the sweat lodge took only a few steps. After the previous day's encounter, I entered the building with trepidation. Nevertheless, I was determined to seek another vision and to find enlightenment regarding the meaning of the terrifying vision from the previous day. I stepped down into the entrance of the Clan Shrine House and knelt on a sleeping fur to cushion my knees for the ordeal ahead. Cougar Walks then used a bison robe to close the entrance to the shrine house, leaving me in the darkened space.

Alone in the darkness of our Deer Clan sacred shrine, I again prayed to the Divine Ones, imploring them to grant me another vision and to offer me insight into the murders and the meaning of my previous one. I tried to empty my mind, leaving me open to be filled with insight. But nothing happened. I knelt silently in the shrine house, not moving or breathing hard, for what seemed like days. And still, nothing happened. Finally, the discomfort of kneeling in the same position on the hard, packed earth floor became too great, and I moved to a sitting position. Despite the purging and the sweat, I knew the gods would not grant me another vision.

If I did not receive further guidance from the Divine Ones, it was my responsibility to decipher the meaning of the vision and then act using that information. After a time, I came to the conclusion that the farmers walking out of the Temple were the poor farmers occupying farmsteads throughout the lands of the Sun King. But who or what did Underwater Panther represent? I did not know. However, I was sure that Muskrat Waits was right about the murders being a threat to the Sun King's rule and to the safety of Cahokia's people, and that a great evil was loose in the land, seeking to destroy us. Satisfied that, although the Divine Ones had not granted me another vision, I knew at least a little more about what I was facing, I left the shrine house with Cougar Walks and returned to his home.

When we reached the ramada, I was annoyed to find Spotted Lynx sitting by the fire, speaking amiably with Pleasant Dove and eating a plate of maize cakes. Showing up at a woman's hearth and charming her into something to eat appeared to be one of Spotted Lynx's talents.

"What are you doing here?" I asked irritably. "I told you to wait for me at the Temple."

"I am looking for you," he replied equally vexedly. "I waited for you at the Temple until well past the sun's high point. I expected you to be there in the morning, so when you did not show up, I decided to come looking for you. Where have you been?"

"The sweat and vision quest took longer than I expected. Let me eat something, and then we will speak with the Priests."

"So your vision quest was successful then?" He asked.

"We will talk about that later," I snapped. "Right now, I am starving."

I was weak and famished from the purging, the sweat, and the vision quest, so it was a delight to see Pleasant Dove hand me a massive plate of maize cakes covered in blackberry syrup. I attacked and devoured the maize cakes ravenously, much to the delight of my hostess.

Smiling at me, Pleasant Dove said. "It is rewarding to a woman to see a man eat heartily. Cougar Walks does not eat much anymore."

Through a mouthful of maize cakes, I said. "You are a wonderful cook, Pleasant Dove. These maize cakes are fantastic. Do not tell my wife, but I think you might even be a better cook than her, and that is a huge compliment because she is the best cook I know. She says I overeat."

Pleasant Dove blushed slightly at the compliment and said, "Nonsense, it is good for a man to eat well and keep up his strength. A weak man cannot work hard or satisfy his wife." She did not know I loved eating and was always a big eater. Although I was not fat, no one who looked at me would ever confuse me with someone who was starving, either. Once I finished downing the maize cakes and a large cup of sassafras tea, Pleasant Dove handed me two pairs of frog legs that had been roasting over the coals. The white, salty meat was tender and delicious, and I devoured them in seconds. I was still hungry, but work was still to be done before the day was finished, and the sun was rapidly slipping toward the western horizon.

"It is far too late to make it home before dark, so we will be spending another night here if that is all right," I told Cougar Walks and Pleasant Dove.

"Of course, of course," replied Cougar Walks happily. "We are glad to have you."

"I am going to sleep under your ramada tonight and not in the shrine house so Spotted Lynx can spend the night with us. That way, he can ensure I get up before sunrise, and we can be on the road early. I guess he can eat here too if he wants." I said begrudgingly. Spotted Lynx grinned.

"We still have time to speak with the Priests before sundown, so let us go," I motioned to Spotted Lynx, and we started toward the Temple Mound.

Chapter 6

From Pleasant Dove's ramada, we walked through the maze of family shrine houses, sweat lodges, and tiny homes. It was only about 200 steps to the base of the Holy Mound. From the front of the mound, we walked to the rear of the complex and found the Priest's lodgings. "Is this where you spent the night?" I asked Spotted Lynx. He nodded. "Who is the best person to speak with here?"

"Singing Mountain is the High Priest of the Emerald Acropolis," he replied. Spotted Lynx walked up to an elderly Priest seated beside the Priest's house in the shade of a ramada. The Priest rose, and Spotted Lynx handed him a parchment with symbols drawn in red and black ink— another pass from Muskrat Waits, I assumed.

The High Priest walked to where I stood, and Spotted Lynx introduced us. Singing Mountain greeted me civilly and then said, "You must be engaged in a critical matter if you carry the seal of Muskrat Waits. What can I do to help you, Walking Stick?"

This was the moment I had been dreading. "Muskrat Waits told me that he ordered the bodies of several people brought to your charnel house. I need to see them."

The High Priest nodded almost imperceptibly. "I thought it might have something to do with the bodies. It is not every day that the Sun King's Minister of Security sends bodies to the Emerald Acropolis and instructs me that I am to tell no one and that my Priests and I are not to discuss the presence of the bodies in our charnel house among ourselves. Very well, follow me." Singing Mountain motioned to a young Priest to accompany us.

We walked to the front of the mound and up the ramp to the charnel house. The young Priest, Gray Crane, assisted old Singing Mountain up the steps. The stench from the charnel house was almost overpowering the moment we reached the top of the Holy Mound, and the smell inside the charnel house was nearly indescribable once we entered the building. In addition to the other dead being prepared for burial by the Priests, the five murder victims—dead now for more than five sunrises—lay on a slab of logs in the center of the room.

The bodies of the murder victims, four men and one woman, were in dreadful condition. Four had been decapitated. Two of the men had their genitals sliced from their bodies. The woman was only recognizable by her genitalia because the murderer had removed her head and breasts. She had also been violated. Some victims were missing arms and legs. All the bodies were bloated from the heat, with flies and insects hovering around their orifices and open wounds. The others in our party seemed to be unaffected by the grisly sight. Singing Mountain and Gray Crane were used to working with decaying bodies in the charnel house, and Spotted Lynx had seen even worse carnage on the battlefield. However, I had never seen anything so ghastly in my life. I could only bring myself to stay in the charnel house for a few heartbeats before the stench and macabre scene drove me from the building, where I immediately doubled over and retched on the Holy Mound.

The others followed me out of the building. Singing Mountain's countenance showered disapproval of my weakness and sacrilege at despoiling the Holy Mound. Although Spotted Lynx had the decency not to comment, he wore an amused expression. Only Gray Crane looked upon my frailty sympathetically. The young Priest helped me to my feet, and I used the back of my hand to wipe the vomit from my mouth. "Can we go into the Temple and talk?" I asked.

Singing Mountain did not look thrilled about commoners entering the Temple. However, the authority I wielded through Muskrat Waits' seal outweighed any reluctance he might have had to allow us entrance, so he begrudgingly led us into the Temple. Despite its proximity to the charnel house, the Temple was mercifully free of the horrid smell of the dead, and the building was cool and quiet. It took my eyes several moments to adjust to the dim interior. I had never been inside a Temple before, so when my vision returned, I examined the interior of the building. The Emerald Acropolis Temple was larger than most and T-shaped, featuring a main hall and a smaller inner sanctuary located at the rear of the T. The most prominent feature I noticed in the hall was a series of masks on the walls. Colorful painted masks representing the Thunderbird Storms-as-he-walks covered the north side of the building, and Underwater Panther masks covered the south side. The opposing forces embody the harmony between the North and the South, and between the Above World and the Below World.

The rear of the main hall contained the pit of the eternal flame. The Priests maintained a small fire in a stone pit to honor Morning Star's eternal vigilance on behalf of Humankind. The Priests kept the fire burning day and night throughout the year, until it was ritually extinguished with water from the sacred spring at each winter solstice moonrise, and then relighted with great reverence. If the eternal fire were extinguished or allowed to go out by accident, it would be a great calamity for the people of Cahokia.

An intricately carved wooden statue of Morning Star in the form of Red Horn, also known as He-who-wears-human-heads-as-earrings, or He-who-gets-hit-with-deer-lungs, sat in a place of honor in the center of the building. The skilled woodcarver portrayed him with long hair arranged in an occipital bun, painted red, double-braided, wrapped around his neck, and running down onto the left side of his chest. Human-head effigy earplugs, painted yellow, hung from each earlobe. He was clothed only in a brown turkey feather cape and a breechcloth adorned with the forked eye falcon motif representing the Above World. In his left hand, Red Horn held the severed head of a *Wage-rucge* giant, and in his right hand, a mace, a symbol of his prowess as a warrior.

I sat on one of the benches lining the Temple's walls. My head was still spinning, but time was slipping away, and I still had questions to ask. "That was awful. The mutilation was so extreme. You cut up dead bodies all the time. After looking at those bodies, what can you tell me about the way these people were killed?" I asked the High Priest.

"Whoever did this knows how to kill people," said Singing Mountain. "The cuts were exact. There was no slashing with a knife or hacking with an axe. There was just one clean cut. Did you notice that whoever killed them removed their hearts?" I did not. "The cuts were so clean, there was very little blood. There is no way to know which wounds were the fatal ones and which came after the victims were already dead. Almost any of the wounds could have been fatal."

"Are you saying they were sacrificed?" I asked.

"I do not know," replied Singing Mountain. "I suppose it is possible the killer removed the hearts as part of a ceremony. But I do not know who would do such a thing. Only the Priests know the ceremonies. Even then, a person would need to beseech a specific deity. There have not been any human sacrifices since the return of Morning Star over a hundred cycles of the seasons ago. I think human sacrifice is highly unlikely."

"It is also possible that removing the hearts was meant as a warning." Spotted Lynx interjected. "To spread terror through the community. You said the deaths of these farmers could destabilize the countryside. Think about it. If a series of murders can cause panic, a series of grisly murders can cause even more panic."

"He is right," said Singing Mountain. "That might be why the killer removed the limbs, breasts, heads, and genitalia as well." I had to agree. The effect of those mutilated bodies on my emotions was far more traumatic than if they had been just killed with a single blow or cut.

"Can you tell me anything else about how they were killed?" I asked.

"The murderer used good-quality weapons. Sharp. The cuts are clean." Replied Singing Mountain.

Spotted Lynx nodded. "I agree with Singing Mountain. The cuts were precise, made with good weapons and lots of force—cutting through bone and cartilage is not easy."

"Strong, skillful, good weapons. Soldiers have good weapons. They are strong, and their leaders train them how to kill. Warriors are also mentally capable of killing. What do you think?" I asked the others.

Spotted Lynx shuffled nervously and said, "Yes, it is possible. Warriors have all the skills necessary to commit murder. But why? Why would a soldier kill these farmers? They were not a threat to anyone, at least not that we know, which brings us to another problem. We do not even know who these people are or where they lived. Locals found the bodies outside of Cahokia in the farmlands, but they were moved to the road for some purpose, most likely so they would be seen by as many people as possible. Perhaps to spread terror."

"Have you identified any of the victims?" I asked Singing Mountain.

"No," he replied. "The Warriors who brought the bodies here did not know who the people were."

"Did they tell you where they found the bodies?" I asked.

"Yes," said Singing Mountain. "The Warriors found four of the bodies on the Great Northern Road from Cahokia to North Star Town, close to Deer Toes Lake Town. They found the other body, the one that was not decapitated, east of Deer Toes Lake, on the road to the highlands and eventually Silver Maple Town." North Star Town was a large village with a Temple Mound and many smaller mounds, and it was about a day's journey north of Cahokia. It served as the administrative center of the northern part of the Sun King's domain. Deer Toes Lake Town was much smaller, with only four mounds, and a man could walk there from Cahokia in less than half of a sunrise.

"We will have to question the Priests there," I said. "They might know if any people in their community are missing. If that does not work, we will have to try talking to the locals. For that, we might need an interpreter."

"I can speak the language of the Waapaahshiiki River people," offered Spotted Lynx. "My parents did not speak Cahokian well, but they made sure their children did. So I learned to speak Cahokian and Waapaahshiiki as a child."

"Gray Crane can speak the language of the Oho people," commented Singing Mountain. "Like you, Spotted Lynx, his parents came from the East to bask in the glory of Cahokia. He can also assist you with the Priests at Deer Toes Lake Town and any other Temples where you may need to speak with them. That seal from Muskrat Waits grants you enormous authority, but Priests can be a prickly lot, and Gray Crane can help smooth the way for you. I will prepare a seal for you as well. Although technically, I have no authority over the other Temples, the position of High Priest of the Emerald Acropolis does lend me some influence."

"Thank you for all your help, Singing Mountain. I will tell Muskrat Waits everything you have done for us." I said

Singing Mountain grunted, "You can tell that old scoundrel, my cousin, that I did not help you for his sake but because I want to see these murders solved. And because you seem like a good sort. Even if you did defile the Holy Mound."

"I am sorry," I stammered. "But the bodies, the smell—I have never experienced anything like it."

The High Priest chuckled and patted my shoulder. "There is something else you need to consider." He said.

"What is that?"

"We have been speaking about a murderer," he began. "However, there is a possibility that more than one person was involved. Especially considering that someone moved the bodies. Even a strong man would have difficulty carrying a dead body very far. And a body slippery with blood and gore at that." I felt slightly nauseous again at the thought.

"That brings us back to my idea that Warriors might have committed the murders," I commented, looking at Spotted Lynx. "Soldiers are strong, used to blood and gore, and do work in groups."

Spotted Lynx frowned, exasperated, and said, "Yes, of course, all those things are true. However, I still do not see a reason why. We need to discover who these people were and the reason why someone killed them. That is the only way we are going to find the killers."

The sun was beginning to set, and I was feeling unwell again, so I decided it was time to go. I stood up and prepared to leave. "I think we have done about enough for today. With your permission, Singing Mountain, we will stop by the Priests' house at sunrise tomorrow and pick up Gray Crane. Thank you again for all your help."

"Very good. I will send a messenger to Muskrat Waits to inform him of what we discussed today and where you are headed tomorrow. Best wishes on your quest, Walking Stick," he said. "Gray Crane will be ready, but an old man needs his rest, so I will still be asleep when you leave." A man after my own heart, I thought.

Curious, I asked, "So you know Muskrat Waits well?"

Singing Mountain snorted. "We grew up together. Our mothers were sisters. That one is a demon, more treacherous than Throw-Away-Boy. Whatever you do, do not trust him, Walking Stick."

I did not intend to.

* * *

From the Temple Mound, Spotted Lynx and I went back to Pleasant Dove's ramada to spend the night. On the walk through the village, I could tell Spotted Lynx was annoyed with me for insisting that Cahokia Warriors could have committed the murders. I did not care. I had had an uneven day, beginning with the repulsive purge. The sweat was invigorating, but my supplication in the shrine house had gone unanswered, and the experience in the charnel house was ghastly. I wanted nothing more than to slip under my blanket and sleep.

Pleasant Dove had steaming bowls of goosefoot leaf, wild onion, and squash stew waiting for us when we arrived at her ramada. I took a few sips of my stew, but was not hungry for one of the few times in my life. Spotted Lynx quickly downed his bowl of stew. Pleasant Dove then gave him a plate with a piece of acorn bread and a slice from a haunch of venison. The haunch of meat was still roasting over the coals, and after my experience in the charnel house, it was too much. I put down my bowl, drank a glass of cool sassafras tea, and then excused myself.

I lay under the ramada, thinking about the murdered farmers. I could hear the others talking around the fire. Spotted Lynx was regaling the old couple with tales of his exploits in the army. Probably exaggerations, I thought uncharitably. After a time, Pleasant Dove approached where I was lying and offered me a glass of hot tea.

"This is yarrow leaf tea," said Pleasant Dove. "It will make your stomach feel better and help you fall asleep. You have had an eventful day. Whatever happened with the Priests—and Spotted Lynx would not tell us—must have been unpleasant. Drink that tea, and I will have a good meal for you in the morning." She left me and returned to the fire to hear more of Spotted Lynx's wild tales.

At least Spotted Lynx could keep his mouth shut when he was supposed to, and I did not have to deal with the embarrassment of my weakness on the Temple Mound becoming common knowledge. I drank my tea, and soon, as Pleasant Dove predicted, I fell sound asleep.

Chapter 7

Spotted Lynx woke me well before sunrise the next morning. Thanks to Pleasant Dove's yarrow leaf tea, I had slept through the entire night. We packed our few belongings, and by the time we finished, Pleasant Dove told us the morning meal was ready. After a night of purging and no evening meal, I was famished. Pleasant Dove, as always, did not disappoint.

She had smoked the remaining deer haunch through the night and already picked the meat from the bone by the time we got up. She made a stew of smoked venison and ground hickory nuts, served with fresh maize cakes. Spotted Lynx is a big eater, but that morning I surprised even him. I finished three bowls of stew and five maize cakes before I finally handed my plate to Pleasant Dove, finally satisfied.

"You must be feeling better this morning," she said, pleased. "Your appetite has certainly come back."

"It has," I told her. "Your stew and tea worked wonders."

I thanked Pleasant Dove and Cougar Walks for everything they had done. "The next time you travel to Cahokia, visit my shop. I will take you home to meet my wife, Whispering Doe. She would be thrilled to welcome you both."

Cougar Walks shook his head with a smile. "I am afraid our traveling days are behind us, Walking Stick. We are too frail to make the journey to Cahokia, so we will stay here at the Emerald Acropolis. But we hope to see you again—perhaps at the fall equinox. Bring your wife. Pleasant Dove enjoys the company of young men, but she would appreciate women's talk too."

We left the two of them by their fire and walked to the Priests' house as the sun crept over the horizon. Gray Crane was waiting for us outside. He gathered what little he needed for the journey, and then the three of us set off on the road toward Deer Toes Lake Town.

The morning air was cool and pleasant, and I was in good spirits after sleeping well and eating even better. We had a long walk ahead to Deer Toes Lake Town, where I hoped to question the Priests before making it home by sunset. I set what felt to me like a brisk pace. Gray Crane could have walked faster, and Spotted Lynx could probably have run the entire way, but for an old man with sore legs, I was doing well enough.

The long walk gave me a chance to get to know Gray Crane. He was young—probably younger than Spotted Lynx—and very tall, though thin as a sapling. His breechcloth, cape, and rattlesnake-master shoes were simple. Like Spotted Lynx, he bore no Clan tattoos, but he carried the markings of his profession: Birdman tattoos across his body, symbols of First Man and the Upper World, and other signs of the Priesthood. His hair was tied in a topknot, and he wore bone ear spools and a necklace of rounded creek stones.

As we crossed the upland prairie, I asked him about his family. He told me he was born near North Star Town. His parents and grandparents were immigrants from the Oho Valley, and his family still spoke Oho at home. His grandparents had never learned Cahokian well, but his parents had made sure their children did.

His knowledge of immigrant customs piqued my interest. It might prove useful in our investigation.

"How did you become a Priest?" I asked.

Gray Crane laughed. "By necessity. I am the youngest of four sons. My parents could not secure enough farmland for all of us, so when I was eight cycles of the seasons old, they took me to the Temple at the Emerald Acropolis. I have been with the Priests ever since."

"How old are you now?"

"Eighteen cycles of the seasons."

I felt a sting of sadness at that. To be taken from one's family so young—well, it wasn't the life I lived, and I felt grateful for it.

Spotted Lynx tried to cheer him. "Perhaps you will be the High Priest here someday."

Gray Crane laughed again, louder this time. "Not likely. The high positions are reserved for Priests from the Noble Clans. Singing Mountain accepted me because he took pity on my parents. I will never hold high office. But I enjoy being a Priest. I am learning the rituals, and I want to be a good one. That is enough."

We walked down a steep slope to Silver Maple Creek, drank our fill, and refilled our water bottles before crossing into Silver Maple Town. Instead of taking the Sacred Way toward Cahokia, we turned northwest on a narrower road leading to Deer Toes Lake Town. A steady stream of travelers used it—farmers, hunters, and traders. None of them paid us any attention, which was just as well.

54

Before the sun reached the middle of the sky, we arrived at the bluffs overlooking the Valley of Cahokia. From the top, we could see the Great Pyramid clearly in the distance, with smoke from thousands of fires drifting above the city.

A spring flowed from the base of the bluffs beside the road. We were parched from the long stretch of dry prairie, so we stopped to drink and fill our water bottles again. I decided we might as well eat before moving on. Gray Crane had not brought food, so Spotted Lynx and I shared what we had packed from home.

We ate quickly, and when we were finished, we continued northwest across the flat valley floor. Despite the growing heat, the walking was easy, and we made excellent time. By the time the sun reached its zenith, the Temple of Deer Toes Lake Town was visible across the fields, rising above the village and the lake that gave the town its name.

Before long, we reached the edge of the village.

Chapter 8

Deer Toes Lake Town sat along the banks of its shallow lake, larger than many of the villages in this part of the valley. Four mounds rose above the houses, including the Temple Mound and the mound where the Chief lived. Many immigrant farmers lived in the lands north of Cahokia, and Deer Toes Lake Town stood along the main road between Cahokia and North Star Town. It was a common resting place for travelers.

Our first stop was the Chief's house atop the largest mound. A young Warrior met us at the base of the ramp. After examining Muskrat Waits' seal, he led us to the top. The Chief was waiting there.

He was a large man with a protruding stomach and thin arms and legs—Eagle Clan, from the look of his facial markings. The Eagle Clan was minor nobility, so it was common for one of their members to serve as Chief of a provincial village like Deer Toes Lake Town. He wore a tunic with red and gold stripes, copper arm bands, and a feathered headdress. He did not introduce himself, but I learned later that his name was Running Deer. I disliked him almost at once.

"My name is Walking Stick," I said plainly. I motioned to Spotted Lynx, who stepped forward and handed over Muskrat Waits' seal. "This is War Captain Spotted Lynx. We are here on behalf of Muskrat Waits, the Sun King's Minister of Security, to investigate the murders in this region. I assume you have heard of them?"

Running Deer flinched slightly at Muskrat Waits' name, a sign of the Minister's influence even in the hinterlands.

"Yes, of course, I know of the murders," he said with irritation. "The bodies were found in my lands. What do the murders have to do with me?" he asked.

His response stunned me. "Presumably the victims were your subjects," I answered. "Have you tried to learn who they were? Or find their families? Or discover who killed them?"

The Chief shook his head. "The dead were not from this village. From what I can tell, they were peasant farmers."

"And you do not care about peasant farmers?"

"Not particularly," he admitted. "The loss of a few farmers is of no consequence. They can be replaced."

I glared at him. He glared back. He did not like me any more than I liked him.

"Do you care that Muskrat Waits cares?" I asked sharply. "Or that the Sun King cares? These murders must be investigated."

That seemed to get through to him. "What do you want from me?" he asked.

"I want to know what you have learned," I said. "What have you done to investigate. And who else in your village might be able to help us?"

"When I first heard about the murders, I sent my Warriors," he said. "But by the time they arrived, the Sun King's soldiers had removed the bodies. My men made inquiries, but no one from Deer Toes Lake Town is missing. Once I learned the dead were not from any of my villages, I stopped investigating."

His indifference was infuriating, but arguing with him would have done no good.

"Is there anyone else here who might know something?" I asked.

"Try the Priests," he said with a sneer. "They pry into everything."

On the way to the Temple, I muttered, "That man is a worthless Noble. Men like him give the whole class a bad name."

"I would like nothing better than to cut his throat and throw his body down the ramp of the city mound for all the inhabitants to see. I bet his people despise him as much as we do." Spotted Lynx said calmly. He was not joking. Gray Crane looked horrified at our disrespect for a Noble.

We left the Chief's Mound and walked to the Temple Mound along the lakeshore. We climbed the ramp to the T-shaped Temple on top. A Priest met us outside. Gray Crane presented both Muskrat Waits' and High Priest Singing Mountain's seals. That was enough. The Priest showed us inside.

The Temple resembled the one at the Emerald Acropolis—Thunderbird masks on the north wall, Underwater Panther masks on the south, and a statue of Morning Star as Red Horn in the center. Benches lined the long hall. On the Temple's exterior, a carved wooden First Man mask rested above the lintel, its long, sharp nose angled upward, pointing reverently toward the Above World.

We took seats along the north wall. Gray Crane asked to see the High Priest, and before long, he appeared from the inner sanctum. His name was Blue Wolf. He wore a Moon Clan tattoo—one of the highest Noble Clans in Cahokia. Blue Wolf's Moon Clan outranked Chief Running Deer's Eagle Clan, which must have been a constant embarrassment to the Chief.

Blue Wolf greeted us formally, and we explained our mission.

"Yes, I know of the bodies," he said. "The farmers who discovered them came to me. I sent word to Chief Running Deer and to Muskrat Waits. The soldiers came soon after and removed the bodies. I was instructed not to discuss the matter with anyone."

"Do you know the names of the victims?" I asked.

He shook his head.

"Has anyone come to you about missing family members? Perhaps farmers from the countryside?"

Again, Blue Wolf shook his head. "I have heard nothing since the soldiers removed the bodies."

I pressed him. "Someone must know something. These victims came from somewhere. Is there anyone among the immigrant families whom people trust?"

Blue Wolf considered this for several heartbeats before answering.

"The immigrants are not fully integrated," he explained. "Many still speak their native languages. Some cling to their old religions. Trust does not come easily."

Gray Crane asked, "Is there an elder among them? Someone respected?"

"Perhaps one man," Blue Wolf said. "Bold Warrior. He came here from the Oho country many cycles of the seasons ago. He was once a feared Warrior but became a man of peace when he embraced Morning Star. He is old now but highly respected. If he cannot help you, I doubt anyone can."

"Where can we find him?" I asked.

"Follow the lake north from the back of the Temple Mound for about five hundred steps. You will reach the canoe landing. His daughter's house is nearby."

We thanked him and left the Temple.

We walked along the lake until we reached the canoe landing. Several men were coming and going. I watched the scene and chose an older man walking alone. He seemed approachable.

"Grandfather," I said gently. "I am Walking Stick of the Deer Clan. These are my companions, Spotted Lynx and Gray Crane. We are strangers here. Can you help us?"

The man studied us. "My name is Wood Duck. What do you need?"

"We are looking for Bold Warrior. The High Priest told us to come here."

"I know him," Wood Duck said. "Why do you seek him?"

"We need advice," I said.

He shrugged. "Very well. Come."

Wood Duck led us a short distance into the village until we reached a small home, where a woman ground maize beneath a ramada. An older man sat nearby, knapping arrowheads.

"There," Wood Duck said, nodding toward the flint knapper. He left us.

I approached. "My name is Walking Stick of the Deer Clan," I said. "My companions are Spotted Lynx and Gray Crane. We are searching for Bold Warrior. The High Priest said he might help us. Are you he?"

The man nodded.

"Do you speak Cahokian?" I asked.

Bold Warrior and his daughter exchanged amused looks. Then they laughed.

"Of course, we speak Cahokian," he said. "I have lived here nearly 30 cycles of the seasons. My daughter was born here."

"I meant no insult," I said. "We were told many immigrant families have not learned the language."

Bold Warrior frowned. "It is true. Some have isolated themselves. It is not wise. However, I do not believe you came here to talk about the Cahokian language—how can I help you?"

"Several people from this area were murdered recently," I said. "Their bodies were mutilated and left along the roads."

"Yes," Bold Warrior said quietly. "Everyone knows. Horrifying."

I was surprised. "Everyone knows? The murders are not known in Cahokia."

He laughed. "In a small place like this, news travels quickly."

He fixed me with a sharp look. "So why would a coppersmith, a Warrior, and a Priest come here to question an old man?"

There was no point denying anything. "The Sun King has tasked me with solving the murders. To do that, I must know who the victims were. No families have come forward in Cahokia. That means I must identify missing people here. I need someone trusted by the immigrants to help me discover who is missing."

Bold Warrior nodded slowly. "A good strategy. You would not know where to begin. Many of the families would not speak to you. They might flee if the Warriors questioned them. Whoever sent you was wise."

He folded his hands. "I will help. Give me three sunrises. Even if I do not learn everything, I will send word. When the time comes, I will also send a man to translate for you and act as a guide."

"Thank you," I said. "But how did you know I was the coppersmith?"

Bold Warrior smiled. "Your name is well-known in Cahokia. The Sun King chose well."

We left Bold Warrior and made our way out of the village to the Great Northern Road. The sun was well past its highest point, descending quickly, and I set a quick pace, determined to reach home by sunset.

As we walked through fields of maize, sunflowers, squash, gourds, goosefoot, and maygrass, I thought of the murder victims.

"Somewhere along this stretch," I told the others, "they found four of the bodies."

Spotted Lynx nodded. "I have been watching for signs, but the Warriors likely cleaned everything up."

"It is strange to think of the dead lying here," Gray Crane said quietly.

"I am sorry to keep you from your work at the Emerald Acropolis," I told him. "But I need you to stay in Cahokia until we solve this mystery. You are welcome to stay with my family until we catch the killer."

"Thank you," he said, "but I must report to the High Priest. I will stay in one of the smaller Temples."

Spotted Lynx grinned. "Even so, you should eat at Walking Stick's house. His wife is an excellent cook."

I frowned. He would no doubt try to follow his own advice.

I pushed myself hard, and at sunset, we reached the canoe landing across from the Great Pyramid. I paid a trader to ferry us across Cahokia Creek. From the south bank, it was a short walk to my home.

When we stepped into the Black Bear Clan Common, Willow Tree saw us and ran to greet me. Soon, the whole family surrounded me, talking over one another. Whispering Doe shooed them away and embraced me warmly.

"It is good to have you home," she said. "I was beginning to worry. It has been many cycles of the seasons since we spent a night apart." She noticed the men behind me. "I see you have picked up another companion."

I introduced Gray Crane without explanation.

"Well then," she said. "The evening meal is ready. Are they staying?"

"Yes," I said. "It is too late to find food elsewhere."

Whispering Doe beamed.

We gathered around the fire. Whispering Doe served hominy stew with wild onions, cattail root, and mussels. I devoured my bowl, then the catfish baked with goosefoot leaves that followed. It took another bowl of stew and two slices of sunflower seed bread to satisfy me.

After the women ate, Whispering Doe and Walks in Water cleaned up while we men pulled out our pipes. I filled mine with Whispering Doe's excellent tobacco. Spotted Lynx eyed it jealously until I relented and handed him the leather bag.

"You cannot find tobacco this good anywhere else," I told him.

Whispering Doe sat beside me, proud of her work. She offered Gray Crane some, but he politely declined.

Walks in Water and Spotted Lynx kept glancing at each other across the fire. Whispering Doe noticed, humming thoughtfully as she set a cup of maize beer in my hand.

The evening was pleasant—good food, good smoke, warm fire, and family. Had I known what was to come in the sunrises ahead, I would have tried to hold on longer to the contented and, in some ways, innocent warmth of that evening with my family and new companions.

However, I did not know the tragedy and sorrows my small band would face in the coming sunrises, so after a while I knocked the ashes from my pipe and stood.

"It is time for bed," I said. "Spotted Lynx must return to his barracks, and Gray Crane must report to the High Priest."

Walks in Water tried to protest, but Whispering Doe silenced her with a single look. The young men thanked her for the meal and her kindness, and then left.

Chapter 9

I slept later than I had in many moon cycles, and when I finally stirred, my body felt as heavy as river-sodden driftwood. My back ached from the restless night, and my head felt like it was wrapped tightly in deer hide. Before I could even gather my thoughts, my bladder reminded me what mattered most, so I took the small clay pot Whispering Doe had thoughtfully left beside our bedding and relieved myself. Such quiet foresight from her was not unusual; she anticipated needs like the wife who had lived with me for over 20 cycles of the seasons and knew my routines and peculiarities well.

I rose from beneath the ramada, blinking at the angled morning light. Our family hearth was already alive, its gray smoke blowing from the fire curling through the ramada's roof thatch like early fog on Cahokia Creek. I smelled simmering stew and woodsmoke—simple, familiar scents that stirred my appetite.

Walks in Water knelt near the embers, stirring a clay pot with deliberate, practiced motions, and she was laughing at something Spotted Lynx had said. The sight of the two of them—my daughter bright and hopeful, he tall and confident—tightened my chest in a way that had nothing to do with age.

Walks in Water spotted me first.

"Oh, Father—you are awake! Come. Sit. There is food ready."

I ignored her cheerful tone and looked directly at Spotted Lynx. "What are you doing here?" I demanded. The edge in my voice was sharp.

Before he could answer, Walks in Water intervened, swatting at me with her words as though I were a bothersome fly.

"He is here to take you to see the Muskrat or whatever his name is," she declared. "Now sit down and stop being a grouch so I can feed you."

"Where is your mother?" I demanded.

"She went to the fields with the Black Bear Clan women. She told me to stay so I could warm your meal when you woke."

She said it lightly, but her eyes flicked once, quickly, toward Spotted Lynx.

I had a suspicion—one that made me more uncomfortable than amused—that Whispering Doe had left the girl behind not merely to feed me, but to spend time with the Warrior.

63

When Walks in Water hurried away to fetch my food, I turned my glare upon Spotted Lynx.

"The Muskrat?" I hissed quietly. "You revealed our mission to my daughter?"

He shook his head quickly. "No—no, not like that. She asked where we were going today. I accidentally said the name Muskrat Waits. I did not explain anything else."

"That is enough to invite danger to my family," I snapped. "A Warrior should have better mastery of his tongue."

Spotted Lynx lowered his head in shame.

"You are right. It was careless, and I will not make such a mistake again."

Before I could continue, Walks in Water returned, beaming, holding a steaming bowl of leftover stew.

"There was food from last night," she said proudly. "Mother said to save it for you—that you might want something heartier than maize cakes."

Bless Whispering Doe.

I sat beside the fire, the rough-hewn chair creaking under my weight. Spotted Lynx crouched nearby as though on campaign.

Not long after I began eating, he leaned close with a grin.

"You look terrible, Walking Stick. Was there too much maize beer and Whispering Doe last night?"

"That is none of your business," I growled.

He laughed—genuinely amused—and returned to Walks in Water's side. As they spoke quietly, she smiled in a way that unsettled me. Part of me wanted to shout No! Not him! But the words remained unspoken. Children follow their own paths; a father may only pray they choose wisely.

As I ate, I considered what the day demanded of me. Muskrat Waits would expect an update—immediately, no matter how exhausted we were, or how little progress had been made. After that, we could do nothing until Bold Warrior sent word. I needed rest, counsel, and time—but time is a luxury only the safe may possess.

After finishing my stew and sunflower bread, I cleaned my teeth with a sassafras twig, then washed my face and hair with warm water that Walks in Water fetched. The simple ritual restored clarity.

"Come," I told Spotted Lynx. "Time to see Muskrat Waits." Before he thinks of new reasons to remain near my daughter, I thought.

He said his farewells to Walks in Water—more warmly than necessary—and then followed me out of the Black Bear Clan Common. I turned toward the Sacred Way, deliberately circling the edge of the new East Plaza so as not to pass the copper works. I did not wish to answer questions—not yet.

The air along the Sacred Way tasted of dust, clay, and distant river wind. Traders and pilgrims filled the road: men and women leading pack dogs, people bartering, Priests moving about the people, families headed to Temples for prayers or ceremonies, and merchants hawking their wares. Ordinarily, I admired the vitality of Cahokia, but that morning the noise grated on my ears like rough stone.

When the towering base of the Great Pyramid rose ahead of us, its enormous ramp casting a shadow broad as the largest trading canoes, Spotted Lynx showed the guards his pass without ceremony. They allowed us through, though their eyes lingered on us with curiosity. They had heard whispers—how many others knew of our mission, and were they friend or foe?

We climbed to the first terrace, where Muskrat Waits already sat beneath his ramada like a carved idol, motionless except for the slightest flicker of irritation in his eyes. When we approached, he did not greet us— he struck immediately.

"Where have you been?" he barked.

"We returned from the Emerald Acropolis last night," I answered, my tone sharp enough to draw a few startled blinks from the guards nearby.

"Yes, yes, I know where you were, but not where you are. I expected you right after dawn. Half the day is wasted. I nearly sent my agents to drag you here."

My patience evaporated like rain on hot pottery sitting in a fire.

"I returned from a long journey, Minister. I am no longer young. My bones ache, and my mind needs rest to think clearly. I am not your servant. I agreed to help for my family's sake, not to be barked at like a dog. If my efforts are not good enough for you, find someone else."

Behind me, I heard Spotted Lynx inhale sharply, as though he feared an execution would begin immediately.

Later, I would wonder how close I stood to death in that moment.

But Muskrat Waits did not explode. His eyes narrowed, his jaw twitched, and then—annoyed more than enraged—he said:

"Well. You are here now. Tell me what you discovered at the Emerald Acropolis."

I took a deep breath to calm myself and to steady my voice.

"We learned little at the Emerald Acropolis," I began, "and yet what we learned is deeply troubling. The victims were butchered by someone strong, precise, and accustomed to killing. The blows were clean, the cuts deliberate, and the dismemberment purposeful. The High Priest there, Singing Mountain, believes more than one person was involved."

I paused, knowing what must come next would poison the air like rotting swamp gas.

"And I believe he is correct. These murders were not the work of panicked farmers, starving vagrants, or angry neighbors. They required people familiar with killing. One group of people in Cahokia possesses the necessary skills: Warriors — trained, hardened, and disciplined. I am not accusing the Warriors of these murders. However, I think it is worth investigating their possible involvement."

Spotted Lynx stiffened beside me. Muskrat Waits stopped tapping his copper pendant. His gaze sharpened, his mind turning like a chert blade against antler. No one spoke for many heartbeats. Nothing moved. Even the breeze seemed to pause, wary of what lived in that silence.

At last, Muskrat Waits spoke.

"That is... an unsettling theory, Walking Stick. But perceptive." He gave no praise — only recognition.

He turned to Spotted Lynx. "What do you think of Walking Stick's theory?"

Spotted Lynx did not answer immediately, and to his credit, he did not bluster. He breathed once, deeply, then said:

"Minister, I do not deny that Warriors could kill in such a fashion. That is our craft. And we are capable of unspeakable violence — when ordered, when justified, or when threatened. But I cannot imagine our Warriors doing such a thing. For ten cycles of the seasons in service, I have never seen our ranks murder citizens. And certainly not like this. We swore to protect Cahokia, and we take that oath as seriously as death."

Muskrat Waits studied him as though measuring bone quality for a war club handle.

"Never in your lifetime," he said, "nor mine have our Warriors broken their sacred vows to protect the people and murdered helpless citizens.

Still… an unbroken record does not guarantee an unbroken present." He stroked one of his copper ear ornaments shaped like a human head — an unsettling gesture, whether intentional or not.

No one spoke. Beneath us, smoke rose from the Grand Plaza hearths, easing through the heavy summer air to the Above World. From that height, Cahokia looked peaceful — too peaceful, like a corpse washed clean before burial.

At last, Muskrat Waits said quietly:

"If Warriors are behind this, even a small rogue band, the consequences could shake the foundations of our world. Farmers will flee. Clans will panic. The Sun King will be forced to act, and civil unrest will follow. So we do not speak this theory aloud — not to friends, not to family, not to Priests. Is that clear?"

We both nodded.

"Spotted Lynx," the Minister continued, "you will return to the barracks. Do not interrogate—observe. Listen. Measure the mood, the whispers, the silences. There may be unrest, jealousy, grievance, resentment, or Clan loyalties we do not yet see."

Spotted Lynx swallowed hard, but answered steadily: "Yes, Minister."

Muskrat Waits shifted in his chair. "Now tell me of Deer Toes Lake Town."

I recounted our conversation with Chief Running Deer — arrogant, dismissive, and eager to blame outsiders rather than examine his own community. Muskrat Waits snorted.

"Running Deer is useful only because removing him would cause more trouble than enduring him. His family holds influence in Cahokia. Otherwise, I would have ended his leadership by rope or fire ten cycles of the seasons ago."

Next, I described Head Priest Blue Wolf, who was willing to help but lacked any knowledge of the murders beyond what Muskrat Waits already knew. Muskrat Waits waved a hand dismissively.

"Priests are often blinded by ritual smoke. They see visions and miss footprints. At least he had the sense to notify me when he learned of the murders, or the situation, the panic, might be worse."

Then I recounted our time with Bold Warrior — his wisdom, his influence among immigrants, and his promise to uncover the victims' names and to send us a messenger and guide to help us in our investigation.

67

Muskrat Waits leaned forward.

"Bold Warrior... yes, I remember him. When he first arrived in the lands of the Sun King, we feared he might be a covert leader of a foreign faction. He had followers, strength, charisma — all dangerous things when combined. We listened, observed, and waited. In the end, we found no conspiracy. Age has gentled him into a village patriarch. If he says he will find the families, we can wait."

Waiting — a thing Muskrat Waits loathed.

He clicked his fingernails against the wooden arm of his chair and repeated, "Three sunrises, he said?"

"Yes," I replied. "Even if he learns only part of what we need, he will send the messenger with what he has learned."

"Then we wait," he said, through clenched teeth. "But before Bold Warrior's messenger arrives, continue your work in the city. Talk to the Priests, talk to the Clan elders, but do not reveal the reason for your questions. Be subtle."

As we prepared to leave, curiosity tugged one last question from me: "Singing Mountain said you are cousins, and that your mothers were sisters. Is that true?"

Muskrat Waits smiled, and it was not a warm smile.

"Yes. We were boys together. But his head was always in the clouds. He followed dreams and smoke and became a Priest. I followed power, duty to the Sun King, and the law. He disapproves of me, and I find him foolish. What did he tell you?"

"He said not to trust you."

Muskrat Waits' smile broadened. He was not offended, but delighted.

"He is correct."

He did not explain further, and I did not ask.

* * *

When we left the Great Pyramid, Spotted Lynx and I paused beneath the shadow of the ramp. The river breeze carried the scent of mud, cedar, and cooking fish from the lower plazas. The world looked unchanged — vibrant markets, children chasing dogs, traders haggling over chert, and Priests chanting blessings for safe travel. Yet I felt as though we had stepped out of a council house where one log had been pulled from the foundation — and no one else yet heard the crack. Knowing what I had learned in the past several sunrises, the world looked different.

"We should separate for now," Spotted Lynx said. "I will go to the barracks. I will do as Muskrat Waits commanded—listen and observe. I will go to my own Troupe first and talk to my lieutenants. After that, I will go to the Warrior headquarters and listen to what my fellow War Captains are saying."

He hesitated and then asked, "Do you truly believe Warriors could be responsible for the killings?"

"I believe," I said, "that whoever did this knows how to kill with skill, not rage. That narrows the possibilities."

He lowered his eyes, and for the first time since I met him, he looked young — a man still caught between duty and his identity as a War Captain of Cahokia.

He walked away toward the barracks, and I wondered whether he feared what he would find — or feared that he might recognize the hands capable of doing such work.

Before I set out to gauge the mood of the local Clan leaders, I decided my next step would be to see how Red Hawk was running the copper works.

The air changed as I drew near the workshop — the metallic tang of hammered copper, the ozone-scorched scent of heated furnaces, the rhythmic tapping of bone hammers against stone anvils. The sounds were music to my bones — steady, purposeful, and alive.

Red Hawk was intent on his work as I approached the ramada beside the copper works, busy directing our apprentices and skilled workers. He did not see me at first, so I had the chance to observe my son—tall, strong, and totally in his element. He made me proud. When he finally saw me, a look of relief and affection softened his stern face — though he kept his composure, as any master should.

As I walked through the shop with my son, I saw copper tubes rolled for ceremonial headdresses, a pair of ear spools wrapped in hammered sheet copper, and a newly molded copper plate depicting First Man in his falcon regalia — wings spread, lips parted mid-incantation. The Sun King's diplomatic gifts would travel farther than any Warrior: through marriage alliances, trade pilgrimages, and stories sung in the tongues of distant rivers.

When I finished my inspection, Red Hawk and I exchanged a quiet nod. The shop still lived, breathed, and thrived without me. He was running the business as well as I could. Perhaps it was time to turn over the copper works to Red Hawk, as my Uncle Rattlesnake had turned it over to me when I was ready.

From the copper works, I went to the Deer Clan Shrine House. I climbed the ramp to the top of the mound and found my Uncle Rattlesnake seated in his usual place under a ramada next to the shrine house.

Although Muskrat Waits had instructed me not to discuss the murders with anyone, I had already told Rattlesnake. Plus, I valued his opinions and insights into the life of the East Precinct community.

"What have you learned, nephew?" He asked as I paused to catch my breath after the steep climb.

I told him about my trip to the Emerald Acropolis, viewing the bodies, and what I had learned at Deer Toes Lake Town. Since I had already confided in Rattlesnake, I saw no reason not to discuss the situation with him, despite Muskrat Waits' instructions.

"Such a terrible thing," Rattlesnake lamented. "Not in my lifetime has such an evil walked the land. Powerful forces are at work here, nephew. You must be cautious."

I asked him to use his knowledge of the East Precinct neighborhood and his relationships with the other Clan leaders to discreetly gather information about the murders.

"I will do as you ask, nephew. I do not mind a little excitement, but I warn you, do not involve any other family members. It could be dangerous."

I assured him that I would not involve any other Clan members in my quest.

I returned home to find Whispering Doe and Walks in Water grinding maize beneath the ramada. Walks in Water leapt up to bring me boiled greens and maize cakes, cheerful as a spring bird. She asked whether Spotted Lynx would return that evening.

"I doubt I could keep him away," I muttered.

She smiled brightly.

True to my prediction, Spotted Lynx arrived long before the evening meal. He did not approach as a soldier summoned to duty but as a favored guest of the women. Whispering Doe, ever gracious in the presence of visitors, smiled widely when he complimented her cooking, while Walks in Water hovered nearby pretending to organize firewood, her eyes following his every movement. I wondered whether Whispering Doe saw the same thing I did — or whether mothers carry a gentler lens for their daughters' hopes.

Gray Crane arrived moments before the meal, his face flushed from walking and his clothing dusty, but his manners pristine. I barely had time to greet him before Whispering Doe placed bowls of venison stew into his hands. Spotted Lynx competed for attention with casual skill, earning laughter from both women. Gray Crane ate politely, observing the interaction without comment. The young Priest saw more than he ever said.

I decided to wait until after the meal to speak privately with the two young men. Whispering Doe knew me well enough not to press for conversation, but I felt her eyes studying me as she worked.

After the meal, we slipped away while Walks in Water and Whispering Doe cleaned the bowls with rushes gathered from the banks of Cahokia Creek and rinsed them in hot water. We walked down to the creek where the night air felt cool against our skin, and the torchlight from the Great Pyramid reflected in ripples like broken stars. I sat on an overturned canoe, while Gray Crane and Spotted Lynx stood nearby — one solemn, one restless.

"Tell me what you learned," I said.

Gray Crane spoke first. "None of the Temples were particularly welcoming, so I spent the night at your Deer Clan Shrine House," he began. "Even though I was a stranger, they received me kindly, though they did not know about the murders."

I nodded. "Good. I am glad they received you kindly; otherwise, I would have given them a harsh reproach. Even though they did not have any information, at least the word of the murders had not reached their ears. And if there were rumors about, my Uncle Rattlesnake would have heard them. I have asked him to make discreet inquiries about the murders."

He continued. "Well after sunrise, I attempted to speak with Priests at the High Temple, but they were busy conducting purification rites for a Noble child with fever. They told me they had no time to help. I asked to see the Lord High Priest on an important matter, but they said he was unavailable to a lowly Priest. I must confess, I do not look important enough for an audience with the Lord High Priest."

"Did you show them the seal from Shining Mountain?" I asked.

"Yes, but they did not care."

Spotted Lynx snorted quietly. "Unbelievable," he repeated mockingly. "They do not care about other Priests, much less ordinary people."

Gray Crane did not bristle; humility was a cornerstone of his simple life. "Not all Priests are like the High Temple Priests. They must protect ritual and order; They have a higher calling than other Priests," he said calmly.

Spotted Lynx rolled his eyes and muttered, "And sometimes protocol is simply a thick blanket placed over truth."

The young men eyed each other with the faintest flaring of rival philosophies. I let the tension settle long enough to reveal character but not long enough to nurture resentment.

"After I left the High Temple, I went to two smaller Temples, but the Priests there did not have any knowledge of murdered farmers." Gray Crane stated.

"You did well," I told Gray Crane. "Tomorrow, we use Muskrat Waits' authority and request — no, demand — an audience with the Lord High Priest."

Even Gray Crane did not object to my choice of words.

"What if he refuses again?" Spotted Lynx asked.

"He will not refuse a sealed order from the Minister of Security," I answered. "And if he does… then we will see that the Priesthood knows about the murders and they have something to fear."

The creek gurgled beside us as though adding quiet commentary to our thoughts.

"What do we do after speaking with the Lord High Priest?" Gray Crane asked.

"We wait for Bold Warrior's messenger," I said. "Once we have names, that will be our best place to start. Until we have names, we are just stumbling around in the dark."

Spotted Lynx shifted, uneasy. "Waiting is not action. I wish there were some way to take the offensive against these murderers."

"No," I said, "it is not action, but in this case, waiting may be necessary. Sometimes we can learn by simply waiting and watching as events unfold. If we act rashly, we might make a mistake. It is better to be cautious until we have more facts."

Gray Crane looked north across the creek. "There is another Temple," he said, pointing with his chin. "Across the water, near the North Plaza.

They are not high-ranking Priests, but they are the closest Temple to where the murders took place. They might have heard whispers."

"That seems reasonable," I agreed. "Speak with them after we are finished at the High Temple. We should explore all possibilities before Bold Warrior's messenger arrives."

Spotted Lynx crossed his arms. "I still believe that the fewer who hear of this, the better. Muskrat Waits is already furious that word is stirring through the immigrant quarter."

"Allies are not the same as gossip," Gray Crane replied softly.

I raised a hand, and they stopped.

"We walk two paths," I said. "A path of caution, and a path of inquiry. There must be a balance. If we walk the paths successfully, we will succeed. If we do not, more people will die—maybe we will die—and our way of life is in danger. We must be clever and cautious, but we must continue to investigate here in Cahokia until the messenger arrives."

Both nodded.

The three of us walked back together, but Spotted Lynx slowed his pace as we approached my household. Walks in Water sat under the ramada, mending a torn storage sack, and she instantly brightened when she saw him. He smiled — not mockingly, not arrogantly — but with open fondness.

Whispering Doe glanced between them with that unreadable expression women use when measuring futures not yet spoken aloud.

I thanked the two young men for their efforts and wished them a restful night, though I doubted any of us would sleep peacefully, knowing what secrets the night concealed. When they departed, Whispering Doe sat beside me near the fire.

"What have you learned?" she asked.

"That beneath Cahokia's beauty lies a shadow deeper than we feared."

She did not look frightened. Whispering Doe believed in survival, not avoidance.

"And tomorrow?" she asked.

"Tomorrow," I said, "we confront the Priesthood itself."

She placed her hand over mine and squeezed.

"You will speak wisely," she said. "But remember, men of power hear only what does not threaten their pride. Or their position. The Lord High Priest is dangerous."

We did not speak further about the danger because discussing it for too long could make it real.

Instead, Whispering Doe gathered our children and extended kin for fire-side stories. I was tired, but I still managed to tell a short tale about the five Great Spirits fashioned by the Creator's own hands, sent to earth to make the world safe for humans, who the Spirits call the two-legged-walkers.

"The first spirit sent to the Middle World by the Creator—Earthmaker, Mą'ųna—was Trickster, Wakjąkaga," I began. "Earthmaker hoped Trickster would guide the people, but Trickster was too foolish and unruly. His mischief brought more harm than good, so Earthmaker eventually recalled him to the Above World.

"Next, Earthmaker sent Bladder, Watexuga, down among the people. But Bladder was arrogant, proud of having come from the Above World. Through his carelessness, he lost all but one of his twenty brothers. Because of his vanity and folly, he too was summoned back.

"Then Earthmaker shaped Turtle—Kecągega—and charged him with teaching humans how to live correctly. Turtle worked hard and taught much, but he also brought warfare into the world. So Earthmaker withdrew him as well.

"Finally, the Creator sent Hare, Wašjigega. Hare fought and defeated the dangerous spirits who preyed upon the two-legged walkers. Yet even he made a grave mistake, for it was through Hare that death first came into the world. To redeem himself, Hare created the Medicine Lodges, whose teachings allow their followers to overcome death and achieve immortality. The Medicine Lodges of the Above World are reflected here in our own Clan Shrine Houses, standing in the Middle World as their earthly forms.

"Earthmaker placed Hare in charge of this world, and to each of the three other spirits, he granted a paradise to rule in the spirit realm.

"But Earthmaker sent down one more son—He-Who-Wears-Human-Heads-as-Earrings, also called Red Horn. He walked through the settlements, speaking to the people and trying to guide them. Yet whenever anyone looked at him, the little living faces hanging from his ears would wink, grin, or make silly expressions. The people became so distracted by the tiny heads' antics that they ignored his teachings entirely. In the end, even Red Horn could not complete his task."

Later that night, after the embers were raked and the children nestled into furs, Whispering Doe and I lay beneath the ramada. Smoke drifted gently beside us, keeping mosquitoes and spirits at bay. Above, the sky glimmered with stars — the path through the stars faintly visible, the direction through which the newly-deceased seek the land of the dead.

She whispered, "What will you do if this task grows darker than expected?"

"I will do my duty," I answered.

"And if that duty costs you your life?"

"Then I can only hope that I have done enough to save the copper concession, and my family will continue to prosper. Then I can follow the Path of Souls through the stars to the Land of the Dead, and live in honor with my ancestors, and my children can remember I tried my best."

She turned toward me in the dim glow.

"I do not want a heroic memory," she said. "I want a living husband."

Her words settled deeper than any prayer.

We spoke quietly until fatigue softened our voices. She asked one final question before sleep claimed her:

"Do you trust the men who walk with you?"

I stared at the night sky, remembering Muskrat Waits' final smile, Spotted Lynx's unsettled loyalty, and Gray Crane's earnest devotion.

"I do not know yet," I said.

"That is not good."

"No, it is not."

I closed my eyes.

"I need to finish this before the darkness spreads," I said

A long silence followed. Then the wind shifted, carrying the faint scent of rain from the west — perhaps a storm approaching, perhaps only wind. I knew a different kind of storm was gathering long before clouds appeared on the horizon.

Tomorrow, the High Temple. Tomorrow, hopefully, some answers — or more walls. Tomorrow, a step deeper into the unseen.

I finally slept, but lightly, like a man who suspects his dreams may soon become indistinguishable from his waking life.

Chapter 10

My companions—yes, that was how I had begun to think of them, for better or worse—arrived at my house shortly after sunrise the next morning. Whispering Doe and Walks in Water were already up, working over the hearth, tending the fire with the quiet confidence of women who ran a household like a battlefield. By the time I stirred from my sleeping furs, Dancing Copperhead had already left for the copper works, and Willow Tree had vanished into the East Plaza to chase other children. It warmed me to see him so carefree, still untouched by the fear that had begun to creep through the Valley of Cahokia like a morning fog.

Gray Crane sat cross-legged near the cooking fire, speaking politely with Whispering Doe, who seemed to enjoy the young Priest's gentle manner. Spotted Lynx, for his part, had positioned himself beside Walks in Water, leaning in with that confident smile of his. My daughter giggled at something he said. I did not like how comfortable he was making himself in my home, but Whispering Doe seemed unbothered—a fact that bothered me twice as much.

Still groggy, I threw on my breechcloth and then joined the others near the hearth. Whispering Doe handed me a plate of maize cakes drizzled with honey and a cup of warm sassafras tea, also sweetened with honey. I devoured the meal quickly. My appetite had returned with the sunrise, although my humor had not.

Once I finished eating, I pushed myself to my feet, already weary at the thought of speaking to the Lord High Priest. I was not looking forward to the encounter. "Time to go," I told the two younger men. "The sooner we anger the Lord High Priest, the sooner we can leave."

Gray Crane rose immediately. Spotted Lynx lingered, whispering something to Walks in Water that made her blush. Whispering Doe shot me a knowing look—one part warning, one part amusement—as we set off toward the Sacred Way.

I took us around the eastern edge of the East Plaza again to avoid passing the copper workshop. I did not need more eyes asking where I had been or why two strangers shadowed my every movement. As we walked, I spotted Willow Tree chasing a girl with a stick near the World Tree Pole in the center of the East Plaza. The sight made me smile. It reminded me of the first time I saw his mother, so many cycles of the seasons ago—when the old East Plaza was still alive, and the world felt simpler. I looked to the top of the Deer Clan Shrine House to see if I could spot my Uncle Rattlesnake, but he was nowhere to be seen.

We stepped onto the Sacred Way, its packed clay surface warm already beneath the rising sun. The stockade loomed before us—a tall wall of logs, each the height of five men. The guard nodded as we passed. Once through the gate, the Sacred Precinct opened like a great bowl around us.

Slightly to the left, across the vast sweep of the Grand Plaza, stood the High Temple Mound.

The Great Pyramid towered to our right, casting a long shadow across the plaza. I could not help but wonder if Muskrat Waits watched us from his perch on the first terrace, hawk-eyed and hungry for information. I looked but saw no sign of him.

We followed the Sacred Way to the far end of the plaza and turned left toward the High Temple. The mound was massive—smaller than the Great Pyramid, yes, but far larger than most other mounds in Cahokia. It stood as the beating heart of the Middle World, balanced between the Great Pyramid of the Above World and the charnel house of the Below World. The Priests would say the alignment preserved cosmic harmony. I suspected it also preserved Priestly influence.

A guard in a cape of woven turkey feathers barred our way at the base of the ramp. Spotted Lynx introduced us and showed him Muskrat Waits' parchment. The guard grimaced, then told us to wait while he consulted his superior. After a while, the guard returned with another, older Priest.

The old man addressed Spotted Lynx.

"You wish to see the Lord High Priest, is that correct?"

Spotted Lynx nodded.

"The Lord High Priest is not in the habit of granting audiences to anyone not of the Priestly Class. This seal you have is sufficient to allow you to pass through many parts of the Sun King's domains, restricted to most people, I am sure, but…"

"What is your name?" Spotted Lynx asked in a threatening tone.

"My name?" replied the old Priest.

"Yes, your name. When I tell the Sun King's Minister of Security—not a nice man, as I am sure you have heard—I want to be able to tell him who obstructed our investigation and defied his seal so that he will not garrot the wrong man."

All of the color drained from the Priest's face.

"Your name?" Spotted Lynx asked again.

Without saying a word to my companions and me, the Priest stepped aside after sending a runner up the ramp to alert his master.

The climb was steep. My knees protested with every step. I envied the nobility their ceremonial privilege of being carried in litters. When at last we reached the summit, the wind hit us, cool and sharp, carrying scents from the whole of Cahokia—the smoke of cookfires, the river's moisture, the sweat of thousands moving through the morning's commerce.

Below us, the Grand Plaza teemed with life. Traders opened stalls. I could see one of my workers laying out copper artifacts on a blanket. Pilgrims haggled over pottery and carved shells. Boys rolled their chunkey stones and hurled spears with the bright-eyed frenzy of youth. Old men gambled fortunes on the outcomes of the games.

Ah, chunkey. Few things stirred my heart like that game. As I watched the young men below, I felt a pang of longing. It had been many cycles of the seasons since I had played. I was always so busy. Perhaps, when this dreadful business was finished, I would find my old chunkey stones and spears and teach Willow Tree how to play the game.

We stepped beneath a ramada beside one of the summit buildings. The Lord High Priest sat on a carved wooden chair, speaking to a richly dressed man—Beaver Clan, judging from his facial tattoo. The two ignored our group. Once finished with their conversation, the Noble did not even glance at us as he left the Temple Mound.

When the attendant whispered in the Lord High Priest's ear, the old man looked at us with irritation—as if we were mice scurrying into his granary.

He was older than I expected. His hair had gone mostly gray, and wrinkles sagged across his chest and arms. He wore copper in excess—ear spools, arm bands, a falcon pendant, tubes threading the feathers of his headdress. His tattoos marked him as a member of the Sun Family, though age had blurred them.

His gaze was sharp enough to slice a man in half.

"I see you admiring your work, coppersmith," he said, smirking.

"It is an honor to see it worn, Lord High Priest," I replied, bowing my head. His contempt slithered over my skin like cold water.

"Well," he sighed, "say what you came to say. Muskrat Waits sent you, so I cannot ignore you. But do not expect me to waste my morning entertaining a merchant, a soldier, and a Priest so young he barely knows the color of smoke."

Gray Crane flinched. Spotted Lynx tensed like a bowstring. I steadied myself and spoke.

"My Lord High Priest, there have been murders among the immigrant farmers near Deer Toes Lake Town. The bodies were defiled, left in the open for everyone to see. Fear spreads through the immigrant households to the north of Cahokia. Muskrat Waits believes this fear may bring instability. He tasked me with uncovering the murderers. Your Priests are everywhere in the kingdom, and I was hoping they might have heard something."

He studied me for a long moment. Then, surprisingly, his tone softened slightly.

"Yes. My Priests did mention the matter. I dismissed it as a local squabble. But if Muskrat Waits fears instability..." He tapped his copper pendant thoughtfully. "Tell me what you have learned."

I recounted our journey—my vision—though I did not tell him the details: the sweat lodge, the purification, Singing Mountain's cryptic insights, the interviews with Blue Wolf and Chief Running Deer, and our meeting with Bold Warrior.

The Lord High Priest scowled. "So you have traveled over a good portion of greater Cahokia, talked to several important people, wasted several sunrises, and yet know almost nothing that will help you find the murderers?" Although true, the words sounded accusatory.

"That is correct, Lord High Priest. That is why we have come to you, hoping one of your Priests might have heard something that will help us solve this mystery."

He sighed through his nose. "No, I have not heard anything that might help you."

The Lord High Priest thought for several heartbeats before continuing. "The immigrants are... difficult. Many still cling to their old beliefs. They say they came to be near Morning Star's blessing, but they do not attend Temple ceremonies. They keep to themselves. My Priests have little influence among such people."

"Blue Wolf told us the same," I noted.

"Yes. Yes." The Lord High Priest waved a hand, already dismissing the issue. "If Muskrat Waits insists, speak with my Priests. Some of them might have information that has not reached me yet. But I have nothing more to give you. You may go."

He flicked his fingers toward us. A dismissal. A command. A reminder of our insignificance. I thought perhaps the Noble Clans teach their sons the art of dismissing commoners. The Lord High Priest must practice that skill; he was very good.

We descended the ramp in silence.

Only when we reached the bottom did Spotted Lynx let out the breath he had been holding. "You sure took that well," I joked. "I thought you might do or say something foolish.."

He glared at me. Gray Crane, still pale, muttered, "I thought he was going to have us thrown off the mound."

With nothing else to do until Bold Warrior's messenger arrived, we headed back to my house.

When we reached the Black Bear Clan Common, Whispering Doe and Walks in Water were preparing a midday meal of fresh greens and sunflower seed bread.

I asked Whispering Doe if she had seen a messenger from Bold Warrior, but she had not.

Willow Tree scurried in, breathless, eager to pepper Spotted Lynx with questions about Warriors. Gray Crane tried to interest him in the ways of the Priesthood, but Willow Tree only wanted to know how many men Spotted Lynx had killed in battle.

The young captain answered him gently, even playfully, wrestling with him on the packed earth until Willow Tree squealed with laughter.

After we ate, we sat under the ramada discussing what to do next. But none of us had an idea. Without the victims' identities, the investigation was stuck in the mud.

Gray Crane announced he would visit some of the local Temples, then the North Plaza Temple, before evening. Spotted Lynx declared he would escort Walks in Water to the Grand Plaza market, no doubt pretending to carry her baskets to impress her.

I reminded him—perhaps with more sharply than necessary—that Muskrat Waits had ordered him to observe the mood of the Warriors as well. He shrugged, as if the Minister's orders were merely... suggestions.

81

"I will go to the barracks after I see Walks in Water safely home from the market," he announced.

The girl had been to the Grand Plaza market and back safely hundreds of times without Spotted Lynx's protection, but I decided not to argue.

With nothing else to do at the moment, I entered the house and retrieved my old chunkey spear and discoidal stone. Inspired by the young man playing chunkey in the Grand Plaza, I decided to see how well I could still play. The Black Bear Clan Common was far from ideal, but it would serve as a practice chunkey court. My body remembered the movements even if my muscles complained.

For practice, I ran several steps and rolled the discoidal stone underhand across the packed earth. Shifting the spear into my throwing hand, I ran a few strides more and cast it toward the place where I judged the stone would come to rest. At first, my throws went wide, the spear striking the ground well before or beyond its mark. But with repetition, the old rhythms returned. My steps grew surer, my timing sharper, and soon the spear began to land where I intended.

Red Bud soon toddled over, her cheeks as red as ever, clapping and cheering with all the enthusiasm a girl of three cycles of the seasons could muster. I showed her how to roll the chunkey stone, and she eagerly joined in my practice, taking her role very seriously. According to her, I was the greatest chunkey player who had ever lived—though, admittedly, the only other players she had ever seen were small boys practicing in the East Plaza.

Nevertheless, I had to admit, her encouragement helped.

But my stamina was not what it used to be. I played until sweat rolled off my hot skin and soaked my breechcloth. Exhaustion overtook me, and my throws became more erratic. At last, I put away the chunkey stone, sat heavily under the ramada, took a drink of cool water from the ceramic water pot, and settled Red Bud on my lap. I told her the stories of Red Horn and the Hero Twins—my voice drifting, soft as the breeze.

At some point, my head leaned back, my words trailed off, and my eyes closed.

For a few heartbeats—or perhaps longer—I slept in my chair, Red Bud curled against my chest, the world momentarily free of murder, politics, and the dangerous games of powerful men.

Chapter 11

Whispering Doe woke me at sunrise the next morning.

"There is a young man here to see you," she said, gently nudging my shoulder.

I rubbed the sleep from my eyes, rolled out of my furs, and reached for the pot she had thoughtfully left by our pallet. After making water, I tied on my breechcloth and stepped out toward the cooking fire.

A young man I did not recognize sat cross-legged near the hearth, calmly eating hot maize cakes as if he had been born in our common. It seemed I was feeding half of Cahokia these days.

He finished chewing, swallowed, and looked up at me. "My name is Green Heron. Are you the coppersmith Walking Stick?"

I nodded. "I am."

"I am to tell you that Bold Warrior found several families who are missing family members," he said. "He sent me to show you where those families live, to be your guide and translator if necessary."

At last, something solid, some information we could use. No more inaction.

"Good," I said. "As soon as my companions arrive, you can lead us to the families."

I lowered myself to my usual chair by the fire. Whispering Doe handed me a plate of maize cakes drizzled with honey and a cup of warm sassafras tea. I had not taken two bites when I heard footsteps in the common.

Right on cue.

Spotted Lynx appeared first, as predictable as a crow at a feast. Walks in Water all but flew to the fire, snatching maize cakes off the hot stones and piling them on a plate in front of him. A moment later, Gray Crane slipped into the circle quietly, offered a polite greeting to Whispering Doe, and sat near the edge of the ramada.

Willow Tree emerged from his sleeping furs under the ramada, hair sticking up in wild tufts, still blinking the sleep from his eyes. As soon as he saw Spotted Lynx, he broke into a grin and slid in beside him, claiming his share of cakes.

Four hungry men and a boy, five cycles of the seasons kept the women busy. Each time a maize cake finished cooking, Whispering Doe or Walks in Water used a stick to flip it off the hot stones and pass it to whichever male hand was first held out. By the time we finished, the air smelled of scorched meal, woodsmoke, and honey. After the hearty breakfast and good news, I felt ready for the challenge ahead.

I noticed Dancing Copperhead had already left for the copper works. I had seen little of my middle son the last few sunrises. His brother had the copper works to keep him busy, and I had been spending most of my time with other young men. I worried that he felt excluded. I would have to speak with him when I returned.

When the others finally finished devouring Whispering Doe's maize cakes, I sent Willow Tree off to play in the East Plaza and motioned for them to gather around me. Green Heron set aside his plate and shifted closer.

"All right, Green Heron," I said. "Tell us what Bold Warrior found."

"He located five families with missing members," Green Heron began. "All of them are immigrant families. It was not easy. Bold Warrior knew the families would not speak openly, especially if they feared Cahokian officials. His men could not approach them directly. But he knows the people the immigrants trust—not Priests, and not officials of the Sun King's government. Local leaders. Elders. Those people told him which households had lost someone."

"And you can guide us to these families?" I asked.

He nodded.

"Are you One Who Remembers?" I added.

He nodded again, more firmly this time.

The *Hiperes Jinak*—the Ones Who Remember—are trained from childhood to listen, observe, and memorize words. Some serve as messengers, carrying spoken instructions along the great rivers and roads, repeating them later without a single word misplaced. Others guard the long memories of Clans or the Sun King's officials, preserving genealogies, tribute accounts, and agreements between city leaders.

They differ from the *Woorak Horak*, the Storytellers. The Storytellers keep our epics: the deeds of Red Horn, Old-Woman-Who-Never-Dies, First Man, and the Hero Twins. They recite and perform our sagas in plazas and Temple courtyards, training young storytellers to take their place. They also serve the Sun King. Instead of sending armies to conquer distant lands, the Sun King sends his *Woorak Horak*, who carry tales of Cahokia's greatness and Morning Star's blessing to foreign cities. In that way, stories,

84

rituals, and song stretch our influence as surely as spears and war clubs ever could.

The Ones Who Remember deal in precise facts. The Storytellers deal in meaning. Both are powerful in their own ways.

"Bold Warrior told me the names of the missing people," Green Heron continued, "and how to find their families. I will take you there. But you must be careful. If you are too forceful, they will close their doors and their mouths."

At last, a path forward.

"All right," I said, turning to Spotted Lynx and Gray Crane. "Gather what you need to be gone for several sunrises. I will ask Whispering Doe to pack my traveling bag and some food. We will want to be on the road before the sun is too high."

Green Heron frowned. "I do not think you will need to stay away from home overnight," he said.

"It will take longer than a day to question five families," I replied. "And it is a morning's walk to Deer Toes Lake Town. Just going and coming back is almost a full day, even if we speak to no one. We will be gone several sunrises."

Green Heron shook his head. "The missing people did not live near Deer Toes Lake Town."

"What?" I stared at him. Spotted Lynx and Gray Crane looked equally confused. "The bodies were found along the road near Deer Toes Lake Town."

"That is true," Green Heron said. "But that is not where the missing people lived. That is not where I am taking you."

My head began to ache. "Then where are you taking us?"

He pointed vaguely north. "The missing people farmed the land just beyond the common fields worked by your Cahokian Clans. On the far side of your wives' and daughters' fields."

For a heartbeat, I could not breathe.

My wife's Black Bear Clan tended plots in those common fields north of the city and east of Cahokia Creek. Whispering Doe and my daughters worked there almost every day during the growing season.

"That cannot be," I whispered. "Whispering Doe and my girls are in those fields nearly every sunrise. You are telling me the murdered farmers lived beside the very lands where they work?"

85

Green Heron nodded. "That is what Bold Warrior told me."

My stomach twisted. I thought of Whispering Doe, walking the rows with her hoe; of Walks in Water and our older daughter, Passing Doe, weeding and harvesting squash, laughing with other women, children running between the mounds of earth.

"If that is true," I said slowly, "then whoever killed those farmers—and it must be more than one person—dragged their bodies away from the edge of Cahokia and carried them to Deer Toes Lake Town. A half-sunrise walk. Why move them so far?"

Green Heron spread his hands. "I do not know, Walking Stick. I only know what Bold Warrior learned, and where the missing people lived."

Behind my ribs, my heart pounded. Part of me wanted to sit down and never leave my family again, to tell Muskrat Waits to do his worst; another part wanted to run north immediately and confront the families of the murder victims and demand they tell us how to find the killers.

I exhaled slowly. "All right. We might as well get started. Lead the way, Green Heron."

Whispering Doe appeared with my ceramic water bottle. I took it from her, then reached into the small chest where I kept scrap copper and slipped several small pieces into a pouch on my belt. Copper could buy many things on short notice—information, food, a bribe, or silence.

Before we left, I caught Whispering Doe's eye and jerked my head toward the back of the house. She followed me behind the wall, away from the others.

"I do not want you working in the Black Bear common fields," I said quietly. "Not until I tell you it is safe."

She frowned. "The maize will ripen within the next moon cycle. We must keep the weeds down. And some of the squash is already ripe for picking. If it grows too big, it will be too tough to eat."

"I do not care about the squash," I said. "Listen to me." I stepped closer so only she could hear. "The murdered farmers lived and worked just north and west of your fields. Perhaps only a few hundred steps away."

The color drained from her face. "That close?"

"Yes."

Her eyes darted toward the north, as if she could see through the houses, through the trees, across Cahokia Creek to those fields. "That is only a short walk from where we work."

"Exactly. That is why you will stay away from those fields until I say otherwise. You are the Clan Matriarch. Do not tell the others why, but order all the Black Bear women to stay away from the common fields for now. Think of an excuse—a pest problem, a curse on the fields, anything you like. Just keep them away."

She swallowed hard. For the first time since this whole business began, I saw real, raw fear in her eyes. It angered me more than anything Muskrat Waits had said. Fear did not belong in my wife's eyes.

"This is bad, is it not, Walking Stick?" she asked quietly.

"Yes," I admitted. "It was bad before. Now it is worse. So far, they have killed only immigrants. I do not know why they are targeting them, but they are. I do not think they will attack Clan women working together in the open—too risky, too visible. But I will feel better if you stay near home until we catch whoever is doing this."

She nodded slowly, jaw tightening as she regained control. "I will do as you say. I will think of something to tell the women."

Just then, Willow Tree dashed into the Black Bear Clan Common, breathless from running. I called him over.

"Yes, Father?" he panted.

"I want you to run to the copper works," I said. "Tell Dancing Copperhead I must see him immediately. Tell Red Hawk that Dancing Copperhead will not be at the shop for the next few sunrises. Remember those words."

Willow Tree repeated the message, then sprinted away again, legs pumping, hair flying. For such a small boy, he ran like a deer.

"I am leaving Dancing Copperhead here with you until we catch the murderers," I told Whispering Doe. It appeared that I would have that talk with my middle son sooner than I expected.

Dancing Copperhead soon appeared, jogging into the common with a worried look on his face. "What is wrong, Father?"

"I want you to fetch your bow and arrows from the house," I said. "String your bow and keep it strung. Do not leave the Clan common unless I say so. Watch everyone and everything. I do not want strangers wandering in here. If you see anyone you do not recognize, confront them, and tell your mother and tell me when I return. Is that clear?"

His expression tightened. "Yes, Father. I will do as you say. But what has happened?"

I hesitated, then decided he had earned the truth. "There have been several murders near the Black Bear common fields—just beyond them, in the immigrant plots. I do not think we are in immediate danger here, but we must be cautious. I am asking you to guard your mother, your sisters, and your aunts. You are old enough to do that."

He straightened, shoulders squaring. "I will protect them," he said. "No strangers will walk into this common without my seeing them."

He turned and ran toward the house, already retrieving his bow.

I faced Whispering Doe again. "I will be back tonight, if all goes well," I said. "And I intend to have Spotted Lynx, Gray Crane, and Green Heron sleep here, in the Black Bear Clan Common, until we catch whoever is doing this. Extra eyes and weapons will not hurt."

A small, mischievous smile tugged at her mouth. "That will make Walks in Water happy," she said.

"Yes, well." I grimaced. "When this is over, you and I need to talk about that."

She only smiled wider, as if she knew something I did not. Then she reached out, squeezed my arm once, hard, and turned back toward the hearth to start issuing orders.

I watched her for a heartbeat—the Black Bear Clan Matriarch, my wife, my anchor—and then I turned to follow Green Heron, Spotted Lynx, and Gray Crane toward the canoe landing at Cahokia Creek and the fields where death had been walking, unseen, just beyond the edges of our lives.

* * *

She stood just inside the doorway of her house, half-hidden in the shadows, watching as the men finished their morning meal. Her eyes followed them as they stepped out of the Black Bear Clan Common and started down the path toward the canoe landing, their voices low, their movements purposeful. Where were they going? What business drew them away from the city, and why did no one in the Black Bear Clan know their purpose?

She intended to find out—and hopefully use them to further her plans, and put a stop to theirs.

Chapter 12

We left the Black Bear Clan Common and headed for the canoe landing on Cahokia Creek, following a well-worn trail of packed earth past other Clan common areas. The morning air was already warm, thick with the smell of damp soil and woodsmoke drifting from cook fires. Somewhere behind us, in the direction of the common fields, I could hear women singing as they hoed the rows of maize—a sound I suddenly heard with new unease.

We entered an open area between house compounds and Cahokia Creek, passing the backs of workshops where men were already shaping clay, chipping stone, and twisting cordage. The trail led us between a large Temple mound on our right and the towering Great Pyramid on our left. The canoe landing lay directly behind the Great Pyramid. Although not as large as the canoe landing in Traders Town, which has a larger canoe landing and dozens of warehouses near the Messipi, the canoe landing at Cahokia is always busy.

The landing was its usual chaos when we arrived. Traders were clustering along the bank like ducks along a log, shouting, laughing, cursing. Their huge trade canoes bumped and slewed against one another as men and women loaded and unloaded bundles of hides, sacks of shell-temper, baskets of dried fish, fragrant bales of tobacco, and herbs. The air smelled of wet wood, mud, and sweat, overlaid with whiffs of bear grease and smoked meat. A pair of young men argued over whose turn it was to unload a cargo of chert nodules. A dog wove through the crowd, tail bobbing.

Our family canoe was gone, still somewhere downriver along the Messipi on a trading run. I scanned the landing and spotted a boy with a sturdy craft—big enough for our small party and still sitting high in the water.

"You there?" I called. "Do you have time for a short crossing?"

He looked up at Spotted Lynx first, as most boys do when there is a Warrior present, then at me. "Across the creek?"

"Yes," I said. "Four of us."

He grinned. "I can take you—if you can afford a real boat." He ducked the mock-slap Spotted Lynx aimed at his head and laughed.

I fished in the small pouch at my belt and flipped him a thumb-sized scrap of hammered copper. His eyes went wide, and he snatched it from the air.

"Get in!" he said eagerly.

We stepped carefully into the canoe, settling our weight while the boy pushed off with his paddle. Cahokia Creek was not wide, but here, near the Sacred Precinct, the banks were steep, and the water was deep enough to float even the largest trading craft. The paddle bit into the smooth brown surface; little whirlpools spun out and drifted away. Behind us, the Great Pyramid loomed higher and higher as we moved toward the far bank, its terraces stepping up toward the sky where Morning Star rose in glory every dawn.

The crossing took only a few dozen heartbeats. The boy beached us neatly against the northern shore. As we climbed out, he held the copper between finger and thumb and said, with what he probably thought was adult dignity, "If you need to come back, look for me. I am here most sunrises."

"We will remember," I said.

* * *

On the north bank, the ground rose gently into the North Plaza, one of the five great open spaces that frame the great city. It was not the grandest—that honor belonged to the massive Grand Plaza in front of the Great Pyramid—but it was still a formal space, bounded by a few low mounds and scattered houses. Compared to the glittering chaos south of the creek, the North Plaza always felt quieter. Separated from the city by Cahokia Creek, the North Plaza lived in the city's shadow rather than its heart.

From here, the Great Pyramid's bulk reared above us, but what we saw was its backside: the steep packed-clay slope of its northern face, without the busy terraces and ramadas of the southern side. It did indeed look as if it had turned its back on the people who lived up here. A petty thought, perhaps, but one I suspected many northerners had entertained as they gazed across the water at the Sun King's house and his private world of Priests and Nobles.

From the landing, we picked up the road that led north toward North Star Town. It cut straight through the plaza, a hard-packed track worn by generations of feet roaming the Valley of Cahokia's alluvial soils. About a hundred steps north of the plaza, we passed a low mound topped by a modest Temple—nothing like the High Temple across the creek, but still a proper house for the spirits. The Temple was solidly built in the familiar wattle and daub style, its walls carefully finished. Above the doorway hung a large Underwater Panther mask, its fierce presence looming over the North Plaza community.

"Is this the Temple you visited yesterday?" I asked Gray Crane.

He shook his head. "I did not make it over here," he said. "Talking with the other Priests took more time than I had hoped. You know how Priests like to talk." He grinned, then added, "And there was no easy way to cross the creek. By the time I could have found a canoe willing to take a poor Priest across, spoken to the Priests here, and gone back, it would have been long after dark. Another day."

"Yes, everyone knows how much Priests like to talk," I said.

"And they have nothing to trade," Spotted Lynx snorted.

While we spoke, the houses thinned around us. We passed through a small village where a few Cahokian Clan families had their homes just outside the city: a cluster of houses, storage racks, and little mounds, all tied by kinship and common fields. Beyond those lay the broader patchwork of Clan common lands, including the Black Bear Clan Common fields to the east of Cahokia Creek, where my wife and daughters spent so many days together, shoulders bent, hands in the dirt. I looked toward them as we walked past and felt the twist of unease in my belly again. The singing I had heard earlier came unbidden to my mind.

Ahead of us, the world opened. Hundreds of small farmsteads spread across the floodplain like beads strung on invisible cords, stretching all the way toward North Star Town and beyond. Each little holding was a universe of its own: a house or two, a storage pit, perhaps a small granary, surrounded by maize, squash, and sunflowers. Many of these farms belonged to immigrants who had come to Cahokia seeking land, peace, and the blessings of Morning Star.

"Here," Green Heron said shortly after we passed the common fields. He led us off the main road along a narrower path that threaded through stands of ripening maize and towering sunflowers. We walked between rows of squash vines, their broad leaves brushing our legs, until a small house came into view.

* * *

The house, by Cahokian standards, was barely more than a hut—four steps long, two steps wide, with a simple ramada leaned against one side for shade. At a glance, it looked like any other home: its floor cut below the ground surface for warmth in winter and coolness in summer; its walls formed of upright wooden posts with saplings woven between them, all plastered with clay and chopped grass; its steep roof of thatched prairie grass shedding rain.

Still, something about it made my skin prickle.

No smoke curled from the little hearth in front of the house. No tools lay scattered near the doorway, no children's toys, no basket of maize ears waiting to be husked. The ramada's shade was empty. The silence around the place felt wrong, as if the air itself were holding its breath.

"Wait," I said. I stepped up to the doorway and peered inside. The interior was dim, so I let my eyes adjust for several heartbeats, and then crouched, looking more carefully at the line where earth met wood.

"Look at this," I said. "Here, where the posts meet the ground."

Spotted Lynx crouched beside me. "I see it," he said. "Each post is set in its own hole, and the saplings are woven in afterward. That is the way my parents built their first house, back before they knew better. Once it began to rot, we rebuilt with trench walls in the Cahokian style."

He straightened and looked around. "These people have seen how Cahokian homes are built. Why build in the old, slow, inefficient way?"

When Morning Star returned to the Middle World and blessed our city, the Priests and builders said the spirits taught us better ways to build. The new way was simple: dig a narrow trench around the house's footprint, build each wall as a single frame elsewhere, and drop it into the trench when ready. Faster, stronger, easier to repair. For more than a hundred cycles of the seasons, all proper Cahokians had built this way.

Yet this house, almost in the shadow of the city, clung to the older pattern like a memory that refused to fade.

"There is no one here," Green Heron said quietly. He had been looking, nose wrinkled, at the cold hearth and the floor. "No fresh tracks, no new ash. It has been empty for several sunrises."

Spotted Lynx nodded once. "He is right. The place is deserted."

Gray Crane stood just outside the doorway, arms folded as if he were cold despite the heat. "You can feel it," he said softly. "Homes hold the breath of the living. This one is empty. Their spirits have gone."

"Who lived here?" I asked Green Heron.

"A man named Black Locust," he replied. "His wife, Blue Petal. Their children. His parents, too. Black Locust is one of the men Bold Warrior believes may be among the murdered."

"His parents lived here?" I asked. That certainly was odd.

In Cahokia, a man marries into his wife's clan. When I wed Whispering Doe, I moved into the Black Bear compound to live under her mother's authority. Our children belong to Black Bear Clan, not my Deer Clan. When Red Hawk took Morning Dove as his wife, he went to live among her Sky kin; their children will be Sky Clan. When Passing Doe married Bear Claws, he moved into the house next to ours, under the eyes of Whispering Doe and her sister. That is how it has always been, as the myths say, First Man and Old-Woman-Who-Never-Dies set it down. For a man's parents to live with him in his wife's house was unusual.

Gray Crane answered the question on my face. "Many immigrants keep the ways they learned from their ancestors," he said. "Including tracing descent through the father. Even after they move to Cahokia, they pray to Morning Star and live in our lands, but their spirits still walk in the old paths."

"Where was this family from?" I asked Green Heron.

"From Waapaahshiiki country," he said. "Far to the east."

Spotted Lynx flinched as if stung. "That is where my parents came from," he said quietly. "Before they settled in the valley of the Wide Muddy. Black Locust's kin might be my own."

"Your family followed the father's line?" I asked.

"Yes," he said. "My parents taught my brother and sisters and me the names of our grandfathers and great-grandfathers, all the way back as far as they could remember. I never saw those elders; I only knew them as stories. When my parents came to Cahokia, they changed. They said we would live as Cahokians do, and that is how they raised my siblings and me: my brother went to live with his wife's family when he married, while my sister's husband came to live with my parents. Perhaps one day we will join other immigrants and form a true Clan."

I thought that was unlikely—forming a Clan is not like starting a new craft stall in the market—but there was no kindness in saying so aloud.

We were still looking around the silent little farmstead when Spotted Lynx suddenly turned his head like a hunting dog catching a scent and sprinted into the maize field beside the house. Stalks rustled and slapped aside in his wake. The rest of us stood blinking, startled, until the maize rustled again and Spotted Lynx emerged, one large hand clamped around the arm of an old man.

"Who is this?" I asked.

"I do not know," Spotted Lynx said. "But he was moving in the maize, watching us."

"No, no," the old man protested, pulling back against the warrior's grip. "I was not spying!"

"Let him go," I said. Spotted Lynx released him, though he did not move far away. I softened my voice. "Grandfather, who are you? And if you were not spying, what were you doing in the maize field so close to this place? Are you Black Locust's father?"

Even as I asked, I knew he was not. A faded Duck Clan tattoo marked his cheek—Cahokian through and through.

"I am not Rabbit Ears," the old man said quickly. "That is Black Locust's father. My name is Dark Ash, of the Duck Clan. I live on the other side of this field, about two hundred steps that way." He pointed east. "Black Locust's people are gone. The old couple took Blue Petal and the children and went back to where they came from."

"When did they leave?" I asked.

"Three sunsets ago," he said. "In the dark. They walked north on the road to Deer Toes Lake Town. Past the place where they say they found Black Locust. I told them they were fools to walk the road at night after what happened to him and those other men." He shivered, a twitch that went through his shoulders and jaw.

"So you know about the other murders," I stated.

"Oh yes," he replied. "Everyone knows. The talk runs faster than runners. We are all frightened. But what can we do? We are farmers."

"Did you know the family well?" I asked.

He nodded. "Rabbit Ears and I talked almost every day. He did not speak Cahokian well, but we understood each other. Two old men, our backs bent, our arms not so strong as they used to be, but our tongues still working. They were good people. They worked hard. They never caused trouble."

"Was Rabbit Ears born here?" I asked.

94

"No," Dark Ash said. "If I recall, his parents brought him as a boy from the Waapaahshiiki country."

Before I could ask my next question, Spotted Lynx spoke. "You said they never made problems," he said. "But how did they fit with the rest of the people here?"

Dark Ash understood the hidden meaning. "They were... different," he said slowly. "They kept mostly to themselves, except with a few families like their own and with me. They did not come to many rituals. They did not join in the festivals. They lived as if they still lived in the Waapaahshiiki country."

"When was the last time anyone saw Black Locust alive?" I asked, reclaiming the direction of the questioning.

Dark Ash frowned, counting in his head. "His wife told me he went to visit his sister's family late in the afternoon more than ten sunrises ago now. He ate the evening meal there and left shortly after dark to walk home. He never arrived. The next morning, Blue Petal went to look for him. When she reached the Great Northern Road, people were already running toward her with the news: a body had been found up by Deer Toes Lake Town. By the time she reached the place, the Warriors had taken it away. No one could tell her why he had gone so far north. Three moonrises later, the family left. We have heard he was butchered like an animal." Dark Ash swallowed. "Is that true?"

The stench of the Emerald Acropolis charnel house rose in my mind: the sickly-sweet rot, the sour smoke, the swarm of flies that rode every breath. I had seen Black Locust's remains without knowing his name. My gorge rose.

I did not answer the question. "Do you know of anyone else missing from this area?" I asked instead.

Dark Ash shook his head. "Not by name. I have heard talk. Families say a cousin or a brother has not been seen, but they do not speak loudly. I have heard there were more bodies found, cut up like Black Locust. People are whispering that Cahokia is cursed."

I glanced at my companions. "Anything more you want to ask him?"

Spotted Lynx said, "Do you know anyone who might have wished harm on Black Locust? Disputes over land, women, trade?"

Dark Ash shook his head. "No. As I said, he and his people were quiet. We are all farmers here. We have enough trouble with the weather, insects,

95

and weeds. We do not quarrel among ourselves if we can help it. Even though they were not of our Clan, we helped one another."

"If there are no more questions," I said, "we should move on. We have other families to visit, and I want to be home before nightfall."

Dark Ash hesitated. "Can you at least tell me who you are?" he asked. "And why do you ask these things?"

"It is safer if you do not know," I said. "Go home. Forget you saw us. And tell no one what we talked about. I speak seriously when I say that what happened to Black Locust could happen to others if the killers think they know too much, whether they do or not. Do not bring death into your house."

He swallowed again.

"But if you hear something truly important," I added, "send word to Bold Warrior at Deer Toes Lake Town. He will get the message to me."

"I will not say a word to anyone," Dark Ash said. "I promise. May I go?"

I nodded. He scurried off through the maize, shoulders hunched, not looking back.

When he was gone, I turned to the others. "We did not get to speak to Black Locust's family," I said. "But Dark Ash told us more than I expected."

"He is probably the neighborhood gossip," Spotted Lynx said dryly. "He talked plenty. We know more about the family. I am not sure we are any closer to knowing why Black Locust was killed."

"Perhaps not yet," I said. "But we have pieces now. Once we have spoken with the other families, we can see what they have in common. Patterns, if there are any, might lead us toward a reason—and to the killers."

I shaded my eyes and looked up at the sun. It already stood closer to mid-sky than I liked. "We have reached high sun and have not yet spoken to a living victim's family. We need to move. What is the next name?"

"Black Oak Tree," Green Heron said.

"How far?"

"Not far. This way."

* * *

We followed Green Heron east along a maze of narrow farm paths, angling toward Cahokia Creek again. Up here, north of the city, the creek rises from springs in the hills and cuts south through the floodplain before swinging sharply west toward the Messipi just north of Cahokia. The land rolled gently, and the fields pressed close to the water, taking advantage of the rich silts.

We found the next house, set back from the creek by about 200 steps. Like the first, it was built in the old style: individual postholes, wattle-and-daub walls, thatched roof. Unlike the first, this one was not empty. A woman sat beneath the ramada, grinding maize with a mano and metate, her shoulders working in a steady rhythm.

She looked up as we approached. Her hands stilled. At first glance, she seemed ready to bolt like a deer; her muscles tensed, her eyes fixed on Spotted Lynx's weapons and on the unknown faces of strangers.

Before she could flee, Green Heron stepped forward, hands spread. "Sister," he called in Cahokian, "do not be afraid. We are only here to talk. Please, stay."

She did not move. Her eyes flicked from him to me, and finally to Spotted Lynx. Her jaw tightened. There was no understanding in her eyes.

Spotted Lynx then stepped forward and spoke in the lilting tongue of the Waapaahshiiki Valley, the language his parents had carried with them to Cahokia. The woman's shoulders dropped a fraction. She answered in the same language.

After a brief exchange, Spotted Lynx turned back to me. "She speaks only Waapaahshiiki," he said. "Her name is Water Lilly. I told her we are here to help. She is still frightened, but willing to listen."

"Gray Crane, Green Heron—step back," I said. "Fifty steps at least. Fewer men will make her feel less cornered."

They obeyed, retreating to the edge of the clearing. I raised my empty hands and walked slowly toward Water Lilly. She stayed put, though every line of her body was coiled, ready to flee if threatened.

"Are you the wife of Black Oak Tree?" I asked, through Spotted Lynx.

Fear flickered in her eyes, but she did not run. She looked from me to Spotted Lynx, measuring us both, and after perhaps twenty heartbeats, she gave a single, tight nod.

I inclined my head, as if she had done me a favor. "We are not here to harm you," I said gently. "We are here to help if we can. My name is Walking Stick. This is Spotted Lynx. His parents came from the same country as you. The Sun King has heard that people have gone missing in his lands. He has sent us to learn what happened. Will you help us?"

She hesitated, then nodded again.

Water Lilly disappeared briefly into the house and emerged with two deer hides. She spread them neatly under the ramada and gestured for us to sit. Hospitality first, even in grief. She poured elderberry tea into two cups—her only two—and set one before each of us.

Only after this ritual of welcome was complete did I begin my questions.

"When did you last see Black Oak Tree?" I asked.

"In the afternoon, about ten sunrises ago," she said through Spotted Lynx. Her voice was level, but her hands were wound together in her lap. "He went to the fields at dawn and worked all day. He did not return for the evening meal. That had happened before, when he stayed to finish work, so at first I was not afraid. When it grew dark, and he still did not come home, I waited. I stayed awake all night. In the morning, I sent the children to look. They searched the fields. One of them found his hoe and digging stick on the path, near where he had been working. There was no sign of him."

"Was he having trouble with any neighbors?" I asked. "Did he have enemies? Have you seen any strangers near your farm?"

She shook her head. "We do not know the neighbors well," she said. "Few speak our language. We keep to ourselves. We do not bother anyone. And no one bothers us. I have not seen strangers nearby."

"Do you have family of your own close by?" Spotted Lynx asked, then translated for me.

"No," she said. "My parents live near North Star Town. Black Oak Tree came here from Waapaahshiiki about ten cycles of the seasons ago, with other young men. My mother's brother gave us this land, and we built our house here. Black Oak Tree has no kin close at hand."

"How many children do you have?" I asked.

Her face softened for the first time. "Three living," she said. "Two boys, one girl. Eight, six, and three cycles of the seasons. Strong, healthy." The word living sat between us like a stone. Whispering Doe and I had lost three babies before their naming time. Most families had.

We weren't learning much that would help us catch a murderer. I took a breath, bracing myself for the question we both knew was coming.

"Have you heard of the bodies found along the Great Northern Road near Deer Toes Lake Town?" I asked.

"Yes," she said.

Her composure was shattered. Tears welled and spilled down her cheeks; her chest hitched. She bent forward, pressing her hands against her eyes, and wept. Not the loud keening of ritual mourning, but a quieter, rawer sound. I let her cry. There are times when pressing a question is not just unkind but useless.

When the worst of it passed, she wiped her face with the heel of her hand and looked at me. "You think Black Oak Tree is one of those men," she said.

I hated Muskrat Waits in that moment, hated the way he had pushed this task onto me and sat above the city with clean hands while I carried the filth. I would rather have gone back to the Emerald Acropolis charnel house and stood among the rotting bodies than keep digging in this widow's pain. But I could not lie.

"Yes," I said. "I believe he is."

She cried again, more softly. When her tears slowed, she stood abruptly. "I have not been a good host," she said. "It is past mid-sun. You must be hungry. Let me bring food."

Spotted Lynx leaned close. "She cannot spare the food to feed us," he whispered. "Without a man to work the fields, they will struggle to raise enough to live on, let alone to sell. They will eat everything they grow this year."

"It is all right," I said. "I brought copper. I will pay her for the meal—and more, so she can face the winter."

In my belt pouch, a handful of small copper scraps chimed softly. To me, they were waste from the workshop, too small to hammer into sheets or mold into plates. To a poor farmer, they were wealth beyond imagining.

Water Lilly glanced toward the path where Gray Crane and Green Heron waited. "Ask your friends to join us," she said.

I waved them over. As they stepped into the clearing, Spotted Lynx made the introductions in Waapaahshiiki. Water Lilly's gaze fell on Gray Crane's chest, where the Birdman tattoo marked him as a Priest of the Emerald Acropolis. Her face twisted, and she recoiled as if she had seen a snake.

"What is he doing here?" she screamed, pointing at Gray Crane. "I do not want him here! I do not want that sort of Priest anywhere near my house!"

Spotted Lynx started translating the words, then realized Gray Crane did not need them; the fury in her voice was clear enough. To his credit, the young priest backed away without argument, his face pale. Green Heron followed him beyond the edge of the clearing.

When Water Lilly's breathing slowed, Spotted Lynx said gently in her language, "What is wrong? Have you ever seen a Priest with a Birdman tattoo? Have the Priests harmed you?"

"He is one of those Priests," she said bitterly.

"What Priests?" I asked.

She folded her arms tightly across her chest, staring toward the creek as if watching a memory. "A Priest came here," she said. "With Warriors. He had that same Birdman tattoo. He and the soldiers stood right where you sit now." She jabbed a finger at the ground. "He demanded to know why we do not go to the Temple rituals like the other families."

"What did Black Oak Tree tell him?" I asked.

"He said we had gone, at first," she replied. "But the rituals here are not the same as those in our homeland. The Priest did not speak our language. One of the soldiers tried to translate, but he spoke badly. Black Oak Tree told him that we honor Morning Star in our own way, in our own tongue. The Priest grew angry. He shouted that we were proud, that we thought ourselves better than other people. Then he left. He was very angry."

"Did you see him again?" I asked.

"No," she said. "He came only once."

"But the soldiers?" I pressed.

Her eyes narrowed. "They came back," she said. "Several times. They lingered on the road, watching the house. They did not speak. They did not smile."

Spotted Lynx's jaw tightened as he translated. He did not like my focus on the Warriors, but he did not soften any of my words.

"How long ago was the Priest's visit?" I asked.

"Three moon cycles," she said.

So: a Birdman-tattooed Priest from the Emerald Acropolis, accompanied by Warriors, visits an immigrant family that does not attend rituals properly. Three moon cycles later, the husband vanishes and likely turns up as a mutilated corpse along a road a long walk from his home. And in between, the Warriors keep coming back.

100

It might have been a coincidence. I did not believe in that many coincidences in a row.

Water Lilly turned back to her fire and began preparing food for us. I watched her moving among her pots and baskets and felt hunger gnaw at my own belly.

"Where are your children?" I asked.

"In the maize," she said warily. "Hiding. Do you need to see them?"

"No," I said. "If it makes you feel safer, let them stay there. We do not need to speak with them."

"I am not afraid of you now," she said, glancing toward the path where Gray Crane had disappeared. "It was the Priest's tattoo that frightened me. Call your friends back. They should eat, too."

"Thank you," I said. "The young Priest, Gray Crane, is a kind soul. Not all Priests are bad. Most do their best to bring the blessings of Morning Star to the people."

I beckoned to Gray Crane and Green Heron. They reappeared somewhat sheepishly and sat at the edge of the fire circle. Water Lilly busied herself baking maize cakes on the flat stones, handing them out as soon as they finished. They were good—crisp-edged, soft inside, with a faint smoke taste—but I still preferred Whispering Doe's, and always would.

When we were chewing steadily, Water Lilly went to the edge of the maize field and called in her language. After a moment, three naked children emerged, creeping out like little deer from cover. They sat where she pointed and accepted maize cakes in both hands, eating in silence while they stared wide-eyed at us. I doubted they saw many strangers.

As we ate, Water Lilly tossed a handful of dried nettle into a pot of water over the coals. When the tea had steeped, she poured it into a single bowl, then carefully divided it between two cups.

"We only have two," she said, embarrassed.

She handed one to me and one to Spotted Lynx. We drank, then passed them to Gray Crane and Green Heron.

When the meal was finished, and everyone's hands had been licked clean and wiped on their thighs, I sent Gray Crane and Green Heron to entertain the children as best they could. Gray Crane made little birds from blades of grass, and Green Heron demonstrated how to balance a stick on one finger. The children watched the strangers with the solemn intensity of the young.

I turned back to Water Lilly. "Is there anything else," I asked, "that seems strange to you? Anything you have seen or heard that might help us understand what happened to your husband?"

She looked down at her hands. "I do not understand any of it," she said. "Men disappear. Bodies are found. Priests and soldiers come and ask questions, then go away. I do not know why Morning Star allows this. I only know my husband is gone."

Neither did I understand, but it was my task to find out.

I reached for her right hand and took it gently in my left. She flinched, but did not pull away. With my other hand, I drew out ten small copper scraps and placed them in her palm.

Her eyes widened. Her breath caught. Her fingers closed around the metal as if it might vanish.

She started to speak, but I shook my head.

"The Sun King loves his children," I said. "Take this gift and care for yours."

I lied. The Sun King had never set eyes on this woman and could not care less about her family or their problems, but the lie served a purpose for us both.

"Take your children and go back to your parents," I went on. "If they cannot afford to feed you, show them some of the copper—some, not all. Keep the rest hidden. Black Oak Tree is dead. There is nothing for you here now but fear and hunger. Take what you can carry and leave tomorrow."

Water Lilly lowered her head. She already knew the truth; she had simply been waiting for someone to say it aloud. "You are right," she said. "I knew he was dead. But I did not want to say the words out loud. We will leave tomorrow. My parents will take us in." Then she looked up with a small, crooked, knowing smile that was more sad than glad. "And whoever gave you this copper—thank him from me, for I do not think the Sun King cares about us."

We left the little family standing beside their small house, all of them framed by the high walls of maize that had sheltered them and now would see them off. They would never return to it once they stepped onto the road away from Cahokia.

"It is time to go home," I said. "We started late after I saw to my family's security, and now we have spent the rest of the day talking to people at two farms. We are so close to Cahokia that I thought we might speak to all the families today. It will take several sunrises at this pace."

* * *

We walked in silence for a long time. The path bent and joined the Great Northern Road. No one spoke. We did not need to. The abstract notion of murdered immigrants had become two sets of very specific absences: a deserted house, an old man fretting in his neighbor's field; a widow and three children preparing to walk away from the only home they had known because their protector was now a mutilated corpse in a charnel house.

At last, I said, "Tomorrow I will go to Muskrat Waits and tell him what we have learned."

Gray Crane walked with his hands clasped behind his back, his gaze on the road. "Who commands the Warriors of Cahokia?" he asked quietly.

"The Sun King is head of the military," Spotted Lynx said immediately. "But if you mean who handles daily orders, reports, patrol routes, and punishments, that would be Muskrat Waits."

I stopped walking. The others took a few steps before realizing and turning back.

"What are you saying?" I asked Gray Crane.

He shrugged slightly. "I am only thinking aloud," he said. "At the Emerald Acropolis, we spoke of how these killings required strength, discipline, skill with weapons—things Warriors have. Now we have learned that the Warriors have been visiting at least one of the victims' families. If Warriors are involved, someone commands them."

"Red Horn save us," I muttered. A sour taste rose in my mouth. "Are you suggesting Muskrat Waits is part of this? That he is using me for some game I do not even understand?"

"That is mad," Spotted Lynx burst out. "I know Muskrat Waits is a cruel, scheming old demon, but if he were behind these murders, I would know."

We all looked at him.

Until that moment, I had mostly thought of Spotted Lynx as my shadow—sometimes a shield, sometimes a nuisance. A young War Captain with no Clan, good with a spear, too quick with his tongue, far too interested in my daughter, and occasionally helpful. But as Gray Crane's speculation hung in the air, another question rose with it: how much did my "bodyguard" really know?

Spotted Lynx saw our faces and flushed dark. "You are all insane," he shouted. "Do you really think I would spend my days slogging through fields, listening to women cry, if I were part of some plot to butcher poor farmers?"

"I do not know what to think anymore," I said. "Everyone who has ever spoken to me about Muskrat Waits has told me not to trust him. He himself told me not to trust him."

Spotted Lynx turned away and strode down the road alone, his shoulders rigid. The rest of us followed at a distance. Gray Crane's brows were drawn together in worry. Green Heron's jaw worked as if he were grinding stones between his teeth.

We walked in silence until the city's shape began to rise before us. At last, Green Heron moved up to walk beside me.

"I do not like this," he said. "Something is wrong here, Walking Stick. I do not trust that Warrior. He knows more than he says."

I chewed on that for a while before answering. "I would not be surprised if Muskrat Waits is somehow entangled in all of this," I said. "But I do not think Spotted Lynx is."

"How can you know?" Green Heron asked.

"I cannot," I said. "Not for certain. But I have spent several sunrises with him. If he were part of a scheme to mislead me, I think I would have seen some sign of deception, a hesitation when there should not be one, a question he ought already to know the answer to, some slip in his story. Instead, he has been the opposite: quick to offer help, sometimes too quick to speak, yes, but not sly. No, I believe he truly wants the killers caught."

Gray Crane, who had been listening, nodded. "I agree," he said. "I have seen nothing in him that feels false. I think he hates these murders as much as we do."

Green Heron sighed. "I hope you are right," he said. "Our lives may depend on it. Still, I will keep my eyes and ears open. Something strange is happening here."

By the time we reached the canoe landing opposite the Great Pyramid, the sun was sinking toward the western horizon. Spotted Lynx had stopped walking and was sitting on an overturned canoe, elbows on his knees, staring at the muddy water as if it might offer answers. He rose when we approached.

"I am sorry I lost my temper," he said to me.

I set my hand on his shoulder. "For what it is worth," I said, "I do not believe you are involved in these murders. Let us cross the creek and see what Whispering Doe has for our evening meal. A few maize cakes at midday are not enough to keep an old man going all day."

He caught my arm lightly to stop me before I stepped away.

"I swear to you," he said, looking me straight in the eye, "I had nothing to do with the killings. I do not know who did. But…" he hesitated, then went on, "I think Gray Crane might be right about one thing. Muskrat Waits does not care about me. He does not care about you. He cares about Cahokia—and about his power inside Cahokia. I always thought he liked me because I was a good Warrior, because I did my duty. Today, I realized he would throw me into the fire without a second thought if it served his plans. He would do the same to you. To any of us."

He glanced up at the Great Pyramid, where, on the opposite side of the mound, the Sun King's Minister of Security liked to sit beneath his ramada on the first terrace facing the Grand Plaza and watch the city.

"We need to be careful," Spotted Lynx said quietly.

"Then we agree," I replied.

Chapter 13

The evening meal was a somber affair. My companions sat around the fire like men who had walked too far and seen too much. No one had much to say. Spotted Lynx was so lost in his thoughts that he did not flatter Whispering Doe's cooking or flirt with Walks in Water. Green Heron sat a little apart from the others, shoulders hunched, staring into his bowl as if he might find answers in the stew.

My family felt the change. Whispering Doe and Walks in Water exchanged quiet glances but did not press us with questions. Even Red Bud, usually a chattering little jay, hovered near Whispering Doe's side without singing out. Only Willow Tree behaved as usual, poking at Spotted Lynx, tugging at his arm, demanding to hear again the story of how a single Warrior could hold a ford against ten enemies. Spotted Lynx roused himself enough to wrestle the boy in the dust for a moment, but his heart was not in it.

Only Gray Crane retained his usual calm expression. He listened more than he spoke, smiling faintly when someone made a small joke, offering to refill water cups, watching all of us with that quiet, Priestly attention. I think everyone, including the women, was relieved when the bowls were empty, the last maize cakes eaten, and it was time to clean up.

* * *

After the fire was raked and the pots set aside, I drew Dancing Copperhead away from the others, into the dim edge of the Black Bear Clan Common where the night wrapped around us more closely.

"I know it is no pleasure to sit here all day," I began. "Guarding against something that will probably never happen. But I want you to understand that what you are doing is important, and that I am grateful."

He watched my face, serious.

"If there is even a small chance that someone might try to harm your mother or your siblings, we must be ready," I continued. I lowered my voice and glanced back toward the ramada to make sure no one was listening. "We learned things today that make me believe this is more than a string of murders and an ordinary investigation. I will not share the details, but I am afraid something worse may be moving behind them."

"Is that why everyone was so quiet during the meal?" Dancing Copperhead asked. "All of you looked nervous, like your backs were full of thorns."

I smiled at my bright son. "Yes. Today was sobering. The families we spoke with tore the cloak away from what had felt like a distant story. And we began to suspect that the man who gave me this task may be using me for a purpose I do not understand. That unsettles all of us. Tell me what happened here today."

Dancing Copperhead lifted one shoulder. "Very little," he said. "Walks in Water ground maize into meal. Mother took a sack of acorns to the creek to wash out the bitterness. The women brought water, then worked together to prepare the evening meal. I went with Mother to the creek to guard her, then walked around the common, speaking with the women and the children. Passing Doe and Daughter came with some doeskin. The women cut the hides and worked side by side, sewing leggings for Bear Claws and a winter dress for Daughter. I gave Willow Tree a chunkey lesson in the afternoon and practiced with my bow when I had the chance."

"It sounds like a very dangerous day," I said dryly.

He snorted in disgust.

"I want you to stay here again tomorrow," I added. "I know it is dull work, but I still believe there is some danger to the women and children."

"I will do as you ask, Father," he said, and gave me a crooked smile, resigned to his duty.

"Good," I said. "Now, go to sleep. Tomorrow will be a long day."

As he walked away, I thought of how my little band had come together almost by accident. Spotted Lynx had been forced on me by Muskrat Waits as a bodyguard. Gray Crane had fallen in with us at the Emerald Acropolis, bearing Singing Mountain's authority. Bold Warrior had sent Green Heron to guide us among the immigrant farmers. Somehow, over the last few sunrises, they had become my people, whether I had wanted that or not.

* * *

I found them sitting in a tight circle near the fire, faces lit by the last coals, discussing the day in low voices. As usual, Spotted Lynx had taken the role of storyteller. He spoke with his hands, tracing paths through the air, sketching houses, roads, and suspicions. He was a natural leader and a clever young man. The thought that such a man could become an enemy made the back of my neck prickle.

They looked up as I approached. Instead of sitting at once, I stepped into the house, retrieved a small leather tobacco pouch, and returned to the fire. I passed it wordlessly around the circle. Even Gray Crane accepted a pinch this time, cupping the sacred leaf with both hands before filling his little clay pipe.

Green Heron took several deep puffs of Whispering Doe's tobacco, then leaned back and sent a thin blue stream of smoke rising toward the Above World, where Morning Star dwelt among the Divine Ones.

"This is marvelous," he said when he could speak. "I have never tasted tobacco like this. It is the finest I have ever smoked."

"You are welcome," Whispering Doe called from under the ramada, where she was pretending to be busy herself with tidying baskets.

We all laughed. Time had certainly not dulled her hearing. Sometimes I thought her name ought to have been Listening Doe.

"Whispering Doe grows the tobacco herself," I explained proudly. "She has a small plot next to the house. She hangs the leaves to dry on racks near the fire and tends them as carefully as any Priest tends a shrine. You will not taste a better leaf anywhere in Cahokia."

"I had the pleasure of smoking it once already," Spotted Lynx said. "On our journey from the Emerald Acropolis. Walking Stick speaks the truth. It is the best."

The familiar ritual of pipe and pouch, the sharp, good smell of the tobacco, and the gentle puffing did what I had hoped. I could see the tension slowly ease from shoulders, the lines of worry soften around eyes and mouths.

"What are we going to do tomorrow?" Spotted Lynx asked, his tone more friendly than earlier, though his eyes were still shadowed.

"I am not entirely sure," I said. "I had planned to report to Muskrat Waits about what we have learned in the last few days. But if he is using me for his own purposes, is it wise to give him every piece of information we acquire? Could he twist it to serve his own plans, in ways we do not see? This task has always confused me, but now that we suspect Muskrat Waits may be playing some game of his own, with me as one of his game pieces, the situation feels more dangerous."

I rubbed my face.

"On the other hand," I went on, "if I do not report to him regularly, he may grow suspicious or angry. Both are bad options."

Spotted Lynx chuckled softly. "As if the puzzle were not tangled enough," he said, "I had another thought. The Sun King employs spies and assassins. There are always tasks that cannot be done openly. Why should Muskrat Waits be any different? What if his spies have been watching us all along? What if he already knows where we went, whom we spoke to, and what we learned?"

"Red Horn, have mercy on me," I muttered. "Every time one of you has another idea, this mission becomes worse."

The others laughed. I did not.

"Muskrat Waits did command me to protect you," Spotted Lynx pointed out. "Even if he is as cunning and deceitful as the Hero Twins, that does not release me from my duty. If I were in his position, and I were using you for some hidden purpose, I would not rely on your word alone. I would have someone watching. That way I could respond quickly to whatever you discovered, and I could be sure you were telling me the truth."

"If Muskrat Waits and the Sun King have spies," I said, "why would he send a tired old coppersmith like me to investigate these murders at all? I understand that he does not want Warriors in armor roaming the countryside and frightening farmers, but spies work in secret. Why not use them instead of me?"

Spotted Lynx thought for a moment before answering. "Spies live in the shadows," he said. "To investigate these murders as we have done requires speaking openly to families, being seen, being invited into houses, asking questions that are already unwelcome. Men trained to kill quietly are not always the right men to comfort widows and coax details from frightened neighbors. They would still stand out. And there is another possibility."

"What is that?" I asked.

"Muskrat Waits may be using his spies already," Spotted Lynx said. "Not to replace us, but to watch us and to help us in ways we do not see. Perhaps we worry over nothing."

"I do not think we are worrying over nothing," I said. "But go on."

"In any case," he said, "I believe you must see Muskrat Waits tomorrow. If you avoid him, he will suspect something. He might send Warriors to fetch you. Or worse, to fetch me. If you go, tell him the truth about what we have learned, but do not tell him that you suspect him of anything. There is no need to put that thought into his head."

110

I sat quietly for several heartbeats, then nodded. "You are right," I said. "I need to see him, if only to keep him from growing suspicious that we are growing suspicious. What a tangle. Morning Star, save me."

That earned another round of laughter.

"What will you three do tomorrow while I pay a visit to our charming Minister of Security?" I asked.

"I must go to the barracks," Spotted Lynx said. "I have a Troupe of Warriors who deserve to see their War Captain once in a while, or they will mutiny." His mouth twisted into a grin.

Green Heron smiled more slyly. "I am going to visit my mother's brother," he said. "His daughter has a friend who wishes to meet me."

"So that is how the great Ones Who Remember are snared," I said. "By a cousin's friend and a plate of food."

Gray Crane looked thoughtful. "I will cross the creek to the Temple near the North Plaza," he said. "I wished to go there before, but I lacked a way to cross. I will speak with the Priests and see if any news from the countryside has filtered to them. Perhaps they have heard of other missing men."

"Good," I said. "Let us meet back here tomorrow before the evening meal. Then we can share what we have each learned and decide our next move."

The fire was burning low now, its light a dull red glow among the coals. The long day sat in my bones like a weight.

"I have had enough of death and scheming Nobles for one day," I said. "Whispering Doe has sleeping furs for all of you. Find places to lie down. After what I saw and heard today, I am glad to have you near my fire."

* * *

Spotted Lynx, Gray Crane, and Green Heron stretched out on the packed earth near the fire, wrapping themselves in their furs. I joined Whispering Doe under our ramada, where the familiar scent of smoke and dried herbs hung in the rafters. She was awake, lying on her side, facing the dim glow of the hearth.

I slipped out of my breechcloth and eased into our sleeping furs beside her and snuggled close, breathing in the warm smell of her skin and hair.

"Something is wrong," she said quietly. "Your investigation is not going well."

"No," I answered. "There are complications."

111

She did not say anything more, but her silence pressed me harder than any spoken question.

"Complications named Muskrat Waits," I said at last. "I do not think I can trust him."

She made a soft, impatient sound in her throat, as if to say that should have been obvious from the beginning.

"Of course, I always knew that in the abstract," I went on quickly, before she could speak. "Everyone has told me not to trust him. He himself told me not to trust him. But today we began to suspect that he might be using me as a pawn in some game he has not bothered to explain. And worse, I am no longer entirely sure that I can trust Spotted Lynx either. I do not want to believe that he would deceive me on Muskrat Waits' behalf, but I am no longer certain whom I can rely on."

Whispering Doe sat up, the furs falling from her shoulders. Even in the darkness, I could sense the sharpness of her gaze.

"That is foolishness," she said. "Spotted Lynx is loyal to you."

"How do you know that?" I demanded. "Because he likes your maize cakes and flirts with you whenever he thinks I am not looking?"

She giggled; the sound was quick and wicked. "You are being silly," she said. "Although he is fun. I think I am a good judge of people. I chose you, did I not?"

I could not deny that this was an excellent argument.

"Tell me," she said, settling back down but still frowning. "Tell me what makes you think Muskrat Waits is using you, and why you doubt Spotted Lynx."

So I did. I described our visit to Black Locust's deserted farm, Dark Ash's stories, Water Lilly's fear, the Priest from the Emerald Acropolis with the Birdman tattoo, the Warriors who returned again and again to watch her house, our conclusions along the road home, and our suspicions that Muskrat Waits might be standing somewhere behind it all, tugging strings.

When I finished, Whispering Doe did not answer at once. For a heartbeat, I thought she had fallen asleep. Then she spoke softly.

"You are right to suspect that Muskrat Waits is up to something," she said. "He is too ambitious and too clever. And yes, the connection to the Warriors is troubling. It puts a shadow over Spotted Lynx as well."

She reached out and placed her hand on my arm.

"However," she continued, "I still believe Spotted Lynx stands on your side. Listen to him. Watch him. But trust him."

I lay there in the darkness, feeling the warmth of her hand and the weight of her words. I trusted Whispering Doe. I had trusted her since the first time she threw a stick at my head in the East Plaza, when we were hardly older than Willow Tree was now. I realized, with a chill that made my skin pebble despite the heat, that there might not be many others I could trust so completely.

I had begun to understand that in Cahokia, trusting the wrong person was not just foolish.

It could cost a man his life.

Chapter 14

Everyone else was awake when I rolled out of my sleeping fur the next morning. My three companions were already gone. Near the fire pit, Whispering Doe, Walks in Water, Passing Doe, and my wife's sister, Prairie Flower, knelt around shallow woven trays where acorn meats lay in the weak morning sun.

The women turned the pieces with quick, practiced fingers. Whispering Doe had leached the acorns in Cahokia Creek the day before, washing away the bitter tannin that makes raw acorn meat both unpleasant and harmful. Fire can do the same work if you boil the acorns and change the water often, but that method requires more wood than most households can spare. For large batches, it is easier to crush the nut meats and leave them in running water for days, until the tannins wash away. Acorns are a gift from Old-Woman-Who-Never-Dies, and they are as crucial to Cahokian families as goosefoot or squash.

When Walks in Water noticed that I was up, she jumped to her feet and hurried to the cooking fire. She returned with a ceramic plate heaped with maize cakes, a handful of blackberries, and a roasted deer rib that had been resting near the coals to keep warm. As I settled into my chair, she placed the plate on my knees and then brought a cup of hot sassafras tea sweetened with honey.

"How are you feeling this morning, Father?" Walks in Water asked.

"I feel very well after a long night of sleep," I said, "and even better now that I have food in my hands. Thank you."

She did not smile. Her brow puckered the way it had when she was a little girl who could sense thunder before anyone else.

"I know something is worrying the others," she said quietly. "They were polite during the morning meal, but they did not talk. Even Spotted Lynx was quiet. I asked him what was wrong, but he would not tell me anything."

That, I thought, was an improvement. Perhaps the Warrior had finally learned not to share everything in his head with every pretty girl he saw.

I smiled at my daughter. "You are not a foolish girl," I said. "You can see that something is happening that we cannot discuss. Do not distract the others. Especially Spotted Lynx. When this is over, I will tell you everything."

Walks in Water pouted, but she did not argue. She went back to the trays of acorns and rejoined the work of the women.

I had not finished my meal when Red Bud came dashing across the common from her house next door, bare feet slapping the packed earth.

"Good morning, Grandfather!" she shouted. "Guess what?"

"What?" I asked, amused by her bright eyes and tangled hair.

"Father is home! He was not there when I went to sleep, but he was beside me when I woke up this morning."

"That is wonderful," I said. My voice was warmer than my heart. I did not dislike Bear Claws. He was a good husband to Passing Doe and a good provider. It was not easy to accept that my little girl had a husband at all. The fact that his work often took him away for several sunrises at a time had done much to improve my feelings toward him.

Bear Claws was a forester. During certain seasons, the foresters lived half their lives on the rivers. In summer, they went upstream along the Messipi, the Wide Muddy, and the Great Northern rivers, felling trees in the deep forests. They tied the trunks together with vines and ropes, forming huge rafts that could be floated downstream. At Cahokia, Traders Town, River Bluff Town, and other settlements, the rafts were broken apart and sold log by log to traders who fed greater Cahokia's endless hunger for wood—for houses, for shrines, for carvings, and above all for the countless cooking fires that never went out in the Sun King's lands.

As I spoke with Red Bud, Bear Claws ambled over from my wife's sister's house next door, where he, Passing Doe, and Red Bud lived.

"Greetings, Father," Bear Claws said.

"Greetings, Son," I replied. "Welcome home. How was your trip?"

"Very successful," he said. "We went up the Messipi for two sunrises, then turned into the Buffalo River, where our crew had never harvested. The trees along the banks are enormous. We spent three sunrises cutting and trimming the trunks, then binding them into rafts. It was one of the easiest jobs I have had. The trees grew right at the river's edge, so we did not have to drag them far. It took four sunrises to float the rafts down to River Bluff Town. We broke them up at the landing and sold the logs to traders. Once the last log was gone, several of us took a canoe downstream to Cahokia Creek and followed it to the landing behind the Great Pyramid. I arrived well after sunset. Everyone was asleep. Passing Doe was already grinding maize when I woke. I was exhausted. I would still be asleep if Daughter had not jumped on me to wake me."

"That sounds like a fine trip," I said. "It is beautiful on the river. I loved going south on trading missions in my younger days. I have never seen the Buffalo River country. It has been many cycles of the seasons since I went on a long journey. I am older now. I will probably never see those places." I shrugged. "What is your next job?"

"I will remain at home for three sunrises," he replied, "and then a group of us will go back to the Buffalo River. There are enough trees in that country to keep Cahokia in firewood for many cycles of the seasons."

"That is good to hear," I said. "Red Horn knows Cahokia always needs wood. Without men like you, families could not cook and would freeze in winter."

His chest swelled at my praise. The compliment cost me nothing and made him happy.

After we had talked about the forestry work for a while, I said, "I need to tell you something, and you must not tell anyone. There have been a series of murders north of here, not far from the Black Bear Clan common fields. I told Whispering Doe to keep the Black Bear women inside the common for the next few sunrises, until we catch the murderer. I have Dancing Copperhead carrying his bow and watching over the compound, but if you could keep an eye on things while you are home, I would be grateful."

"I will be glad to keep watch, Father," Bear Claws said at once. "If there is anything else you need me to do, just ask."

I thanked him, as Red Bud tugged at his hand until he let himself be dragged away to inspect a caterpillar she had discovered.

I could not delay any longer. It was time to face Muskrat Waits.

I stopped by the copper workshop and exchanged a few words with Red Hawk. He told me everything was going well, and by the sound of the hammering and the rhythm of the shouting, he spoke the truth. I did not linger. The less my craftsmen knew about the murders and my involvement, the safer they were. From the workshop, I walked to the Sacred Precinct and the base of the Great Pyramid.

Only when I reached the gate did it occur to me that I had no pass. Spotted Lynx had always been at my side on previous visits, flashing his parchment seal the way a hawk flashes its talons. Now I stood alone.

The young Warrior at the gate leveled his spear, but did not look especially hostile. I said, "I am Walking Stick. I am here to see Muskrat Waits. I do not have a pass of my own, but he told me to report to him regularly. Can you send a runner to tell him that I am here?"

"There is no need," the Warrior chirped. "Muskrat Waits told me that if you came to the gate, I am to escort you to him at once."

That unexpected courtesy did not make me feel safer, but it smoothed my way. I followed the gate guard up the ramp that climbed the south face of the Great Pyramid to the first terrace, where Muskrat Waits sat in his usual place under his ramada, like some squat, dangerous idol.

"Well, coppersmith," he said without preamble. "Have you made any progress?"

"Bold Warrior found the families of the murder victims," I replied. "He sent a *Hiperes Jinak*, Green Heron, to guide us. Yesterday we went to question two of the families. One had already left, but we spoke with a neighbor. The second family was still there. The wife is frightened. She is taking her children and returning to her parents near North Star Town."

"So they have already begun to leave," Muskrat Waits said. His tone was flat, but his eyes sharpened. I nodded.

"Green Heron also told us something else very interesting," I said, letting the words hang.

"And that is?" he asked impatiently.

"The victims were not from Deer Toes Lake Town," I said. "They lived just north of the Cahokian Clan common fields, close to the city. That means someone, certainly more than one person, carried the bodies all the way to Deer Toes Lake Town. There is only one reason I can see for moving the bodies so far from where they were killed."

"To conceal the true place of death," Muskrat Waits finished smoothly. "And to hide where the victims lived. Undoubtedly, to confuse anyone who tried to investigate." He fell silent for many heartbeats, his fingers drumming on the arm of his chair. "The question is why," he said at last. "Tell me what else you learned from the two families."

So I did. I told him about the deserted farmstead, the odd old-style house, Spotted Lynx catching Dark Ash hiding in the maize, and the old Duck Clan man's account of Black Locust's family and their flight back toward the Waapaahshiiki. Then I recounted our visit with Water Lilly, her fear, her children, and her plan to depart for her parents' home. I did not mention the copper I had given her, nor that I had suggested that she leave at once. Muskrat Waits did not need to know everything.

"There is something else," I said when I had finished.

He raised his eyebrows.

"Water Lilly told us that Priests from the Emerald Acropolis had harassed her family, and Cahokia Warriors passed through the area several times," I continued. "She said they were openly hostile toward her family. That is another connection to the Cahokian military."

"Yes," he said blandly. "That is troublesome."

His lack of reaction irritated me. "The last time we spoke," I said, "you seemed alarmed when we suggested that Warriors might have committed the murders. Now you seem unconcerned when I tell you that we have more evidence tying the Warriors to the victims. I intend to pursue the possibility of Warrior involvement. Is there anything that you can tell me that might help?"

Muskrat Waits frowned. "What exactly would you like to know?" he asked.

"If you know anything at all about Warriors being involved in these killings," I said, exasperated. "Anything."

A strange look passed across his face. It might have been anger, or amusement, or both. It was gone so quickly that I could not be sure.

"Do you not think I would tell you if I did?" he asked in a dry, mocking tone.

"I am not sure you would," I said just as dryly.

"Obviously, I want these murders solved," he snapped. "You have seen what panic can do when farmers believe that we cannot protect them. You examined two families yesterday, and already one has abandoned Cahokia. How many others have already fled, or are preparing to leave? It sounds as if the fear is spreading. And where is Spotted Lynx?"

It struck me as odd that he had not asked after the young Warrior sooner, or that he asked at all. Perhaps that was a good sign that he was not conspiring with the young Warrior.

"He has gone to his Troupe's barracks," I said. "He is speaking with his Warriors and the senior War Captains to see if anyone knows anything about soldiers harassing farmers north of Cahokia."

Muskrat Waits made a face as if I had just told him the stew was burned. "Do you have anything else to report?" he asked.

"I do not," I said.

"What are you going to do now?"

"We will question the other three families," I said. "Spotted Lynx is trying to determine which Troupe of Warriors has been operating north of Cahokia during the time of the murders. Gray Crane is speaking with his fellow Priests at the North Temple. It is the closest Temple to the farms where the victims lived."

"Who is Gray Crane?" Muskrat Waits demanded. "And how many people are you adding to this band of yours? I gave you Spotted Lynx, and now you have gathered a *Hiperes Jinak* and a Priest. I told you to keep a low profile."

His question took me by surprise. "Gray Crane is a Priest from the Emerald Acropolis," I said. "Singing Mountain sent him with me as an interpreter in case we needed to speak with immigrants from the Oho country, and to assist us in dealing with other Priests. I must not have mentioned him during our last conversation."

"No," Muskrat Waits said sourly. "You did not. Although I do recall that Singing Mountain mentioned sending one of his Priests with you after you left the Emerald Acropolis." He waved a hand. "And the *Hiperes Jinak*? What is his name?"

"Green Heron," I replied. "Bold Warrior sent him to show us where the victims' families live."

"Very well," Muskrat Waits said, still clearly displeased that the circle of people with knowledge of the murders was widening. "Question the remaining families, then report back to me."

The dismissal was as abrupt as ever.

* * *

I descended the Great Pyramid, walked along the Sacred Way, and turned toward the East Plaza. On the way home, I stopped once more at the copper workshop. Red Hawk assured me again that all was well. I wandered through the shaded work area beneath the big ramada, watching the craftsmen.

Our oldest artisan, Little Mink, perhaps two cycles of the seasons older than I was, sat hunched over his work, fashioning a pair of human-head earrings. The Priestly class favored such ornaments, copper-covered faces that echoed the earrings of Red Horn himself. A single pair was worth more in trade than a peasant farmer would see in his entire lifetime.

Although I had grown up in the copper workshop, I had never been an artisan. My father had trained my hands for counting, directing and evaluating the work of others, and dealing with traders and Nobles. From the time of my naming ceremony at four cycles of the seasons, it had been assumed that I would manage the business. I learned to judge the quality of copper work, to bargain with Nobles and traders, and to calculate profits and losses. But if you had placed a hammer in my hand and asked me to make a plate, I would have produced something fit only for the scrap heap.

From the workshop, I crossed the new East Plaza. The old plaza where Whispering Doe and I had played as children, where I had first learned the joy and sting of chunkey, had disappeared when the Sun King ordered the stockade built. The palisade ran just west of the copper works and the Deer Clan Shrine House and lodge. The new East Plaza lay beyond, and by fortune or divine design, the Deer Clan Shrine House now stood at its west edge in a more prominent position than before.

It was past full sun when I walked into the Black Bear Clan Common. I noted with satisfaction that Dancing Copperhead was taking his duty seriously, circling the compound with his bow in hand, eyes scanning the entrances and the lanes between houses. He must have been bored enough to wish for a small invasion.

Whispering Doe saw me and hurried to ladle a bowl of hominy, wild onion, and fish stew. She added a thick slice of acorn bread and filled a cup with maize beer. I sat in my chair beneath the ramada, eating slowly, savoring the simple food. When the bowl was empty, the warmth and the steady murmur of children at play began to lull me. My eyes drifted shut.

I jerked awake with a shout when something jabbed me in the ribs. Dancing Copperhead stood beside my chair, bow in hand, laughing so hard that he almost dropped it.

"What do you want?" I snarled.

"I wanted to see if you were awake," he said, still chuckling.

"What are you doing over here?" I demanded. "You are supposed to be watching the family, not disturbing me when I'm resting."

He knelt beside my chair, still smirking. "I wanted to know what you were doing," he said.

"I was about to take a nap until you stabbed me with your bow," I said. "Is there anything interesting happening that I should know about?"

He shook his head. "Nothing. Women working, children running around, men coming and going. Two men came into the compound earlier to talk to Bear Claws about a job cutting timber in a few sunrises."

My grogginess faded. It felt good to have strength in my limbs again.

"Let me fetch my bow," I said. "We will practice. It has been a long time since I loosed an arrow."

"I already have a target," he said and ran off.

I went into the house and searched under one of the sleeping benches until I found my bow and quiver wrapped in a deer hide. I carried the bundle back to the common, where Dancing Copperhead was tying a cloth bag stuffed with prairie grass to a simple tripod made of poles.

I unrolled the deer hide and pulled out the bow. My bow was a weapon of exceptional quality, one carved from the hard, fine-grained, yellowish wood of the bow-tree that grows west of the Messipi. The wood and sinew string were dry and needed oil and care, but they were sound. The arrows, made of river cane and fletched with red-tailed hawk feathers, were tipped with triangular chert points of the type that had made Cahokia famous from one end of the Messipi Valley to the other. Those points, chipped from the white stone quarried in the hills west of the Messipi, were as much a trade item as copper. Men in distant towns shot Cahokian points at deer and enemies alike.

Bowed Willow, my old tutor, had trained all of his students in the arts of war and sport: archery, chunkey, spear throwing, running, war club drills, and wrestling. I had excelled in archery and chunkey. Among Bowed Willow's students, I was the best with the bow, and on the chunkey court, only Prince Raging Fox, the younger brother of the Sun King, had bested me.

Dancing Copperhead finished tying the bag and, with a bit of charcoal, drew a small circle in its center. I pulled an arrow from my bark and hide quiver, nocked it, and drew the bowstring back until the feathers brushed my cheek. I let my breath out and loosed the arrow.

The bowstring twanged. The arrow shot forth and struck the target just beside the little charcoal circle.

Dancing Copperhead's jaw dropped. I laughed.

"I remember you used to be a good shot," he said. "But you have not shot your bow in many cycles of the seasons. That was beginner's luck. Let us see if you can do it again."

I did. Several times. We each shot six arrows. When we walked up to pull them, all of Dancing Copperhead's shots were in or near the circle, but every one of mine had pierced it cleanly.

"Well," he said, a little grudgingly, "I suppose you still have it, Father."

We were about to shoot again when Whispering Doe strode over from the fire, hands on hips.

"It is good to see you standing up instead of sinking into that chair," she said. "I think you have lost a little weight since you started working on this mystery."

I had noticed it too. All the walking had made my legs ache, but my belt had grown loose.

Then she saw the target and froze. "Is that my bag?" she asked in a dangerous tone.

She yanked the bag from the tripod and stared at the holes, her eyes blazing.

"I found it in the house, Mother," Dancing Copperhead said defensively. "It was folded under the bench. It looked like it had never been used, so I thought no one wanted it."

"It looks as if it has never been used because it has never been used," Whispering Doe shouted. Nothing was whispering about her now. "I made that bag last winter. I was going to use it for nuts, arrow-leaf tubers, rattlesnake master leaves, and everything else I gather. Now it is ruined. When the Black Bear women go out to collect rattlesnake master leaves on the highland prairie a moon cycle from now, you are coming with us. You will walk with the women and the girls and carry leaves like a girl. Then we will see if you pick up any more of my bags without asking."

Still furious, she turned on her heel and stomped back to the fire.

I winced. For a young man, walking with the women to gather plants was a punishment worse than digging a new latrine. But I could not deny that she had cause. Making a fiber bag took many sunrises of labor. Women and girls walked to the highland prairie to strip spear-point shaped leaves from rattlesnake master plants by the basketful. In winter, when families stayed indoors, they split the leaves, teased out the fibers, twisted them into a string, and wove the string into cloth on a loom. From that cloth, they made clothing, shoes, blankets, and bags. Every thread represented much patient work.

I put a hand on Dancing Copperhead's shoulder. "I am sorry, boy," I said. "I do not remember seeing your mother so angry."

"You were not very helpful," he snapped.

"Are you mad?" I asked, chuckling, which made him glare all the more. "I am not foolish enough to step between your mother and something she has worked long and hard to complete."

As we were speaking, Willow Tree slipped into the common, returning from whatever secret world occupies the feet and mind of a five-cycles of the seasons-old boy. He took one look at Whispering Doe's back and came straight to us.

"What is happening?" he asked. "Mother looks angry, so I did not talk to her."

"Smart man," I told him. Dancing Copperhead only scowled. "Never bother a woman when she is angry. And when you want to use something that does not belong to you, ask the owner first."

Willow Tree nodded as if I had just revealed a profound mystery.

"Well," I said, looking at the torn bag. "It is ruined now. We might as well make more use of it."

"I am finished," Dancing Copperhead said and stalked away.

So I gave Willow Tree an archery lesson instead. He had a small practice bow of his own, but this was the first time he had tried to draw an adult bow with a heavy pull. He did well for his first attempt. When we finished, I had him untie the battered bag and hide it behind the house, out of Whispering Doe's sight but close enough to serve as a target again.

I went back to my chair. Sweat trickled down my neck. Whispering Doe noticed and brought me a fresh cup of maize beer. She knelt by my side.

"The women want to know when we can return to the fields," she said. "It has been two sunrises. We have weeds to hoe and crops to harvest. We cannot stay locked inside the common forever."

I sighed. "You are right, but I am still uneasy. Perhaps there is a way to do both. What if the women return to the fields, but I send Bear Claws and Dancing Copperhead with them? Everyone goes out together and returns together. The men can stand guard while you work. I would feel better if I knew that someone I trust is nearby."

Whispering Doe's face brightened. "That is an excellent idea," she said, and rose at once to start planning.

I went to find Bear Claws. He sat outside his house, drinking cool maize beer and watching Passing Doe and Soft Elk prepare the evening meal. When I explained what I wanted, his chest swelled again.

"I will be glad to take charge," he said. Bear Claws was a large, powerful man. He would make an impressive guardian standing at the edge of a field with a bow in his hands. Satisfied, I returned to my chair and sat for a few moments, trying to decide what to do next.

* * *

Spotted Lynx appeared first, dropping onto a stool near me, dust on his boots and a thoughtful look on his face.

"Did you learn anything at the barracks?" I asked.

"I learned that War Captain Black Elk's Troupe has been operating north of Cahokia," he said. "He knows that there have been murders, but he has no details. He says his men have been doing routine patrolling, nothing special. Aside from the murders—which he claims to know nothing about—he has seen nothing unusual. He claims his men have not harassed any farmers."

"Did you talk to the Warriors in your own Troupe?" I asked.

He nodded. "I spoke with my second-in-command and several of my men. They have not heard about the murders, and they do not know of any Warriors from other Troupes harassing farmers."

I was not surprised. If the military had anything to do with the murders, no Warrior was going to admit it to a War Captain who might be considered too honest. Without pressure from above, questioning the ranks would only make them wary.

Spotted Lynx wandered off toward the ramada where Walks in Water worked. Gray Crane arrived soon after and took his place on the stool.

"Did you learn anything of use?" I asked.

Gray Crane frowned. "No," he said. "Not really. I went to the Temple near the North Plaza, but the priests there had no knowledge of the murders. They were friendly, and we spoke at length, exchanging news. The High Priest, Blue Falcon, showed great interest in our investigation, but regretted that he was unable to offer any help."

"You had an interesting day, but I do not see how it helps us find the killers."

"Neither do I," Gray Crane said.

Whispering Doe's voice called us to the evening meal. The only one missing was Green Heron, but he arrived just as she began to ladle venison stew into bowls, and Walks in Water handed out pieces of sunflower seed bread. I noticed that Spotted Lynx seemed to receive a larger slice of bread than I did, though he took a huge bite before I could be certain. I wondered whether all young men possessed some special sense that led them unerringly to the fire at precisely the right time. Spotted Lynx and Green Heron certainly did.

As is our custom, I was served first, then our guests, then Dancing Copperhead (the next-oldest male), and finally the women and children. Feeding three additional young men every day was not cheap. I feared that this mystery would devour our food stores even if the murderers did not kill any more farmers.

* * *

After the meal, my companions and I gathered behind our house, where curious eyes and ears were fewer. I spoke first, summarizing what Spotted Lynx, Gray Crane, and I had learned that day, so everyone shared the same knowledge.

Then I turned to Green Heron, who had vanished before I woke up that morning and had not returned until just before the stew was served.

"Where did you go, and what did you do today?" I asked.

"I went to find the other three families," he said. "I wanted to make sure they had not fled Cahokia. I located all three. One family has already disappeared. The other two are still living in their houses. I did not speak to them. They did not see me. I watched from a distance. Nothing seemed unusual.

"After that, I wandered the countryside," he continued. "I talked to people—Cahokians and immigrants. People are afraid. Some families have already returned to their homelands. Others are preparing to go."

"You said that you spoke with immigrants," I said, curious. "You can speak their languages?"

Green Heron laughed. "Yes," he said. "I speak Oho, Waapaahshiiki, and Dhegihan from the Oho country. I also speak Southern tongues—Caddoan from the Ochre River country, Muskoegan from the Tanasse, and Ogahpah from the hill lands to the southwest. That is another reason Bold Warrior sent me to you."

"Has anyone heard of any other people who have gone missing?" I asked the group.

No one had.

"That is good," I said. "Perhaps the madness has ended. But we still have five dead immigrants and no answers. Tomorrow we will leave early, visit the two remaining families, and see whether they can tell us anything that will help. With a little luck, we can speak with both before nightfall. Honestly, I do not feel that we have learned much that points toward the killer's identity. Unless one of you can see something that I cannot."

"I have thought of one connection between the two victims we heard about yesterday," Green Heron said gravely.

We all turned toward him.

"What is that?" I demanded.

"They are both black trees," he said in the same solemn voice.

I stared at him.

"Black Locust. Black Oak Tree," he said.

The others burst out laughing. Green Heron grinned at me, pleased with himself. So he meant to be the jester in our little band. I did not bother to respond.

"Let us go back to the fire," I said.

We returned to the central hearth. Passing Doe's family joined us. Red Bud crawled into my lap. I told her stories of Red Horn and the Hero Twins while Spotted Lynx helped Walks in Water fetch firewood. Gray Crane and Green Heron murmured to one another in a language I did not know. Whispering Doe explained to everyone how the Black Bear women planned to leave at dawn to work in the fields with Bear Claws and Dancing Copperhead standing guard.

I realized, watching the young men talk, that I knew very little about Green Heron. Spotted Lynx, I understood—at least I thought I did. Gray Crane's story, I had heard in bits and pieces over the past few sunrises. But Green Heron was still a stranger.

I am about fifteen and one-half fists tall. Whispering Doe is a fist shorter. Spotted Lynx is taller than the average Cahokian, perhaps seventeen fists, broader in the shoulders than most Warriors. Gray Crane is even taller but thinner and less muscular. Green Heron is shorter than most Cahokian men, compact, with a dark complexion and small brown eyes. He seems about the same age as Gray Crane, perhaps eighteen cycles

127

of the seasons. Like Spotted Lynx, he ties his hair back with a leather string and has no Clan tattoo.

"Green Heron," I said. "We do not know much about you beyond the fact that you are a *Hiperes Jinak* with an extraordinary memory and a talent for languages. Tell us about yourself."

He looked embarrassed, but after a moment, he nodded.

"I was born in a small village north of Deer Toes Lake Town," he began. "My parents are farmers. My father's family came from the Caddoan lands far to the south several generations ago. My mother's family came from the Oho country. As a child, I grew up hearing Cahokian, Caddoan, and Dhegihan around the hearth. I discovered that I had a gift for learning languages as easily as other children learn games.

"I was also born with a perfect memory," he continued. "One day, a man came to our house and asked to speak with me. Someone had told him about my memory and my skill with tongues. He spoke to me in Oho, then in Dhegihan, then in Waapaahshiiki. When he finished, he asked my parents whether I could go with him and learn to be a *Hiperes Jinak*. He said that I had a gift. I was twelve cycles of the seasons old. My parents were very proud. I went with him. For the last six cycles of the seasons, I have trained as a *Hiperes Jinak*. This work with you is my first assignment on my own."

"And the man who came to your house and took you to be trained," I said, already sure of the answer, "was Bold Warrior."

Green Heron smiled. "Yes," he said. "Bold Warrior has been my teacher and mentor."

I had known that Bold Warrior was an influential leader among the immigrant farmers in the lands between Cahokia city and North Star Town. I had not realized how far his influence spread—far enough to recruit gifted children, train them, and place them as his agents. He would be a very valuable ally.

Or a dangerous enemy.

"Will you tell us a story from one of the far lands?" Whispering Doe asked.

"I am not a *Woorak Horak*," he said modestly. "But I have heard many tales told by the elders near my parents' village, and I enjoy retelling them. Would you like to hear the story of how Evening Star received her Companion Star?"

The tale was new to us. Everyone, even Bear Claws, leaned closer.

"This tale comes from the Caddo people who live to the south along the Ochre River," Green Heron began. "Many cycles of the seasons ago, a boy lost his mother, father, and siblings in a terrible accident. He had no other family, so the Clan gave him to another family who treated him cruelly. They forced him to do all of the hard work for the family, and he was not allowed to play with other children or to learn how to hunt. Even though he did all of the hard work for his adoptive family, they did not want him. Several times, the family tried to leave him behind when they moved. However, the boy was always able to follow their trail and find their new camp. The Orphan Boy did not like his adoptive family, but he had nowhere else to go, and he could not survive on his own.

"One spring day, the Clan paddled in canoes to a large island in the middle of a lake to hunt ducks and geese and to gather their eggs. After a time, everyone lay down to rest because their canoes were filled with birds and eggs, and they were tired from the work. However, it turned out to be a trick. The others were only pretending to be asleep, and when Orphan Boy dozed off, the others got into their canoes and left him on the island. Orphan Boy was now truly alone.

"Although Orphan Boy had never learned to hunt like the other boys, the island was filled with game easily caught, roots to dig, and berries to pick, and he was able to survive. Even though Orphan Boy despised his adoptive family, they were the only other humans he knew. On the island, he was very lonely and wanted badly to find a family he could live with. Day after day, he sat on the bank of the island and stared at the rocky shore of the mainland far across the lake. He thought about swimming across the lake, but he had never learned to swim, so he was marooned.

"One evening, as he stared across the lake, a giant turtle-like creature appeared in the water near the island. Orphan Boy was terrified, but fascinated at the same time, so he stood on the shore and watched as the beast came closer. When the giant turtle reached the shore, it spoke to the boy, saying 'Orphan Boy, I have come to save you. I know how the wicked people of your Clan abandoned you on this island. If you climb onto my shell, I will swim across the water to the land, and you will be free.'

"So the Orphan Boy did as the giant turtle instructed and climbed onto his shell. Before leaving the island, the giant turtle said, 'Watch the skies for me. If you see a star, you must tell me immediately, or we will perish.' They had barely entered the water when the boy saw a star appear in the western sky. He told the turtle what he had seen, and the beast immediately turned around and took Orphan Boy back to shore.

"The giant turtle came again the following day, but once again, when they were still in the lake, Orphan Boy spotted a star in the western sky, and they returned to the island in despair.

"The Giant Turtle came every day for six days and tried to take Orphan Boy off the island. Each day, they came closer to shore, but each day a star appeared in the western sky, forcing them back to the island. Orphan Boy was becoming desperate. On the sixth day, they were almost to the other side when Orphan Boy spotted the star. The shore was so close, and Orphan Boy so frantic that he did not tell the giant turtle that he had seen the star.

"As Orphan Boy and the giant turtle neared the shore, a black cloud trundled across the sky, hiding the star. Terrified, Orphan Boy jumped off the giant turtle's back. Luckily, the water was shallow, and he was able to walk the last few steps to the lake shore. No sooner had he jumped from the turtle's back than a lightning bolt pierced the sky with a great roar, striking the giant turtle, killing him instantly.

"Once on shore, Orphan Boy noticed a young woman walking toward him. As he got closer, the young woman said, 'Thank you, Orphan Boy. For many moon cycles, I have tried to kill the giant turtle without success. However, when you kept him in the water until the dark cloud hid the star, I could see him and strike with my lightning bolt. My name is Evening Star, and I dwell in the sky. As a reward for your help. You can come with me and be my companion, and you will never be lonely again.'

"However, Orphan Boy was troubled. 'I feel bad for the Giant turtle. He was helping me escape the island, and now, because of me, he is dead.'

"Evening Star laughed. 'Do not be troubled, Orphan Boy. The giant turtle was not your friend. Once he had you on land, he would have taken you to his nest, where you would have been food for his children.'

"Orphan Boy was relieved and told Evening Star that he wanted to go with her and live in the sky forever, and never be alone again. So he and Evening Star ascended into the sky, where he remains to this day as the small Companion Star who keeps Evening Star company each night. If you step away from the fire, find Evening Star, and you will see Orphan Boy next to her, who dwells in the skies forever."

The story settled over the fire like soft ash. Red Bud snored, her head against my chest. Walks in Water rested her cheek against Spotted Lynx's shoulder. Willow Tree sat cross-legged, eyes wide. Dancing Copperhead absentmindedly stirred the embers with a stick. Whispering Doe smiled, her face peaceful for the first time in days.

It should have been a perfect evening—family and friends sharing food and a story beneath the watchful eyes of the Divine Ones. Yet I felt no peace. The weight of my task pressed on my chest. Every time I looked toward the shadows beyond the fire, I seemed to see the mutilated bodies again and the frightened eyes of Water Lilly, and the empty house of Black Locust. Immigrant families were already slipping away from the lands of the Sun King.

Unless I found the killers, more would die.

And I could not shake the feeling that something terrible was moving toward us through the dark, like a giant turtle rising from deep water.

* * *

There are three of them now. What are they doing? Why did the Black Bear Clan women not go to the fields for two sunrises, only to have to go tomorrow as a group with guards? She watched from the dark, her presence protected by the fire's shadows. She hated them. She would find out what they were doing and, once she learned the truth, she would strike.

Chapter 15

Everyone was awake before dawn the following morning, me included. I was not happy about rising before the sun, but we had a long day ahead and needed an early start. I was equally unenthusiastic about a cold morning meal, yet the women were leaving for the Black Bear Clan common fields at first light, and Whispering Doe did not have time to cook. Instead, we ate cold stew and leftover sunflower seed bread from the evening before, chewing in silence while the world around us still lay in shadow.

Shortly after sunrise, my small band and I left the Black Bear Clan Common and walked to the canoe landing. We crossed Cahokia Creek, passed through the North Plaza, and went by the North Temple until we reached the Great Northern Road. Green Heron led the way into the rich agricultural lands of the Great Valley of Cahokia.

Although there were no hills, the country was not truly flat. The floodplain rose and fell in long, gentle undulations, which farmers call ridge and swale. Narrow ridges, perhaps twenty fists high, alternated with shallow swales only a few hands deep. Squash, maize, sunflowers, tobacco, and gourds crowded the low ridges, their leaves whispering in the faint morning breeze. In the damp swales between them, farmers tended plots of starchy and oily seeds—goosefoot, little barley, marsh elder, maygrass, and knotweed. While the starchy and oily seeds produced less grain than maize, they were more nutritious.

As I walked through the rich farmlands surrounding Cahokia, my thoughts returned to the vision I had received at the Emerald Acropolis. Since leaving that sacred place, I had turned the vision over in my mind countless times, examining it from every angle, and I had begun to draw certain conclusions. I was already confident that the farmers emerging from the Temple in my vision represented murder victims. But other images still troubled me—the people gathered around the plaza, the maize field bursting suddenly into flame, and, most of all, Underwater Panther.

As I watched farmers moving steadily through the fields, bending to tend maize, squash, and sunflowers, a new thought took shape. The people slain by the *Wage-rucge* in my vision must have been the immigrant farm families who had come to Cahokia after the return of Morning Star. In the vision, they stood beside the maize field at the center of the plaza as it

133

erupted into flames. The *Wage-rucge* themselves could only represent the killers—brutal, inhuman forces cutting down the helpless. And the burning maize was unmistakable. It symbolized the destruction of Cahokian agriculture itself, especially maize, the sacred crop upon which the city's survival depended. And finally, the burning World Tree Pole represented the fall of Cahokia.

Yet one crucial piece remained elusive. In my vision, if the *Wage-rucge* destroyed the farm families, then Underwater Panther was responsible for the five murders. But who in the Middle World was represented by Underwater Panther? And what part was the demon playing in the mystery? He is a creature of deception, born of the Below World, feeding on fear and delighting in disorder. Wherever he moves, balance collapses, and harmony turns into chaos. Try as I might, I could not place him within the pattern of the murders. He loomed over the vision like a shadow whose shape I could not define.

Even as the meanings of the figures in my vision grew clearer, I still did not understand how this knowledge was meant to guide me toward solving the mystery of the immigrant killings. The vision felt important—urgent, even—but its wisdom remained just beyond my grasp.

So deep was my reflection that I failed to notice I had stopped walking altogether.

A hand touched my shoulder.

"Are you all right, Walking Stick?" Gray Crane asked gently.

Startled, I nodded, feeling suddenly foolish. "Yes. I was only thinking about the vision I received at the Emerald Acropolis."

"That is good," Gray Crane said, his voice calm and reassuring. "Visions are gifts from the Divine Ones. They must be considered carefully and patiently. In time, their meaning will reveal itself."

"I know," I replied, "but I lack the understanding of a Priest. It would be a relief to share the vision with someone wiser than I."

Gray Crane shook his head. "No, Walking Stick. That vision was meant for you alone. Visions are both a blessing and a burden. You must discover its meaning yourself."

We had wasted enough time talking about my vision, so I turned to Green Heron. "Let us visit the families who are still here first. If time remains, we can stop at the farm of the family that has already fled."

`He agreed, and as it happened, our first stop was not far. We soon reached the farm of a man named Bright Eagle. His family's home stood in a tight cluster of four small buildings around a packed earthen common. Several naked, dirty children played there under the dubious supervision of a thin girl of perhaps ten cycles of the seasons. No adults or older youths were in sight.

As we approached, the girl snatched up a drum that lay on a stump and began to beat it furiously. The children ran to her at once, eyes wide with terror.

"Stop. Do not go any closer," Green Heron ordered quietly. "Stay here. Wait for the adults to come, or there may be trouble."

Spotted Lynx immediately moved to the front of our little party. Without seeming to do so, he placed his body between me and the village, shoulder to shoulder with Green Heron. His posture looked relaxed and unthreatening, but he had arranged himself so that he could move in any direction at a heartbeat's notice. His hands did not hover near his weapons, yet they were free and ready to seize a war club or a bow in an instant.

It did not take long for the adults to answer the alarm. Men and older youths burst into the common from the fields, brandishing hoes. The blades were made with heavy, rough-grained chert. Used as weapons, the hoes could be deadly. Green Heron lifted both hands in the universal sign of peace. The newcomers did not lower their tools. Their eyes were fixed on Spotted Lynx.

He did not snarl or posture, yet they recognized him at once for what he was. Death. Warriors in Cahokia look a certain way. They had seen such men before.

"Everyone, remain calm," Green Heron said in a firm, carrying voice. Facing the man who appeared to be the leader, he spoke first in Oho. "Greetings. My name is Green Heron. This is Walking Stick," he said, indicating me. "He has come from the Sun King to speak with you. Will you hear him?"

They stared back without comprehension. Green Heron shifted to Waapaahshiiki and repeated himself. No reaction. Next, he tried Caddoan. Still nothing. Finally, he spoke in a fourth tongue I did not recognize, and one man stepped forward and replied in the same language.

Green Heron smiled. "They speak Dhegihan," he told me. "It is a language from the Oho country. Many Dhegihan families have come to

135

Cahokia over the cycles of the seasons. They live together in small communities like this. They adopt some aspects of our religion but keep their old language. They dwell in greater Cahokia, yet in many ways they remain a people apart."

After another brief exchange in Dhegihan, the man gestured for us to enter the compound.

They had no chairs or benches, so they motioned for us to sit on the bare earth in the common. I noticed at once that there was no World Tree Pole. In Cahokian compounds, even poor families often raise at least a small pole as a symbol of the three worlds, connected by the World Tree Pole here in the Middle World. These people had none.

When we were seated, I addressed them formally. I spoke one sentence at a time and then waited while Green Heron rendered my words into Dhegihan. I kept my eyes on the man who had answered for the group.

"Greetings," I began. "My name is Walking Stick. I come from Cahokia. The Sun King has ordered me to investigate the disappearance of Bright Eagle."

"Have you come to tell us my sister's son is dead?" asked the leader in Cahokian. Although he spoke with an accent, I could understand him clearly. We later learned that he was called Beaver Swims.

At this, a woman began to sob.

I nodded. "We cannot be certain, but we believe so. From what we know, he vanished at the same time that the Sun King's Warriors found several bodies near Deer Toes Lake Town. When was the last time you saw Bright Eagle?"

"It has been many sunrises now," Beaver Swims replied. "We were working in the fields until it grew dark. The rest of us came home to eat the evening meal. Bright Eagle chose to stay and work a little longer. He never returned. After we ate, I took a torch and went back to look for him, but the darkness was thick, and I did not find him. The next morning, we all went together to the fields. He was gone."

"Did you find anything that might tell you where he went or what happened to him?" I asked.

The woman who had been crying earlier began to sob again.

"Blood," Beaver Swims said at last. "There was blood in the field where Bright Eagle had been working—a great deal of blood. Maize plants had been torn out of the ground, and the soil was churned up over a wide space.

Bright Eagle was a strong youth, sixteen cycles of the seasons, and he must have fought hard. We saw several sets of footprints leading away from the field. We followed them and the blood drops for hundreds of steps until the trail ended at Deer Toes Lake. It looked as if someone had launched a canoe there. We did not know what else to do. So we went home."

"Did you tell the Chief at Deer Toes Lake Town? Or the Priests at the Temple?"

He shook his head. "We do not speak with the Priests in this area. They do not like us. We do not trust the Chief at Deer Toes Lake Town. He does not care about people like us."

"Have you asked for help from anyone? Do you have other family here?"

"This is all of us," Beaver Swims said, gesturing to the circle of thin men, women, and children. "This is our family. We have no one else."

I studied the people gathered in the hard-packed yard. They were a sad sight. The children were naked, dusty, and thin. The adults were gaunt, their faces hollow, their eyes dull with exhaustion. Maize is the staff of life in Cahokia, but a diet of almost exclusively maize slowly starves the body of what it needs. I saw no evidence of meat, fish, or greens. Their houses, too, were small and built in the old style, with individually set posts rather than trench-set walls.

"Where did your people come from?" I asked.

"Our parents came from the Oho country about forty cycles of the seasons ago," Beaver Swims said.

"And everyone here is kin?"

He nodded.

"What will you do now?" I asked.

Beaver Swims lifted his hands and let them fall. "Nothing. What can we do? We have nowhere else to go. And now we have one less strong back in the fields."

I decided it was time to raise another issue. "Have you seen Warriors near your farm?"

"Yes," he replied. "Warriors come through this area often. They do not speak to us, but we know they are there. They do not hide themselves. I do not think they like us either."

"Will you show us the field where you found the blood and the torn maize?"

A flicker of fear crossed Beaver Swims's face, but he masked it quickly. "Yes," he said. "I will take you there. We have not gone back since we knew Bright Eagle was gone."

"That is good," Spotted Lynx said. "It has not rained since the murders... since the disappearances. Perhaps the ground still has something to tell us."

We left the rest of the family clustered in their cramped farmstead and followed a narrow farm path through the patchwork of fields to the place where Bright Eagle had vanished. As the trampled maize came into sight, Spotted Lynx halted and raised a hand.

"Stay here," he told us. "If you all walk through the field, you will trample what remains. Let me read the ground first."

We obeyed without argument. Spotted Lynx moved forward alone, a big man but light on his feet. He circled wide at first, studying the disturbed soil from a distance. Only after a time did he step closer, picking his way carefully to disturb the ground as little as possible. Finally, he beckoned for me to join him.

"Careful," he warned. "Do not step on any footprints or in the blood."

He pointed to a clear set of bare footprints. "These belong to Bright Eagle. He was working barefoot, as most poor farmers do. Now look there." He indicated a tangled cluster of prints a few steps away. "Those belong to the men who took him, more than one. I would say three. They wore sandals, not bare feet."

He led me to the center of the struggle. Maize stalks lay ripped from the ground. The soil was torn and gouged in every direction for perhaps five steps across, as if the earth itself had been turned in a brief, violent plowing. Dark patches stained the ground and clung to the torn roots.

"This is where he died," Spotted Lynx said quietly.

I shivered. "Are you certain? Could he not have been attacked here and killed somewhere else?"

Spotted Lynx shook his head. "There is too much blood. He died here. Then they carried the body away. Killing him where he fell would have been easier and safer for them. Dragging a corpse is hard work, but trying to drag a living man through the countryside is more dangerous. He could shout and give them away. No. Bright Eagle died here."

Spotted Lynx had seen death many times. I trusted his judgment.

"There is one more thing," he said. "Come here."

He led me ten steps farther into the field, to where a tangle of maize stalks lay crushed. Half-hidden among them was a hoe. It was the ordinary tool of a Cahokian farmer, with a chert blade about three fists long fixed at a right angle to a wooden handle ten hands in length. The blade had the soft sheen of long use, polished by the soil of the Messipi Valley after thousands of strokes over many cycles of the seasons.

The stone itself had been quarried in the hills south of Cahokia, four sunrises by canoe downstream and six by canoe upstream against the current. The Sun King owned the quarries and the workshops that shaped the raw, coarse-grained, grayish chert into hoes and tools. Traders carried the finished blades to Cahokia, Traders Town, and cities up and down the Messipi Valley.

This hoe, however, had something extra. The tip of the blade was stained dark with dried blood.

"Is that the weapon that killed Bright Eagle?" I asked.

Spotted Lynx shook his head. "I do not think so. Beaver Swims, will you come here?"

Beaver Swims hesitated at the edge of the field. I could see the struggle written on his face. At last, he forced himself forward and stood beside us.

"Is this Bright Eagle's hoe?" Spotted Lynx asked.

Beaver Swims glanced at the tool, nodded once, and then turned away, retreating from the scene as quickly as he could.

"If the hoe is Bright Eagle's, and the blade is bloody, what does that mean?" I asked. "Did the killers use his own tool?"

Spotted Lynx studied the ground for a few heartbeats, then shook his head. "No. We know from the other bodies that these murders are deliberate. The killers went out to hunt men. They would not rely on finding a useful weapon lying in a field. They would bring their own. Do you remember the corpses in the charnel house at the Emerald Acropolis?"

I nodded. How could I ever forget them?

"The cuts on those bodies were clean and precise," Spotted Lynx continued. "They came from keen blades, not dull farm tools. This hoe is perfect for chopping soil, but look at the edge. It is rounded and worn. It could break bones, but it would not slice like the wounds we saw on those corpses."

"Then what are you trying to tell me?" I asked, my patience thinning under the weight of the blood and memory.

"Look at the churned ground. They told us Bright Eagle was young and strong. He did not die easily. The blood on that hoe is not his. It belongs to one of the men who attacked him. Bright Eagle struck back before he fell. Somewhere, one of the murderers carries a wound from that blade."

I drew in a sharp breath. "That is a clue at last."

Spotted Lynx gave a grim smile. "It is not much, but it is more than we had. Now we must follow the trail they left from this field to Deer Toes Lake and see what else the ground has to say."

"Can you read their trail?" I asked.

Spotted Lynx walked along the path where the blood drops led away from the field, following it for perhaps a hundred steps before he returned. "Yes," he said. "They made no effort to hide their tracks. If these farmers could follow the trail to Deer Toes Lake, I could also."

We rejoined the others at the edge of the field. I faced Beaver Swims. "I am sorry for your loss. Thank you for bringing us here. I know it was painful for you to return. What you have shown us today may help us find those who killed Bright Eagle. We will follow the killers' trail to Deer Toes Lake and see what we can learn. You do not need to come. Spotted Lynx can follow the tracks."

Beaver Swims looked greatly relieved. He nodded once and hurried back toward his family without a word.

"Let us go," I told my companions, and we set off toward Deer Toes Lake behind Spotted Lynx.

As we walked, Green Heron asked, "Do you truly think we learned something that might help us catch the murderer?"

"Perhaps," I replied. I told Green Heron and Gray Crane what Spotted Lynx had deduced at the scene, how Bright Eagle had likely injured one of his attackers, and how the hoe gave us our first glimpse of the killers' flesh. After that, we walked in silence, heads down, while Spotted Lynx followed the blood and tracks along the narrow farm paths that twisted toward the Great Northern Road.

Although there had been no rain since the killings, many feet had passed along those trails, blurring the footprints of the murderers. Even so, Spotted Lynx was a skilled tracker. We eventually crossed the Great Northern Road itself and soon saw Deer Toes Lake glimmering ahead through the maize stalks.

At the lakeshore, Spotted Lynx signaled for us to hold back while he moved ahead alone. He approached the water's edge carefully and spent some time studying the bank before beckoning us forward.

"Look here," he said, pointing to the mud. "You can see where a heavy weight was dragged into a canoe or out of it. This is where they landed. It is easier to see the footprints here than in the trampled maize. There were indeed three men, all wearing sandals. We already suspected that these murders were planned, not random. This proves it. They landed here, went inland, killed Bright Eagle, carried his body back to this spot, and then paddled away toward Deer Toes Lake Town to stage the corpse near the road."

"We know where Bright Eagle died, and now we know where the killers entered the lake," I said. "We still need to find where they landed the canoe to place the body."

"Exactly," Spotted Lynx agreed. "We will walk along the shore until we find another landing with the same kind of sign. Then we will see where they carried the body from there."

We followed the shoreline north toward Deer Toes Lake Town. After only a few hundred steps, we came to a small farmstead where three tiny houses faced the water. Several dogs erupted into frantic barking as we approached. An old man, three women, and several children came to meet us. One child immediately ran off, no doubt to summon others. The women were tending racks of buffalo fish fillets, laid over smoldering fires to smoke. The old man sat mending a fishing net.

"Do you speak Cahokian?" Green Heron asked politely.

They stared at him as if he had asked whether the sky was wet. After a few heartbeats, one of the women answered, "Of course, we speak Cahokian. What else would we speak?"

Green Heron flushed. "We have met people in this area who still use the language of the land they came from," he explained. "Even if their families have lived here many cycles of the seasons."

The woman who had spoken—likely the matron of the household—sniffed. "That is true. Some people cling to their old tongues. They keep to themselves, mostly. We do not mix with them."

Spider Clan tattoos marked the women's faces. Spider is not one of the great Noble Clans, but it is a Cahokian Clan. These people were not newcomers. They were of the Sun King's realm.

A moment later, another group appeared: six men and four women coming in from the fields, several of the men carrying hoes of the same kind Bright Eagle had used to defend himself. One of the men looked us over and asked bluntly, "What do you want?"

"My name is Walking Stick," I said, taking over from Green Heron. "The Sun King has charged me with finding who killed five farmers in these lands. Have you heard of the murders?"

The leader's expression did not change, but fear rippled across the group like a gust of wind across grass.

"Yes, we have heard," he admitted. "No one knows the truth. There are only whispers. But everyone has heard enough to be afraid. People say that all the dead were immigrants. Why are you here? What do those killings have to do with us?"

I decided to tell him part of the truth. He deserved at least that much. But I did not want to panic the entire household.

"If you do not mind," I said, "let us speak a few steps away from the others. What I am about to tell you will cause fear. If you wish to tell them later, that is your choice."

He nodded and walked a short distance from the group with me.

"I will speak plainly," I said. "We believe the men who killed one of the immigrants used a canoe to move his body. We are trying to find where that canoe came ashore, and where the killers dragged the body to leave it by the Great Northern Road. They killed Bright Eagle in his field, carried him to the lake's edge south of here, and then paddled north, past your farm, with his corpse in the boat. They must have landed somewhere along this shore, perhaps near your land, and dragged the body up to the road."

The man's face went pale.

"They passed by here? The murderers and a dead man?"

I nodded. "Yes. That is what the ground tells us."

"Morning Star preserve us," he whispered. "You were right not to say this in front of the children."

"The rumor that the victims were all immigrants is true," I continued. "We do not yet know why they were chosen. Until we find the killers, no one is truly safe. Not immigrants. Not Cahokians."

The man drew a slow breath. "My name is Fisher," he said. "I am sorry I spoke so roughly when you arrived. Everyone is on edge. When four

142

strange men appeared at my door, one of them clearly a Warrior, I feared the worst."

I laughed softly. "Spotted Lynx can be intimidating, it is true. The rest of us are less dangerous. I am a coppersmith. I own the copper concession in Cahokia."

"Copper?" Fisher asked, surprised. "Why is a copper merchant investigating murders?"

"It is a long tale," I said with a sigh. "If I had my way, I would be anywhere else, doing anything else. I want only to learn who killed those people and return to my shop and my family."

"What can we do?" Fisher asked. "None of us will feel at ease until you catch them."

"Let us sit by your fire," I suggested. "Invite whichever of your kin you trust most to join us. We can speak more easily there. I see you have plenty of fish. We will gladly pay your women to prepare a meal for us."

My stomach growled at the thought.

While the women set about cooking, my companions and I sat around the fire with Fisher and several of his male kin. "First," I said, "tell me what people in this area are saying about the murders. After that, think back over the past half of a moon cycle. Have you seen or heard anything unusual at night?"

The conversation lasted some time. In the end, I learned very little that was new. No one in the household had heard strange noises or seen suspicious canoes on the lake. The killers must have chosen a time when the entire farm was deeply asleep. The dogs, too, had apparently slumbered through the night. Another stone was laid atop Spotted Lynx's argument that Bright Eagle had died in his field, not by the lake.

"No one in authority has told us anything," Fisher said bitterly. "The Chief says nothing. The Priests say nothing. They tell us everything is as it should be. All we know are rumors. Some say the victims were all immigrants, because families whisper that they have lost kin. Some say people have already left these lands and gone back to where they came from. No one really knows. There is only fear."

The women finally brought our meal: catfish—my favorite—stuffed with goosefoot leaves. Instead of ceramic plates, each fish rested on a thick maize cake that soaked up the rich juices. I doubted they owned more than one or two pots. I tore the fish apart with my fingers and ate greedily. The flesh was soft and salty, the goosefoot leaves tender, and the maize cake rich with the taste of the lake.

When we had eaten our fill, we refilled our water gourds at the lakeshore. We were far enough from Deer Toes Lake Town that the water was still clear and sweet.

I thanked Fisher and pressed several copper pieces into his hand—a sum worth ten times the value of the meal. I did not need the copper, and a bit of generosity might buy us a friend here.

"If you hear anything that seems important," I told him, "send a message to Bold Warrior in Deer Toes Lake Town. He will know how to reach me."

Fisher promised that he would.

Refreshed, we continued along the shore northward. We passed several more small farmsteads, but none of the people there had anything to add to what we already knew. At last, after some distance, we reached a stretch of bank where the mud showed clear signs of a recent landing.

"This is the place," Spotted Lynx said.

I squinted at the tracks. "How can you be sure?"

He pointed. "Three sets of footprints, all sandal-wearers, just like at the first landing and in Bright Eagle's field. And there—look."

Tiny, dark droplets led away from the water.

"Bright Eagle's blood," I said.

Spotted Lynx shook his head. "No. His blood would have clotted long before this. A corpse does not bleed for this many steps. This is the blood of a living man. The one Bright Eagle struck with his hoe."

I felt a grim satisfaction. "Then we are still on the killers' trail."

Spotted Lynx grinned. "Yes. This is their path." Then his expression darkened. "I see tracks leading away from the water, but none returning."

"Did you see any tracks leaving the other landing?" Green Heron asked.

"Good question, Green Heron," Spotted Lynx said. "No, I saw only tracks going toward the lake, not away. That means there was a fourth man. The three killers met a fourth at the first landing. He waited in the canoe while they went inland to find a victim. They arranged a meeting place, killed Bright Eagle, dragged him to the water, and paddled together to this shore. After he brought them here, the fourth man left alone in the canoe. The other three carried the body up to the road and walked away."

"If you can follow the trail, let us see where they went from here," I said.

Spotted Lynx retook the lead, following the bloody drops and sandal prints away from the lake. We moved east in a slow, careful line. As I expected, it did not take long to reach the Great Northern Road. There, the trail ended abruptly in a chaos of footprints.

Spotted Lynx crossed to the far side of the road and searched there as well, but he found nothing. The road had swallowed the killers' tracks as completely as if the earth itself had decided to protect them.

"When we passed this way several sunrises ago, coming from Deer Toes Lake Town to Cahokia, I saw no sign of a struggle," Spotted Lynx said. "Muskrat Waits's Warriors did a thorough job of cleaning the site where the body lay."

I looked over the stretch of road. "They chose their spot well," I said. "Hundreds of people pass here each day. They left the corpse where it would be found quickly. That spreads fear. Yet they also used this place to disguise where Bright Eagle lived and where he died. Why hide the victims' homes? If they wished only to terrify people, leaving the bodies near the farms would have been more effective."

No one offered an answer.

We had spoken with only one family that day, and the sun was already sliding toward the western horizon. By the time we walked all the way back to Cahokia, Whispering Doe would be ready with the evening meal.

"Let us go home," I said. "We can talk on the way."

We turned south along the Great Northern Road toward Cahokia. No one spoke for a long time. Bright Eagle's desperate struggle had given us our best clue so far, but it also made the horror of the murders feel more immediate and personal.

"We must look for someone who has been wounded in the last few sunrises," I said at last, glancing at Spotted Lynx. "I know you are tired of my fixation on Warriors as the likely murderers…"

"I would call it an obsession," he muttered sourly.

"You may call it what you wish," I said. "I still want you to go to the barracks tomorrow. Ask whether any soldiers have been injured recently. Especially any with a blow that looks like it came from a hoe or an axe. The wounds would appear similar."

Spotted Lynx was silent for several heartbeats. "As much as it pains me to agree," he said finally, "you are right. We need to know if any Warriors have taken such a wound. But not just Warriors. We must also somehow learn whether any commoner has such an injury. That is the difficulty. We are looking for one wounded man in a city of thousands, and in the countryside there are thousands more."

"The Clans," I said. "We can use the Clans. Or rather, Muskrat Waits can. He can put the Clan Patriarchs to work. That means I must see him again tomorrow." I sighed.

Turning to Gray Crane and Green Heron, I said, "While Spotted Lynx and I are busy chasing a wounded man in Cahokia, I want the two of you to go to Deer Toes Lake Town and speak with Bold Warrior. Tell him what we have discovered. Ask him to use his own network to search for a recently injured man. Based on what we know, if the killers are not Warriors in Cahokia, there is a good chance they live somewhere near Deer Toes Lake Town."

Gray Crane brightened. "I will gladly go, Walking Stick," he said. "I do not feel I have been much help so far. Perhaps I can assist Green Heron and Bold Warrior this time."

I assured him that his counsel and presence had been valuable, but I was not sure he believed me.

"There is something else we need to consider," said Spotted Lynx.

We all stared at him expectantly.

"The bodies were all found on the same day," he began. "But it would have taken a great deal of work to murder five people and move the bodies to the Great Northern Road. For example, to find Bright Eagle, kill him, carry the body to Deer Toes Lake, load him into a canoe, and paddle north for some distance, and then carry his body to the Great Northern Road would have taken half a night. It would not have been possible for four men to commit all the murders and move the bodies."

Spotted Lynx was right, but the implications were staggering.

"So there were teams of killers roaming the countryside on the night of the murders," I said, terrified at the thought.

"Again, Warriors are my first suspicion," said Gray Crane. "We have gone from looking for a single murderer to several men, and now teams of killers. How monstrous."

Spotted Lynx said nothing, but he was clearly troubled.

"I will have to think about this," I said. "And I would like all of you to spend the night at my house again. I do not think we are in immediate danger, but I would feel better with you close by, and the women will feel safer as well."

As soon as the words left my mouth, I regretted mentioning the women.

"For the sake of the women, I will make the sacrifice," Spotted Lynx chirped, with just enough mischief in his voice to draw snickers from the others. They tried to laugh softly, but I heard them. I chose to pretend that I had not.

By the time we reached the Black Bear Clan Common, the sky was streaked with red and gold. Whispering Doe and Walks in Water had the evening meal ready, as I had known they would. I lowered myself into my chair, and Whispering Doe set a ceramic plate in my hands, piled with roasted, cracked deer bones, along with a cup of cool maize beer.

Using my knife, I pried the soft marrow from the bones and sucked it out greedily. The marrow was rich and salty, and the grease ran across my plate. After cleaning the bones, I wiped up the spilled juices with a piece of acorn bread and ate it too. Whispering Doe then gave me a bowl of hot maize gruel sweetened with blackberries that Walks in Water had gathered several sunrises earlier. I finished with another long drink of maize beer and leaned back, full and momentarily content.

My young companions also ate with great enthusiasm. As I watched them devour their portions, I wondered if Muskrat Waits had ever considered reimbursing me for the cost of feeding three extra men every night. I decided that such a thought would never occur to him.

* * *

After the meal, when the women had finished cleaning up and the children had scattered to their games, I finally had a moment alone with Whispering Doe beside the fire.

"How did the fieldwork go today?" I asked.

"Very well," she replied. "We harvested the rest of the little barley and picked some of the first tender ears of maize for fresh eating. We brought in more squash. The crops look strong, and we are nearly caught up with the weeding." She paused and then added, "But Walking Stick, I do not know how much longer I can keep the Black Bear Clan women from returning to their normal work patterns. Everyone sees that something

147

strange is happening. Three strangers linger around our house, one of them obviously a Warrior. You vanished for several days. They know you have not gone to the copper workshop. You are behaving oddly. We will have to tell them something."

"You are right," I admitted. "It was foolish to think I could hide my work for Muskrat Waits from the Clan forever. What do you plan to do tomorrow?"

"I had intended to take the women—and Dancing Copperhead—and walk to the highland prairie to gather rattlesnake master leaves," she said. "It is earlier than we usually go, but it will take us all day. By the time we return, the women will have just enough time to cook the evening meal. They will be too tired to sit around speculating about why you are acting strangely or why I insist that they stay together."

Clever, as always. Muskrat Waits should have chosen Whispering Doe for this investigation instead of me.

"Excellent," I said. "That will occupy them tomorrow. The next day, keep them close to the common, but tell them I wish to speak with the women and their husbands in the evening. I will talk with the Patriarch first and explain my plan, so there is less grumbling. There will still be gossip, of course—but at least it will be organized gossip. I probably will not have caught the killers by then, but we can begin to bring the Clan into our confidence."

"Thank you, Walking Stick," Whispering Doe said, nestling against me under our sleeping robes. "I know your work for Muskrat Waits is important, but this secrecy makes things very difficult for Black Bear Clan and for me."

I sighed. "I know, and I am sorry for the trouble I have brought upon you," I said. "Curse Muskrat Waits for dragging me into this. I will tell the Clan what is happening. I can only hope they will understand and help me keep the news quiet, so we do not spread panic through all of Cahokia."

Chapter 16

I awoke earlier than usual, yet Spotted Lynx, Gray Crane, and Green Heron had already eaten and gone. The hearth felt strangely empty without their tall shapes and easy banter. Whispering Doe, Walks in Water, Willow Tree, and Dancing Copperhead were readying themselves to leave.

"You have food by the fire," Whispering Doe said. She kissed me quickly on the cheek and then prepared to leave on the long morning walk to the highland prairie.

While my family prepared to depart, I heard a commotion from the Black Bear Clan Common: hushed voices and footsteps. In the predawn darkness, shapes appeared at the limit of my vision. I stood and braced myself. People were coming. The thought flashed through my mind that our adversaries had discovered we were hunting them, and they had come for us. We were now the hunted.

A large man stepped into the circle of light surrounding our hearth.

Mad Owl, Patriarch of the Black Bear Clan, greeted me respectfully, but cautiously.

"May the blessings of Morning Star be with you, Walking Stick," he said.

I nodded. "And you as well, cousin."

More people entered the space in front of our home and crowded around the Patriarch.

"Walking Stick," he began. "There have been odd things happening here the last several sunrises. Strange young men are staying with your family. You leave with these strange men and do not return until sunset. The Clan tells me you have not been to the copper works in many sunrises. Your wife keeps the Clan women in the common during the growing season, and when they do return to the fields, men with weapons accompany them. The Clan is scared, Walking Stick. There are those among us who would see your family driven from your home. Before I allow it to happen, I need you to tell me what is behind your family's strange behavior."

They had waited to confront us until my companions had departed.

I looked at the people standing behind Mad Owl. They were my wife's Clan. I had known most of them for over 20 cycles of the seasons. They were good people, but they did not like change. New ways frightened them.

Routine was safe. Now my mission for Muskrats Waits had frightened them, and as a result, had placed my family in danger.

I noticed some of the men carried clubs. Bear Claws and Dancing Copperhead stepped beside me. They were both armed. The situation could become deadly very quickly. The Clan looked at us with a mixture of fear and anger. Fear and anger cause people to do terrible things they would not ordinarily consider. I had to think fast. I could not reveal my mission to the whole Clan, but I had to say something, or these frightened people might harm my family.

I stepped forward and addressed the Patriarch.

"Mad Owl, I realize our behavior has been odd lately. However, there is a reason for all that has gone on for the past sunrises. Send the women to the highland prairie to gather rattlesnake mast leaves and the men to their jobs. Have everyone go about the day as if it were any other. I will come to you and explain everything."

"No!" a woman screamed from the crowd. "They must be punished. Drive them out now, before the strangers return. Do not let them work their magic on you. For too long, they have lorded themselves over the rest of the Clan, acting as though they are better than we are."

I recognized the voice at once. It was Red Cardinal, my wife's cousin. She was older than Whispering Doe, and when the old Black Bear Clan Matriarch died several cycles of the seasons earlier, many had assumed Red Cardinal would inherit the role. Instead, the Clan women chose Whispering Doe, judging her to be the wisest among them. Red Cardinal had never forgiven that decision. She resented Whispering Doe's authority and envied the standing my family enjoyed because of the copper concession. Now, she saw an opportunity to strike back.

Mad Owl stood in silence, weighing my request. Low grumbling rose from the people gathered behind him, a restless sound like wind in dry leaves.

"At my word," Mad Owl said at last, "and out of respect for your family and your wife, the Clan Matriarch, I will do as you ask. I will see you again before high sun."

"Do not listen to him!" Red Cardinal shrieked. "I have been watching them these past sunrises. Something is wrong. If you allow them to stay, they will bring nothing but trouble to the Clan."

The accusation struck me hard. She had been spying on my household.

The muttering behind Mad Owl grew louder, and Red Cardinal began to wail, but with a single raised hand, he silenced the crowd.

"You have heard my decision," he said firmly. "Now go."

Reluctantly, the people dispersed. The women gathered their children and began preparing for the journey to the highland prairie, while the men drifted away toward their daily labors. Many were clearly dissatisfied, yet none dared defy Mad Owl's command.

As I watched them leave, an uneasy realization settled over me. Beneath the surface of Clan unity lay resentment and jealousy I had never fully acknowledged. Some among them harbored real anger toward my family—and I knew, with a chill certainty, that a few might even wish us harm.

The thought sent a shiver down my spine.

* * *

After everyone was gone, I ate my maize cakes alone in the deserted Clan common. The silence pressed in around me. A place that usually rang with children's shrieks, women's laughter, and the thump of grinding stones seemed hollow and eerie without them.

After I washed and straightened my clothing, I went to find Mad Owl. As I expected, I found him in the woodworking shop east of the common. The smell of fresh-shaved wood and smoke greeted me even before I stepped through the doorway.

Some woodworkers carve only utilitarian tools, and some devote themselves to bows and spear shafts, but the men of Black Bear Clan have made an art of wood. From local walnut, hickory, oak, and maple, they fashion plates and cups, statues, wall plaques, beds, chairs, and elaborate headboards for Cahokia's elite. The Priestly class commissions Black Bear Clan to carve masks and sculptures of the Divine Ones. The masks that hang along the walls of the Temple at the Emerald Acropolis came from these very hands.

Mad Owl, as Clan Patriarch, worked closely with Whispering Doe, the Clan Matriarch, so I knew him well. Despite his fierce-sounding name and our confrontation earlier, he was a quiet, thoughtful man, slow to speak and careful with his words.

He put down his tools when I entered the workshop

"Will you step outside with me, cousin?" I asked

Mad Owl nodded and followed me into the bright morning sunshine. He was about my height and a few cycles of the seasons older. His hair,

151

once black, was now mostly gray, bound in a neat topknot. The Black Bear Clan tattoo on his face, once bold, had blurred among the lines and creases carved by weather and time. Yet his bearing, calm authority, and easy courtesy made him a respected leader in the Clan and, like my Uncle Rattlesnake, a man of influence in Cahokia's East Precinct.

"Things are happening in Cahokia," I said. "Dangerous things."

He nodded, eyes intent, saying nothing, patiently waiting for the rest. So I told him everything that had occurred during the last several sunrises, leading up to our earlier confrontation. I began with Muskrat Waits' summons and our journey to the Emerald Acropolis, the charnel house, and the mutilated bodies, continued with our trip to Deer Toes Lake Town, and finished with our conversations with the immigrant families north of the city. As I described the murders and my part in investigating them, his eyes widened.

The color drained from his face as I explained why Whispering Doe and I had insisted that the Black Bear Clan women remain together in the common and why we had tried to distract them with extra work while I moved back and forth across the valley. Whatever he had expected to hear, it had not been the brutal killing of five people in the lands just beyond our fields.

"I tried to keep the Clan out of this," I concluded. "I see now that it was impossible. I should have told you from the beginning."

Mad Owl stood in silence for several heartbeats, collecting his thoughts. At last, he said, "No, Cousin. You were right to keep the knowledge from the Clan at first. That sort of news spreads fear like a fire in dry grass. And you were right to keep the women away from the common fields. Morning Star have mercy, those people were killed not far from where my own wife and daughters work almost every day."

"I am sorry I brought trouble to our Clan," I said.

"There was nothing else you could do," he answered, his voice reassuring. "If you had refused the Minister of Security, his anger would have fallen on you and then on Deer Clan and Black Bear Clan. None of us needs that."

"What will you do now?" I asked.

He thought again before he answered. "I will call the Clan together this evening," he said. "I will tell them that you and the young men in your house are working for the Sun King. I will say to them that what you are

152

doing is important and must be kept secret for now. They must go about their daily tasks as if nothing were wrong, treating the strangers as if they were invisible.

"The women will go to the common fields only in groups, and they will be accompanied by at least five men armed with bows, knives, and clubs. And they are not to speak of any of this to anyone outside the Black Bear Clan. That is what I will tell them. What do you think?"

I nodded. "That is a good plan."

He smiled slightly. "There will still be grumbling, and there will certainly be more gossip," he said. "But if I at least admit that something is happening and give them a shape for it, that will ease some of their anxiety. Pretending that nothing is wrong in your household only makes the mystery larger."

"Thank you, Cousin," I said. "I am grateful for your help. Now I must go see Muskrat Waits and tell him what we learned yesterday."

Mad Owl looked at me curiously. "Tell me, Walking Stick, what is it like to work for the Cahokian elite? To be at the center of power?"

I answered him truthfully. "It is terrifying."

* * *

I left Mad Owl and his wood shavings and made the now-familiar walk along the Sacred Way, past the stockade wall and into the Sacred Precinct, across the edge of the Grand Plaza, and up the ramp toward Muskrat Waits' ramada on the first terrace of the Great Pyramid.

I still did not know whether he actually lived in that building on the southwest corner of the terrace or sat there like a spider in its web, pulling the strings of Cahokia's defenses. Either way, he was there, seated in his chair under the ramada when I arrived, watching me approach as if he had expected me to appear at that very moment.

"What news?" Muskrat Waits asked. His tone was almost neutral, not nearly as harsh and sour as usual. For him, that counted as warmth. I wondered if our last conversation had given him a grudging respect for me, or if he was pleased that I had managed to arrive before the sun stood high in the sky.

"We learned something interesting yesterday," I said. "Now I need your help."

"Oh?" he asked, leaning forward a little. "What did you learn?"

I told him about our visit to Bright Eagle's field, how we had followed the tracks to Deer Toes Lake, our talk with the fisherfolk, and our discovery of the second canoe landing. Then I described the bloody hoe and Spotted Lynx's reading of the scene—how Bright Eagle had likely wounded one of his attackers before he died.

"That is logical," Muskrat Waits said, rubbing his chin. "And interesting. What do you need from me?"

"The fact that we know one of the killers is wounded matters only if we can find him," I said. He nodded. "I have sent Gray Crane and Green Heron to Deer Toes Lake Town to speak with Bold Warrior and ask him to use his contacts in the villages and farmsteads around the lake. Spotted Lynx has gone to the barracks to learn whether any Warriors have been injured in the last few sunrises. But Cahokia is a big place. There are thousands of people in the city and many thousands more in the surrounding countryside. We cannot ask every household ourselves.

"If you will use your authority to send word through the Clans, to have the Patriarchs check their people for recent injuries, our chances of finding the wounded man will be much better."

Muskrat Waits nodded slowly. "You are right," he said. "That will increase our chances. I will send my agents to the Clan Patriarchs. They will order the Clan leaders to report any men who have recently been injured. People are hurt every day in farming accidents, arguments, chopping wood, and a hundred other foolish ways. There will be many injured men.

"When my agents identify someone, I will send healers to examine his wounds and judge whether they are suspicious. If they find someone whose story does not make sense, I will send a runner to fetch you. Is that agreeable?"

"Yes," I said. "Thank you." I was honestly surprised by his ready cooperation.

"Is there anything else?" he asked.

I shook my head. I did not dare tell him about the trouble with Black Bear Clan.

"Very well," Muskrat Waits said. "This seems like the best lead you have had so far. Perhaps I did not choose the wrong man for this task after all."

From him, that was as close to a compliment as I was ever likely to hear.

After leaving Muskrat Waits, I stopped briefly at the copper works to speak with Red Hawk and make sure the shop had not burned to the ground or fallen into chaos. Everything was running smoothly. The sight of men hammering, filing, and polishing copper under the broad ramada eased my heart for a few moments.

Then I walked back to the Black Bear Clan Common. It was nearly empty. The men were in the wood shop. The women and children—and poor Dancing Copperhead—were far away on the highland prairie, stripping rattlesnake master leaves from their stalks. I did not expect Gray Crane and Green Heron to return from Deer Toes Lake Town before dark, and knowing Spotted Lynx, I suspected he would not appear until he was sure Walks in Water had returned safely.

Whispering Doe had left maize cakes and a bit of honey for my midday meal. I ate them alone, then, with nothing pressing before me, I grew restless. I took my chunkey stone and spear and walked to the East Plaza.

A few boys were rolling stones and throwing spears in lazy practice. They were surprised enough to see the coppersmith of Cahokia stroll up with his own stone. They were even more astonished when I challenged three of them in turn and defeated each one at chunkey.

After proving that I could still outplay six-year-olds, I returned home. I fetched the practice target Dancing Copperhead had made two days earlier and shot arrows at it until my arms tired and my fingers stung. Then I retreated to my chair under the ramada and let my eyes close.

I must have dozed off, because the next thing I knew, Willow Tree was shaking my shoulder.

"Father, wake up. We are back."

I blinked and pushed the fog from my mind. The Black Bear Clan women were filing into the common, each burdened with a bundle of prickly rattlesnake master leaves. They would store the leaves in the Clan storage building and, during the long winter months, strip the fibers, twist them into cord, and weave that cord into cloth.

"Did you help pick rattlesnake master leaves today?" I asked Willow Tree.

He snorted. "Of course not, Father. The women were picking leaves. Men do not do that work. Since Dancing Copperhead was helping Mother, I was guarding the women," he said with great pride.

"Good man," I told my youngest son. He puffed up and then darted off in search of some new adventure.

Across the common, I saw Spotted Lynx had returned as well. He stood beside Walks in Water, making her laugh when she was supposed to be helping the other women store leaves in the Clan storage building and prepare the evening meal. I caught his eye and beckoned.

Reluctantly, he left Walks in Water's side and jogged over to join me under the ramada.

"Did you find anything useful at the barracks today?" I asked.

Spotted Lynx shook his head. "No. I spoke with the other War Captains. They claim none of their Warriors have been injured recently. Two Troupes are away on operations for the Sun King in the South, but they left before the murders began, so they cannot be responsible. What about you? Did Muskrat Waits agree to help us?"

"Yes," I said, and I told him about my conversation with the Minister of Security.

"That is good news," Spotted Lynx said. "Knowing Muskrat Waits' ruthlessness, if anyone in greater Cahokia has been injured in the last few sunrises, his people will drag that information out of the Clans."

"I hope you are right," I said. "Now we will see whether Green Heron and Gray Crane have managed to persuade Bold Warrior to use his influence the same way." A thought struck me. "The man Bright Eagle struck bled heavily. Is it possible he died from his wound?"

Spotted Lynx considered this. "I do not know whether he died from blood loss," he replied. "If he had lost that much blood at once, he might not have had the strength to help carry a body such a long distance. But I have seen many men die from wounds that did not look serious at first. It is not always the blood loss that kills them. Something happens inside the wound. After a few sunrises, the flesh around it turns a sickly color, the cut begins to stink, and the man weakens and dies. I have seen that many times among Warriors."

"So instead of a wounded man, we may be looking for a dead man," I said.

"Yes," he agreed. "That is possible. And it will make our work harder."

Just when it seemed we had found a path to one of the killers, the path twisted and grew more complicated. Nothing about this task was simple, and my patience was wearing thin.

We spoke a little longer until Whispering Doe came over to us, wiping her hands on her skirt.

"The food is ready," she said. "Shall we wait for Gray Crane and Green Heron to return from wherever you sent them, or do you wish to eat now?"

I prefer food hot, not cold and congealed, while men drift in late. "Let us eat now," I said. "I do not know when they will return, and I am hungry."

The women had just begun to ladle stew into bowls and pass out maize cakes when Gray Crane and Green Heron trotted into the common.

"Good timing," Green Heron chirped happily as he dropped down beside me with a plate piled high.

I only grunted through a mouthful of squash stew. Spotted Lynx and Dancing Copperhead snickered. Everyone was hungry enough that, for a time, we did little but eat. The squash stew and maize cakes vanished quickly.

When the meal was finished, and the women had cleared away the dishes, the Black Bear Clan families began to gather near the Clan World Tree Pole. As Mad Owl and I had agreed, my family did not join them. We stayed under our ramada. I could hear Mad Owl's voice rise and fall as he addressed the Clan, but I could not make out his words. Every so often, heads turned, and eyes slid in our direction. I heard Red Cardinal scream; Mad Owl's decision was obviously not the outcome she had hoped for. After a time, the meeting ended, and the families drifted back to their houses.

Spotted Lynx had watched the gathering as closely as I had, so I told him what was happening and the events of that morning. When the Clan began to disperse, he turned to me. "What do we do next?" he asked.

"Let us hear what Gray Crane and Green Heron learned in Deer Toes Lake Town," I said. I motioned for the two of them to join us by the fire. I did not care if my family overheard. The time for secrets had passed.

"Did you speak with Bold Warrior?" I asked Green Heron.

"Yes," he said. "We spoke with him today. He agreed to send his men into the villages and farming lands around Deer Toes Lake Town to look for anyone who had been injured recently."

"Excellent," I said. I told them about my meeting with Muskrat Waits and how he had promised to send his agents through the Clans to search for wounded men. "With so many people asking questions in Cahokia and around Deer Toes Lake Town, we may yet find an injured man whose story does not fit. If we find one, he may lead us to his fellows. Then we can finish this investigation, and I can return to my copper workshop.

"Until we hear from Bold Warrior or Muskrat Waits, however, we must keep searching on our own. Tomorrow we will speak with the family of the murdered woman and see whether the neighbors of the family that has already left can tell us anything useful."

I felt the faint sag in their shoulders, the unhappiness they did not voice. I shared it. I was tired of tramping through fields and farm lanes, always half a step behind unseen killers. But until we found a wounded man or a dead one whose scars matched a farmer's hoe, we had no choice. The work had to go on.

* * *

Spotted Lynx slept lightly. A Warrior's life depended on always being ready and never being surprised. For ten cycles of the seasons, he had trained himself to drift only into the shallow edge of sleep, to wake in a heartbeat, and to sense danger even when his mind walked the Dreaming Road.

Now that sense flared.

He was awake at once, though he kept his eyes closed. Listening. Breathing slow and steady. There—a faint sound. Movement. Close, but not yet close enough to be a threat.

Spotted Lynx slid from his pallet beside the house and stepped into the deeper shadow just beyond the circle of dim light cast by the cookfire embers glowing in the hearth. He stood very still, every muscle loose, his head tilted slightly in the direction his keen ears had marked.

Nothing.

He waited. Patience.

For a long time, he remained by the wall of the house, listening. Only the familiar sounds of Cahokia at night reached him now: a dog barked once, then yelped and went quiet, a baby wailing for its mother, a distant shout.

There had been something here. Someone. Now, they were gone.

At last, satisfied that whatever danger had brushed past them had moved on, Spotted Lynx returned to his pallet, lay down, and let himself slip back into sleep.

Chapter 17

It was still dark when shouting in the distance tore me from sleep. The voices were faint at first, then grew louder—approaching fast. A moment later, someone grabbed my arm and shook me hard.

"Walking Stick! Wake up—wake up!"

I blinked into the darkness. Whispering Doe had already risen to her elbows, her face tense with fear. Standing over me was a young man from our Clan—my cousin, Black Rope—breathing hard, his eyes wide.

"You must come now," he insisted. "Walking Stick, you must come now."

I pulled myself from my sleeping furs, mind still foggy, and hastily tied on my breechcloth and slipped into my shoes. The noise had roused everyone. My children and the young men staying with us crowded close, confused and frightened.

Before I could relieve myself, take a sip of water, or even splash my face awake, Black Rope seized my arm and half-dragged me from the Black Bear Clan Common toward the East Plaza.

Behind me, I heard Spotted Lynx snap to the others, "Stay here. Guard the family." Then he followed us at a run.

Black Rope led us straight to the Deer Clan lodge at the base of our mound, the shrine house above silhouetted against the faint gray of dawn. Even before I stepped inside, the smell hit me—hot, metallic, unmistakable. A coppery stench that sucked the breath from my lungs.

I had smelled that horror before at the Emerald Acropolis. It was the smell of blood—the smell of death.

I steadied myself, pushed aside the lodge door covering, and stepped inside.

I did not recognize him at first. There was too much blood splattered across the wall, pooled on the floor, glazing his body in a dark sheen. Then I saw the severed ear lying a hand's length from the corpse. Still attached was a copper ear spool engraved with the curling shape of a snake.

A rattlesnake.

My knees buckled. Spotted Lynx caught me before I hit the floor and guided me back outside into the cool predawn air.

"You know who that is?" he asked quietly.

I could barely speak. "It was my uncle. Uncle Rattlesnake."

The truth struck me like a spear thrust. I staggered. "Red Horn, preserve me... several sunrises ago, I asked him to speak with the other Clan leaders in the East Precinct. I wanted to know if anyone had heard whispers about the murders." My voice cracked. "Spotted Lynx—I think I got my own uncle killed."

His jaw tightened, but he said nothing.

A heartbeat later, he spoke. "I did not bother waking you, but we had a visitor last night. I sensed movement in the common. Someone crossed through the shadows. I never saw him, but he was close. Too close. There was an evil to him." His voice dropped. "When I rose to confront him, he slipped away; whoever it was moved with great skill. If I had remained asleep..." He hesitated. "I think he meant to kill you. Or someone in your family."

A cold shiver ran through my body.

A moon cycle ago, I would have laughed at such a tale, brushed it away as a Warrior's superstition. But I had seen too much. The butchered bodies at the Emerald Acropolis. The terror of immigrant families. And now this—my uncle murdered in his own Clan lodge, butchered like the others.

"I believe you," I whispered. "Come. I need to tell my family what happened."

* * *

Spotted Lynx and I walked the Sacred Way through the stockade gate, into the Sacred Precinct, and up the ramp to Muskrat Waits' ramada on the first terrace of the Great Pyramid. He sat in his carved walnut chair, studying me as though he had been waiting all along.

"Back so soon, coppersmith? What news?" he asked. His voice was less harsh than usual. He was curious. Under the circumstances, that felt like respect.

"My Uncle Rattlesnake was murdered last night," I said, unable to mask the accusation in my tone.

Muskrat Waits touched the copper human-head earrings dangling from his lobes, his eyes narrowing as he searched his memory.

"Yes," he said slowly. "I remember Rattlesnake well. He managed the copper concession when I was a young man. A steady man. Honest. What do you mean he was murdered?"

My voice faltered. I could not continue. Spotted Lynx stepped in and recounted what had happened—the intruder in our common, the early-morning summons, the body in the lodge, three dogs killed in the Black Bear Clan Common before they could raise an alarm. Something was hunting us.

When he finished, I added, "If not for Spotted Lynx, I might be dead. Or worse—someone in my family."

Muskrat Waits nodded once toward the young Warrior, an acknowledgment as rare as it was meaningful.

"There is something else," I said. "I asked my uncle to speak quietly with Clan leaders in the East Precinct community, to gather whispers about the murders. He knew many people. They respected him. I thought he might learn something others would not tell me."

Spotted Lynx resumed. "Whoever crossed through the common last night realized I was awake, sensed that Walking Stick was no longer an easy kill. So he punished him by killing his uncle instead. Rattlesnake must have been found asking questions. By murdering him, the killer sent a message: We know who you are. You are not safe."

For the first time since I had known him, Muskrat Waits looked shaken.

"They have brought death into the city. The situation is near collapse," he muttered. "If news spreads that a respected Cahokian was butchered in his own Clan lodge…" He exhaled sharply. "Fear will ignite faster than a wildfire in a drought."

Too late, I thought, word was already spreading.

He fixed his gaze on me. "Walking Stick, you and your companions must act quickly. You must stop these killers before panic consumes the city."

* * *

I spent the remainder of the day with the Deer Clan Council, preparing Uncle Rattlesnake's funeral rites. My heart twisted with guilt. None of them knew the truth—that I had placed him in danger. I lacked the courage to tell them. Perhaps when this is over… if I can solve the immigrant murders… I will tell them he died in the service of Cahokia.

After we met with Muskrat Waits, he quietly dispatched several Warriors to watch over the Black Bear Clan Common. They did not wear uniform tunics or carry shields. Instead, they eased themselves into the East Plaza like ordinary men—leaning against a wall, repairing a net, sitting in conversation. Most residents would never notice them. But I had spent the last several sunrises around Warriors and men of authority. I saw them. And I was grateful.

Muskrat Waits must have been badly shaken to devote his Warriors to protecting a Clan that was not one of the Noble Clans. I wondered what fate awaited him if he failed in this crisis. Was he untouchable because of his rank? Or would he meet his end at the top of the Great Pyramid—garroted and flung down the steep slope like disgraced officials before him?

The evening meal was subdued. Whispers replaced conversation. No one laughed. And when darkness settled, we all retreated quietly to our sleeping furs.

Despite the hidden Warriors posted around our common, Spotted Lynx insisted on extra precautions. He ordered Gray Crane to keep watch until moonrise, then wake Green Heron, who would stand guard until the moon set. After that, Spotted Lynx himself would take over until dawn.

The big Warrior would hardly sleep, but knowing he was watching over us eased the weight pressing on my chest.

Chapter 18

We rose again before the sun, choked down a hurried morning meal, and set off toward the farmlands north of the city. The long days of walking and the short nights of broken sleep were wearing on me. My legs ached, my back complained, and my feet throbbed in my shoes. The three young men, by contrast, strode along as if they had only just begun this journey. I was getting old.

Once we crossed Cahokia Creek and left the crowded houses and shrines around the North Plaza behind us, I fell in beside Green Heron.

"I want to visit the family of the murdered woman," I told him. "What can you tell me about her?"

"Her name was Morning Mist," he said. "I do not know much more about her family, except that they lived not far from Bright Eagle's farm. However, local farmers found her body along the road between Deer Toes Lake Town and the Emerald Acropolis."

"We passed that place when we came from the Emerald Acropolis," Gray Crane observed. "After all this time, there will be nothing left to read. The site where they placed the body will tell us nothing now."

"What do you think?" I asked Spotted Lynx.

The big Warrior shrugged. "Gray Crane is probably right. The villagers who found her and the Warriors who carried her away will have trampled any sign the killers left. Since then, hundreds of feet have passed that way. Any tracks and blood left behind will be gone. And we would still need to find someone who remembers exactly where they found her. It is not worth the time."

I would have liked to see the place where Morning Mist was found, to understand how the killers had chosen it, but Spotted Lynx was right. Even if we could find someone to guide us, it would almost certainly be a wasted effort.

Morning Mist. Her name haunted me.

I did not know the identities of the other victims whose bodies I had seen at the Emerald Acropolis, but I knew which corpse had been Morning Mist. She was the only woman among the dead. The image of her body surged up from the place in my mind where I had tried to bury it. I saw her again on the platform in the charnel house. Bloated. Decapitated. Her breasts removed. Desecrated. Violated. My stomach twisted, and bile burned the back of my throat.

Morning Mist.

"Are you well?" Gray Crane asked. "You look terrible all of a sudden."

I waved away his concern. "I am fine. My stomach is unsettled, and I am tired and sore. That is all."

Spotted Lynx smirked, but—for once—kept whatever cutting remark he was thinking to himself.

"I have ground blackberry root in my bag," offered Gray Crane, ever solicitous of everyone else's comfort. "We can stop and make tea if you wish. It will settle your stomach and ease your joints."

I managed a small smile for the young Priest. "Thank you, Gray Crane, but I will be fine. Let us keep moving."

With Green Heron leading us along twisting farm paths between fields of ripening maize, we soon reached the farmstead of Morning Mist's family—three small houses, built in the old style, clustered around a cramped common. There was no World Tree Pole. The buildings leaned and sagged, badly in need of repair. Flies swarmed over half-filled trash pits next to the houses. Sherds of broken pottery littered the ground.

This was not a prosperous family.

The only person in sight was an old woman sitting in the shade, grinding maize on a worn mano and metate. She did not notice us at first. When she finally looked up and saw four strange men in her common, her face changed from blank concentration to pure terror.

"Mother, please remain seated. We mean you no harm," Gray Crane called in Oho, stepping ahead of us with both hands raised in the gesture of peace.

She did not run, nor did she answer him. She only stared at us, silent and rigid with fear.

Gray Crane tried again. "Mother, my name is Gray Crane, a Priest from the Emerald Acropolis. This is Walking Stick, coppersmith of Cahokia. May we speak with you? You have nothing to fear from us."

For several heartbeats, she studied us, her eyes moving from one face to the next. At last, in Oho, she replied, "What do you want, Priest? We have nothing that you need. Why have you come here?"

Gray Crane translated her words and then motioned for me to step forward.

164

"Mother," I said, "we want nothing from you or your family. We seek only information. The Sun King has tasked us with finding the men who killed several people in this area. We believe that one of the murdered people was named Morning Mist. Is this her family?"

The moment she heard the name, the old woman dropped the mano and nearly toppled over. Gray Crane leaped forward to catch her. She began sobbing, her shoulders shaking with deep, wracking cries. Green Heron grabbed a gourd and scooped water from a pot near one of the houses. He held it out to her, and she halted her sobbing long enough to drink.

We gave her a few heartbeats to compose herself. Then I asked softly, "So this is the home of Morning Mist?"

She nodded. "Morning Mist is my daughter. We have not seen her for many sunrises. She disappeared one night while walking home after visiting a friend who had given birth to a baby. It was a hard labor, but both mother and child lived. Morning Mist went to see the child and took the mother cloth strips stuffed with cattail down, the same kind she used when her own children were babies."

Her voice trembled, but she forced herself to continue.

"Her children—the two who lived—are past their naming ceremonies now, and she no longer needed the baby cloths. She left her friend's house, but she never came home. Her husband, Long Hands, searched the area. No one had seen her. No one knew where she went. Then we heard that someone had found a woman's body on the road between Deer Toes Lake Town and the Emerald Acropolis. At first, we did not believe it could be Morning Mist. Why would she be so far from home? Long Hands went to see, but we heard the news too late. By the time he arrived, the Sun King's Warriors had already taken the body away."

She swallowed, then asked in a thin voice, "She has never come home. We are afraid that the body found along the road was Morning Mist. Have you come today to tell me that the body was my daughter?"

Gray Crane did not wait for me to answer. He took her hands gently and said, "What is your name, Mother?"

"Blackberry," she replied. She already knew what he was going to say.

"We cannot be absolutely certain," Gray Crane said, "but we believe that the body found along the road was your daughter, Morning Mist."

"But why?" Blackberry demanded. "Why would anyone wish to harm my daughter?"

"We do not know," Gray Crane said. "That is why we are here. We are trying to learn what happened to Morning Mist and why."

She drew in a breath and asked, "How did my daughter die?"

Gray Crane's heart was too kind for the truth. "She was stabbed with a very sharp weapon," he said. "The Priests at the Emerald Acropolis said she would have felt a sharp pain and then died quickly. They do not believe she suffered."

The image in my mind called him a liar, but it was a gentle lie.

Blackberry's expression shifted in an instant. Grief hardened into fury.

"What did your Priests at the Emerald Acropolis do to my daughter?" she demanded.

Startled by the sudden change in her mood, Gray Crane answered, "They were preparing her body for burial in the way of our people. They must have already performed the ceremonies to guide her along the Path of Souls through the stars to the Land of the Dead, to take her place among your honored ancestors."

"You fools!" Blackberry screamed. "You do not know what you have done! Your ghoulish Priests, with their foolish ceremonies and their hunger for bones, have defiled my daughter. Without her earthly remains, they have condemned her to an eternity of darkness in the Below World. Leave us! Leave us now! Take your heathen ways away from my home!"

She struck Gray Crane on the head with the gourd dipper, then snatched up the mano she had dropped and hurled it at me. It hit the ground at my feet with a heavy thud.

I could not understand her words, but I understood her meaning very clearly.

I motioned to the others, and we backed away from the common and onto the nearest farm path.

"Come," I said quietly. "We must leave this place now. I do not want to be anywhere near that farmstead when the men return and learn why Blackberry is screaming. We will not gain anything more here."

We walked quickly until the farmstead and Blackberry's wails were far behind us. When we reached the Great Northern Road south of Deer Toes Lake Town, we stopped to rest and drink. Everyone looked shaken.

"I would rather face an armed enemy than go through that again," Green Heron muttered, trying to restore his usual humor. He jabbed Spotted Lynx lightly in the ribs. "What about you, big man?"

Spotted Lynx chuckled. "You are right. That was terrible. I was more afraid of Blackberry than I was of some enemies I faced in battle. She was fierce. What was she shouting, Gray Crane?"

Gray Crane did not smile. In a subdued voice, he explained why Blackberry had reacted the way she did.

"These people are from the Oho country," he said. "I could tell as soon as we entered the farmstead. Their broken pots are of Oho design. That is why I addressed Blackberry in Oho. My grandmother made pottery that looked exactly like the pieces we saw at her home."

He stared down at his hands.

"They have different beliefs about the dead and the Path of Souls. The Priests at the Emerald Acropolis did not follow the ways of the Oho religion. In Blackberry's mind, by cutting and cleaning Morning Mist's body, they condemned her souls to the Below World for all eternity."

No one spoke for many heartbeats. At last, Spotted Lynx broke the silence.

"I do not understand some of these immigrant families," he said. "They come to Cahokia to live near the place where Morning Star appeared to the people of the Middle World, to be part of greater Cahokia. Yet when they arrive, some refuse to practice our religion. They do not speak our language. They cling to old ways of building houses and making pots. Why come here if they will not become Cahokian?"

"I agree," Gray Crane said. "Our religion is the foundation of Cahokian civilization. Morning Star's teachings shape everything. Without our religion, there is no miracle. There is no Cahokia."

"My family came here to be close to Morning Star and become part of Cahokia," Spotted Lynx said. "My parents embraced everything Cahokian. They tried to learn the language. When my brother and sister married, they did so according to Cahokian custom. Our house was built in the Cahokian style, as Morning Star commanded. We celebrated all the festivals. I was raised as a Cahokian, not as an immigrant."

Gray Crane nodded. "My family was the same, except my grandparents preferred to speak Oho inside the house. Now here I am, the grandson of immigrants, a Priest in the service of Morning Star."

"Most immigrant families have adapted," I said. "They have become Cahokian and prospered. Before Muskrat Waits tasked me to solve these murders, I had no idea some families resisted. From what I have seen, those

167

who refuse to adapt live in isolation and poverty. Yet the people who have become Cahokian, like your families, have done well. Why come here and resist the very culture that drew them in the first place? It makes no sense."

After we had rested, Green Heron led us toward our final destination. Along the road, we passed a woman selling maize cakes. I bought two cakes and a handful of blackberries for each of us, and we walked on. A short distance farther, we came upon several boys tending gar that roasted in their tough skins over cedar coals.

I have never been able to resist fish.

Fishermen in canoes speared gar on backwater lakes and slow channels of the Messipi, where the long fish floated near the surface. I paid the boys and accepted a slender gar wrapped in a sycamore leaf. The fire had charred the armor of skin and scales. I slit it along the back with my knife and peeled away the shell to reveal two long strips of boneless meat along the spine, much like a deer's tenderloins.

Gar is not my favorite fish, but I do not think there is any fish that is not good to eat.

We sat by the roadside, watching travelers come and go along the Great Northern Road while we ate. The boys had chosen their spot well; their little business thrived. When we finished, we tossed the bones and scales into an adjacent maize field and continued.

It was a short walk from there to our next stop. Green Heron turned us off the main road onto a side path that led west toward Deer Toes Lake. After we left the road, we did not pass another farmstead. At last, we reached a deserted compound not far from the lakeshore.

"Who lived here?" I asked.

"A man named Three Hawks," Green Heron said. "I do not know where his family came from. I only know that they left after he vanished."

"Let us look for neighbors who might tell us more," I decided. "Gray Crane, you and Green Heron follow the path toward the lake and see if there is a farmstead nearby. Spotted Lynx and I will return to the Great Northern Road and search there. Come back here after you find the closest neighbors. Then we will decide which to visit first and go together."

We split up. Spotted Lynx and I walked back to the road, then north, perhaps a hundred steps, until we saw a well-worn trail heading toward the lake. We followed it between tall maize stalks. Before long, Spotted Lynx spotted a farmstead ahead.

"Do you see anyone in the compound or in the fields?" I asked.

"Yes," he said. "Men are working the fields."

"Stay here and keep watch," I told him. "I will fetch the others."

I retraced my steps to Three Hawks' abandoned farmstead, where I found Gray Crane and Green Heron already waiting.

"Did you see another farmstead close by?" I asked.

Gray Crane nodded. "Yes. There is a farm near the lakeshore about a hundred steps from here. We saw people working in the fields and came back to you rather than approach them ourselves. Did you find anyone?"

"Good work," I said. "Yes, we also found a farmstead. Spotted Lynx is watching them. Come. We will speak with those people first, then visit their neighbors by the lake."

We found Spotted Lynx where I had left him on the path—no longer alone. Three young men stood with him, laughing.

"This is Sparrow Hawk, Blue Catfish, and Green Frog," Spotted Lynx said. "Sparrow Hawk and Green Frog are brothers. Blue Catfish is their cousin. They live in the farmstead ahead. They saw me standing here and came to see who I was. I was telling them some of my Warrior tales while we waited for you."

Their facial tattoos marked them as native Cahokians of the Black Rock Clan, peasant farmers. Sparrow Hawk seemed to be the eldest, and he took the lead when he spoke.

"Spotted Lynx told us why you are here," he said soberly. "We never liked Three Hawks much, but we are not happy he is dead. It could have happened to any of us. His family was odd. They did not mix with others. They spoke poor Cahokian."

"Do you have any idea who might have done this?" I asked.

Sparrow Hawk shook his head. "No. They never made trouble. They had no enemies that I know of. When people spoke of them, they spoke only of how strange they were; that is all. No one I know wished them harm."

Spotted Lynx took over. "When did the rest of the family leave?" he asked.

Sparrow Hawk thought for a few heartbeats. "Several sunrises after Three Hawks disappeared. His father, Walking Deer, came here to ask if we had seen him. His Cahokian was hard to understand, but we think Three Hawks did not come home the previous night. The next day, we heard the

169

Warriors came and carried away some bodies found along the road. Sometime after that, the family vanished. We did not see them for several sunrises, so we went to check. They were gone. No one saw them leave. They must have slipped away in the night."

"Do they have any other family nearby?" Spotted Lynx asked.

"Not that I know of," Sparrow Hawk replied. "We did not interact much, but I never saw strangers visit their farmstead."

"Have you seen anyone around their farm since they left?" Spotted Lynx asked.

Sparrow Hawk shook his head. "No one. People avoid that place now. It may be cursed."

We all fell silent. I could not think of any other useful questions.

"Does anyone have anything else to ask?" I said at last. The others shook their heads.

I turned back to the three young men. "Is there anything else you can tell us that might help us understand why anyone would want to kill Three Hawks?"

They exchanged glances and shrugged. Sparrow Hawk answered for them. "No. We have no idea why anyone would want to kill him. We have not seen anyone take crops from the fields or possessions from the houses. No one has tried to move into their buildings. People did not like them, but that is a long way from murder."

A thought came to me. "Do you know the family that lives on the other side of Three Hawks' farm, toward the lake?"

"Of course," Sparrow Hawk said with a chuckle. "That is my mother's brother, Sky Climber, and his family. Black Rock Clan, like us."

I had no more questions for the three. I thanked them and pressed a small copper piece into Sparrow Hawk's hand for their trouble.

We returned to Three Hawks' empty farmstead, then followed the path west toward the lake. "Gray Crane, lead us to Sky Climber's farm," I said.

"Why go there?" Green Heron asked. "We have already spoken with their clansmen. Do you think they will tell us anything Sparrow Hawk did not?"

"It is possible," Spotted Lynx answered. "They may have had a different relationship with Three Hawks. They may have noticed something their kin did not."

"Or neglected to mention," I added.

"Exactly," said Spotted Lynx.

The walk was short. We soon reached another Black Rock Clan farmstead. In the common, several women were preparing the evening meal. An old man sat under the shade of a ramada, using sandstone to smooth a hematite plummet that would serve as a net weight.

I approached him. "My name is Walking Stick of the Deer Clan," I said. "My companions and I just spoke with your kinsman Sparrow Hawk. He told us this is a Black Rock Clan farmstead and that we could find Sky Climber here."

The old man nodded. "That is true. I will send someone to fetch him."

He rose from his chair and walked to the fire, where the women had paused in their work to stare at us. He murmured to a girl of perhaps ten cycles of the seasons, and she immediately dashed off into the maize field.

We did not wait long. Several men emerged from the rows of maize and walked toward us. A tall man carrying a hoe stepped forward.

"I am Sky Climber," he said. "Which of you is Walking Stick?"

"I am," I replied, stepping forward.

He studied me for a moment, weighing what he saw. I am sure I did not look particularly impressive or threatening. Spotted Lynx, towering and heavily muscled, drew the eye far more readily.

"What can I do for you?" Sky Climber asked.

I told him about my commission from the Sun King and repeated, in brief, the story I had just told Sparrow Hawk and his cousins.

"Yes, we lived beside Three Hawks for many cycles of the seasons," he said. "But we never truly knew them. They did not speak our language well enough for easy conversation. They did not join our festivals or rituals. They were... apart."

"Did you ever have disputes with them?" I asked. "Arguments over land? Fights over men or women?"

He shook his head. "No. We did not mix with them. They were not troublesome. They wanted to be left alone."

"How about other neighbors?" I asked. "Do you know if they had problems with anyone else?"

Again, he shook his head. "Not that I know of."

"When did you first notice the family was gone?" I asked.

"We knew Three Hawks was missing when his family came to ask if we had seen him," Sky Climber said. "Later, we heard that the Warriors had

171

taken away several bodies found near Deer Toes Lake Town. At first, we did not believe Three Hawks could be one of those dead people. It was too far from his home, and the family seldom left their land. But he never returned. We did not see the family for several sunrises, which was not unusual. They kept to themselves. Then, about five sunrises ago, Sparrow Hawk came to tell us the farmstead was empty."

"Have you seen any strangers around?" I asked.

"No," Sky Climber said. "No one. Some of our young people went to look at the deserted farmstead, but I had no interest in abandoned houses."

I decided to ask something more direct. "Will the Black Rock Clan take over the land?"

Even under the heat of the sun, Sky Climber shivered. "No," he said firmly. "I have ordered the young people to stay away from that land and not to touch anything that belonged to that family. The farm is cursed now. The land and all their possessions will bring trouble to anyone who claims them."

"One more question," I said. "Have you seen Warriors operating in the area? Or heard of Warriors threatening anyone here, immigrant or Cahokian?"

Behind me, I heard Spotted Lynx groan softly.

Sky Climber shook his head. "We see Warriors occasionally, but they do not trouble us. I have never heard of them threatening anyone around here, immigrant or Cahokian."

"And you have no idea who might have hated Three Hawks enough to kill him?" I asked.

"None," he said. "But people here are frightened. And not only immigrants. Someone is killing immigrants now, but who knows when they might begin killing Cahokians. We keep our people close to home and set guards at night. I hope you catch the murderers soon, so that we can return to normal life and stop living in fear."

I hoped so as well.

I thanked Sky Climber, and we took our leave, letting the Black Rock Clan return to their work.

By then, I was exhausted and frustrated. As we walked back toward the city, my anger slipped out.

"We keep learning more and more about these immigrant farm families," I said. "We know their names, when they disappeared, where they

172

lived, and how they got along with their Cahokian neighbors. And yet I do not see how any of this brings us closer to the killers. We still do not know who their enemies were. No one we have questioned can give us so much as a hint of who might have wanted them dead or why."

"One thing I find interesting is that every victim was killed at night and away from home," Green Heron said thoughtfully. "None were attacked in their houses."

"Yes, that is interesting," I agreed. "What kind of people are frequently out at night?"

"Bandits," Gray Crane said uneasily. "I have heard they roam the roads after dark, robbing travelers."

Spotted Lynx snorted. "Bandits do occasionally rob travelers, yes. But they target people with possessions worth stealing. Our victims had nothing. In Bright Eagle's case, the killers went well off the main road into the fields to find him, and even then, they left his hoe behind. That is not bandit work."

"Hunters," Green Heron suggested. "Hunters travel at night and carry weapons."

Spotted Lynx shook his head. "Not here. There has not been a deer or other large animal in this valley for many cycles of the seasons. Hunters have to go far into the hinterlands, away from Cahokia, to find game. Around here, only squirrels and rabbits remain, and they are not worth a hunter's time. And before Walking Stick mentions the third possibility, I will. Warriors patrol at night to keep bandits away from the roads." He gave me a pointed look. "But as you already know, I still do not believe the Warriors were involved."

"Then why were the victims killed away from home?" I wondered aloud.

"In the military, we have a saying," Spotted Lynx replied. "A 'target of opportunity.' That is when we have not planned an attack, but some unexpected situation arises in our favor. We strike because the chance appears, not because we were hunting that particular person."

"By Red Horn's hair," I exclaimed. "Are you telling me that the murdered immigrants might not have been chosen in advance?"

"Not exactly," he said. "I am saying there may not have been a single intended victim. The killers could have been looking for anyone who presented themselves as easy prey. The dead may have been in the wrong place at the wrong time."

I was stunned. "So instead of a deliberate attack on the immigrant community, you think the killers might have simply taken random victims because they were convenient?"

"That is a possibility," Spotted Lynx said flatly.

I shook my head in frustration. "Then we may be completely wrong about why these people were killed." He nodded. "Sometimes, despite everything we have learned, it feels as if we know nothing at all."

"You are right," Green Heron said. "Everything is still confusing. What do we do now?"

"At this point," I said, "our best chance is to wait for Muskrat Waits and Bold Warrior to find a man with a suspicious wound. I do not know who else to question. Muskrat Waits told me he would send word when his men found such a person, but I will go see him tomorrow morning to hear what progress he has made and whether he has any new information that might help us."

We walked the rest of the way in silence, each man lost in his own thoughts. I had spoken with the families of the dead and their neighbors. I knew how and where the victims had vanished. Yet motive and suspects remained a fog.

As we crossed Cahokia Creek, I looked up at the Sun King's palace crowning the Great Pyramid, home of the most powerful man in the world. I wondered what would happen to my family and me if I failed.

Despite my weary mood, we received a warm welcome when we stepped into the Black Bear Clan Common. The young men were no longer strangers here; they were becoming part of the household. Whispering Doe left her work by the fire when she saw me approaching.

"You look tired and discouraged, husband," she said softly. "What happened today?"

I gave her a sad smile. "It feels as though we are making no progress. I will tell you everything later, after we are wrapped in our sleeping furs."

Not even Walks in Water had much to say during the evening meal. She sensed something was wrong and kept a respectful distance from Spotted Lynx. When we finished eating, we sat in a glum circle around the fire until Whispering Doe finally broke the heaviness.

"We did receive some good news today," she said brightly.

174

"We could certainly use some," I replied. "What did you hear?"

"The Sun King's messengers visited the Clans today," she said, "and announced that three sunrises from now will mark the beginning of the New Maize festival. On the first day, Priests will hold ceremonies at the Clan shrines to bless the ripening maize. Those without Clan shrines will go to one of the plaza Temples. On the second day, everyone will gather in the Sacred Precinct, where the Sun King and the Lord High Priest will perform the New Maize ceremony atop the Great Pyramid. The third day will be for Clan feasts."

The ripening of maize in summer is one of the year's great turning points. Maize is the staple that supports most Cahokian families. Poor families, especially, depend so heavily on it that their lives rise and fall with the harvest. Although we had already eaten the first tender green ears before this, the fully ripened grain could now be used in countless ways.

Women would grind the dried kernels on a mano and metate into flour and meal for cakes, puddings, and porridges. They would boil maize with wood ash to make hominy, enriching it and making it tender for toothless toddlers and the elderly. When cooked in pots tempered with powdered mussel shell, maize became even more nourishing.

"That is excellent news," I said. "This city needs something to pull its thoughts away from murder. A festival and a feast may help people forget their fear, if only for a few sunrises."

The New Maize Festival could not have come at a better time. I was worn out in body and spirit. Three days of rest and celebration sounded like a blessing from Morning Star.

Feeling lighter, I asked Whispering Doe about the Clan. "How were things today after Mad Owl's talk last night?"

"Much better," she said, smiling. "Everyone now understands why we have been so secretive. In fact, you have become something of a hero among the Black Bear Clan."

"What?" I spluttered. "How am I a hero?"

"You have an important task from the Sun King," she said. "When you find the killers, and all of Cahokia learns that you solved the mystery, it will bring honor to the Black Bear Clan and to the Deer Clan as well."

I was appalled. What if I did not solve the mystery? What if I failed? Instead of honor, I might bring ruin. My wife had more faith in me than I had in myself.

"So you had no trouble getting the women to obey Mad Owl's new rules?" I asked.

"None," she said. "We worked in the fields today. Five men, including Dancing Copperhead and Bear Claws, went as guards. We walked out together, worked close enough that the men could keep an eye on everyone, and returned as a group. No one complained."

"That is a relief," I said. "I was tired of the tension we had created in the Clan, and I know you were also. But people's patience will not last forever. They will grow restless and want their freedom back, and I would not blame them."

"Then you must solve this mystery quickly, husband," Whispering Doe said, sliding closer. "Only then will our lives return to normal."

A thought occurred to me. "There have been no murders in the countryside for more than ten sunrises," I said slowly. "Perhaps the killers have already accomplished whatever they set out to do—even though I still have no idea what that might be. Perhaps the killings have stopped. If there are no more murders and daily life returns to normal, maybe I do not need to find the killers. Muskrat Waits will not be pleased with me, but if the deaths stop, he cannot be too angry. Maybe the murderer of Rattlesnake was the last killing, a final message to us, and the murders will stop."

I exhaled, feeling the tension ease from my shoulders. That must be the answer, I told myself. If there were no more murders, everything would be all right.

Drained, I left the fire with Whispering Doe, and we lay down together under the ramada. All I wanted was for the killing to end and for me to sleep through the night, finally.

I received neither.

Chapter 19

"Wake up! Walking Stick, wake up," Two hands roughly shook me from a deep, dreamless sleep. I opened my eyes to find Spotted Lynx staring at me.

Gaining her senses more quickly than I, Whispering Doe asked, "What is wrong, Spotted Lynx?"

For the second time in three days, I was awakened from a sound, peaceful sleep to face a nightmare.

"There has been another murder."

His words went through me like a spear thrust. Instantly awake, I jumped to my feet. Gray Crane and Green Heron stood behind Spotted Lynx, dressed and ready for the road. I looked at the sky; the moon had not set. It was still the mid-point of the night, and I had been sleeping for only a short time. Whispering Doe put on her skirt and a cape and went to the fire. I pulled on my breechcloth and turned to Spotted Lynx.

"What happened?"

"A messenger from Bold Warrior arrived just a few heartbeats ago." He motioned to a young man standing several steps behind Green Heron. "He woke Green Heron, who then woke Gray Crane and me. There was another murder, this time north of Deer Toes Lake Town. I do not have many details, but Bold Warrior's messenger, Lightning, can tell you what he knows while we walk. Bold Warrior says to come right away before Muskrat Waits learns of the murder and orders the Warriors to remove her body."

"So it was another woman?" I asked.

"Yes," replied Lightning. "A woman. We can talk on the road, but we need to leave now. Bold Warrior said it was very important for you to hurry."

I made water in a pot beside my sleeping furs and grabbed my knife and water bottle. By the time I was ready, Whispering Doe had already warmed some maize cakes on the coals, which she passed out to us. I noticed her hand shaking as she handed me two maize cakes, and tears welled in her eyes.

"Another woman." Whispering Doe said hoarsely. "This is so terrible. When will the madness end?"

I had no answer. She hugged me tightly for several heartbeats and then retreated to the ramada, crying softly. I turned and led our little band out of the Black Bear Clan Common.

"Be careful," Walks in Water called out to Spotted Lynx as we left the common. The tall Warrior turned around, smiled at my daughter, and waved back. Spotted Lynx was almost 20 cycles of the seasons younger than me, a towering figure, and a skilled fighter. And yet, it was he that my daughter urged to be careful. What about her father? Spotted Lynx was only assigned to protect me during the murder investigation, or so Muskrat Waits claimed. May Red Horn give me strength. When I returned from Deer Toes Lake Town, I planned to speak with Whispering Doe and find a way to end the budding romance between my daughter and Spotted Lynx.

Silently, like spirits in the night, we moved through the sleeping city and made our way to the canoe landing. No one was around, so we took a canoe and paddled across Cahokia Creek. The owner would be surprised to discover his canoe on the north side of the creek in the morning, but we did not have time to waste searching for a paddler. We passed through the North Plaza and were soon headed to Deer Toes Lake Town on the Great Northern Road. Sunrise was still a long way away.

Once in the countryside, I turned to the newest member of my small group and told young Lightning, "Tell me everything you know."

"The murder must have happened not long after sunset," Lightning began. "The Woman, Red Feather was her name, was late coming home from visiting a friend near Deer Toes Lake Town when it got dark. The family lives north of town. When it got dark, and she was not home, the family went looking for her. They found her body along the Great Northern Road, not far from their farmstead."

"Was she from an immigrant family?" I asked.

Lightning nodded his head. "Yes, the family was originally from the Oho country. They do not speak Cahokian well. They sent Red Feather to the Deer Toes Lake Town market because she spoke Cahokian better than the other family members, and it was easier for her to communicate with the merchants."

"Why did they not send one of their men with her?" I asked rhetorically. "Five other immigrants have been killed recently. What were they thinking? Surely, they heard about the murders."

"How did Bold Warrior find out about the murder so quickly?" Spotted Lynx asked.

"When Red Feather's family found her body, they began screaming. People living near the road heard their cries and came to see what had happened. One of those men knew Bold Warrior and ran to Deer Toes Lake Town with the news. Bold Warrior immediately sent the man who had come from the murder site to wake me. He told me everything he had seen. Bold Warrior ordered me to run to Cahokia as fast as I could, find you, and lead you back to the murder site."

Spotted Lynx studied me with a peculiar expression. There was something in Lightning's account that troubled him, though he had not yet put his unease into words.

I asked, "Are you a *Hiperes Jinak*, like Green Heron?"

"I am training to be a *Hiperes Jinak*," he corrected. "Green Heron has already completed the training. Someday, I hope to become a *Hiperes Jinak* like him." Lightning clearly admired the older boy. Green Heron still considered himself a novice, but in the eyes of Lightning, who was several cycles of the seasons younger, he seemed so experienced.

We lapsed into silence. The countryside around us was silent and dark. The ripening maize fields crowded the road, creating a tunnel through which we five men passed unseen in the darkness. No lights burned in the homes along the Great Northern Road, and they were invisible to us.

Unsettled by the unnatural stillness, I told Lightning, "You must have run hard once Bold Warrior sent you to bring us. The murder happened earlier this evening. You ran all the way from Deer Toes Lake Town, and yet it is still dark. You certainly earned your name tonight." Even in the dark, I could see Lightning flush with pride.

I pushed myself hard and set a fast pace, and we reached the outskirts of Deer Toes Lake Town just as the sun peaked above the hills east of the Great Valley of Cahokia. I had barely slept that night, and while our night march did not faze my young companions, I was already exhausted. Although we had almost reached the murder site, I nevertheless ordered a rest once we reached the town plaza. I sat down on the ramp to the Temple and drained my water bottle. I lay back and closed my eyes for just a few dozen heartbeats before Spotted Lynx poked me with his foot.

"Let us go," Spotted Lynx ordered. "We need to reach the scene of the murder before our Warriors or someone else moves the body."

I groaned and reluctantly got to my feet, and we continued our journey. While walking towards the north from Deer Toes Lake Town, we encountered some people returning from the murder site. Although some wanted to stop and tell us what they had witnessed, we ignored them and kept walking. After a while, we noticed a crowd blocking the road ahead.

As we got closer to the site, I saw Bold Warrior, who was trying to prevent the crowd from getting too close to the body lying on the side of the road. As soon as he saw us, he signaled to join him. However, we had to push through the curious onlookers threatening to overrun the crime scene to do so.

"Praise Morning Star, you are here at last," exclaimed Bold Warrior as we approached. "The people are getting restless and are desperate to see the body. My men are struggling to control them."

"I will take care of it," declared Spotted Lynx. The imposing warrior pushed through the crowd and stood beside Bold Warrior's men, guarding the body. Green Heron and Lightning followed him while Gray Crane remained by my side. Spotted Lynx was dressed in his red breechcloth, cape, and feather headdress and held his War Captain's spear. He looked intimidating.

Using his commanding voice, he addressed the crowd, "I am War Captain Spotted Lynx of the Cahokia Warriors. You are hindering a murder investigation, and your presence is not welcome. You must all leave immediately!" A few people on the perimeter of the crowd walked away, but most of the curious spectators continued to struggle for a glimpse of the mutilated corpse. Spotted Lynx repeated his previous order. "This is the last time I am going to tell you people; you will all leave the area now! If you do not leave immediately, I am going to start hurting people!"

Although most of the people left the area, others remained, jostling with Bold Warrior's guards. Spotted Lynx handed his spear to Green Heron and faced the remaining onlookers. He gave another menacing look and walked up to the nearest man grappling with Bold Warrior's men. Spotted Lynx punched the man in the head, and he immediately fell to the ground. Before Spotted Lynx had time to reach another man, the stunned crowd fled the scene.

Spotted Lynx appeared pleased with himself and said, "Well, that was not so hard. Now that the rabble is out of the way, let us look at the body."

"You look like you enjoyed that," I told Spotted Lynx.

"I did," he replied without a trace of a smile.

While Green Heron and Lightning dragged the unconscious spectator to the opposite side of the road out of our way, the rest of us went to look at the remains of Red Feather. "We will be lucky to find any evidence after that mob trampled everything close to the body. It is a good thing you brought your men with you." Spotted Lynx complimented Bold Warrior.

Red Feather's remains were in a ghastly condition. Although she had only been dead since the previous evening, the body had already begun to bloat and smell in the summer heat. Like Morning Mist, the other female victim, the killers had cut off Red Feather's breasts and violated her. However, unlike Morning Mist, they did not decapitate her. Instead, her dull, sightless eyes stared out at the world she would never be a part of again. I stayed well away from Red Feather's remains and let Spotted Lynx, Gray Crane, and Bold Warrior examine the body closely.

Red Feather's family—presumably her husband, parents, and children—stood on the far side of the road, wailing, yet not approaching the mangled corpse of their loved one closely. For the moment, we let them mourn in peace.

"I would say she was about 25 cycles of the seasons," Bold Warrior speculated. She was no longer young, but she was not old yet, either. Looking at her children, the oldest of whom looked to be less than ten cycles of the season, I thought his guess was about correct. "She was a pretty girl once. What a shame."

"There is no blood around the body," observed Spotted Lynx. "She was killed elsewhere, and her body was moved here, just like the others."

Gray Crane pointed to her breasts. "Look here, her breasts have been sliced off. Not cut with a dull blade or hacked with an axe, but sliced off smoothly with a single cut by a very sharp weapon, something much sharper than a tool or weapon carried by the average Cahokian."

"Just like Morning Mist's body that we saw at the Emerald Acropolis," Spotted Lynx observed.

Spotted Lynx continued to examine the corpse for clues to her death. "The way she has been mutilated would have been excruciating, but I do not think those wounds alone caused her death."

"I agree," said Gray Crane. "Let us turn her over."

Red Feather had been placed next to the road at a slight angle, resting on her back and left side, but hiding her right side. When the two turned her onto her front, it revealed a gruesome sight.

"Oh, my," said Gray Crane, sucking in a breath. "I think we know how she died."

Spotted Lynx nodded, staring grimly at a savage wound in Red Feather's side.

Looking closely at the wound—about one-half fist long and deep—Gray Crane said. "There is something in the wound." Carefully working his fingers into the deep gash, he pulled out the tip of a knife. Holding up the blade for everyone to see, he said, "And I would say this is what killed her."

"Green Heron, find some water and wash off that blade," instructed Spotted Lynx. Reluctantly, the young *Hiperes Jinak* took the blade and went to find some water to clean the blood and gore.

Gray Crane was still examining the body when he noticed something pressed into the earth beneath where the killers had laid Red Feather. "Did you lose a feather from your headdress when we turned the body?" Gray Crane asked Spotted Lynx as he held up an eagle feather. The feather's quill was covered in bright red cloth and held in place by two bands of golden thread wrapped tightly around the fabric. The threads were broken on one side, as if the feather had once been attached to another object and then broken off.

"I do not think so," said Spotted Lynx as he pulled off his Warriors headdress and searched for a missing feather. None were missing.

Gray Crane held the dark brown eagle feather he found under Red Feather's body next to Spotted Lynx's headdress. The feathers on the headdress were identical. Spotted Lynx turned pale.

"Your headdress is not missing any feathers," observed Gray Crane. "Someone else lost this feather, probably when they moved the body here from wherever they killed her. This feather is from a Warrior's headdress. I am sorry, Spotted Lynx."

Spotted Lynx stood by the body, stunned. Everyone stared at him. For the first—and perhaps the only time I have known him, his shock was so great that Spotted Lynx found himself unable to speak. Finally, he stammered, "It cannot be. The feather must have fallen along the road sometime before the killers placed the body here."

No one believed him

Green Heron returned from cleaning the broken blade and handed it to me. I looked at it in horror, and my gaze snapped instinctively to the knife on Spotted Lynx's belt. I held the blade up to the sunlight. The lustrous, fine-grained, blue-gray hornstone chert glistened in the morning sunshine.

Upon seeing the blade, Spotted Lynx's hand reflectively touched the knife on his belt. "Hand me your knife," I ordered.

As if in a trance, Spotted Lynx pulled his knife from its sheath and handed it to me by the bone and sinew handle. I held both blades to the sunlight; the blue-gray cherts were identical. They were rare, fine-grained hornstone cherts from the hill country south of Cahokia. The weapon that killed Red Feather was a Warrior's knife.

I gave Spotted Lynx his knife back and handed the broken blade to Gray Crane. "Could the killers have used this knife to make the wounds on Red Feather's body?" I asked the Priest.

Gray Crane examined the blade closely with the eye of someone used to witnessing the older Priests dissect bodies. "This is a good blade," he began. "The chert is very high quality and can be worked very sharp. Yes, this knife is sharp enough and large enough to have sliced off her breasts and made the fatal wound in her side."

While we were examining the body, Red Feather's family was watching and wailing about 30 steps away, waiting for us to finish our work. I motioned Gray Crane, Green Heron, and Bold Warrior to join me, and I went to question the family. I left Spotted Lynx standing bewildered by Red Feather's body, and he did not attempt to join us.

"When can we take our daughter?" an older man asked in Oho as we approached the family.

"His name is Red Hand," Bold Warrior told me. "He is Red Feather's father. He will do the talking for the family."

Using Gray Crane to interpret, I told the man we were almost finished. He said, "Good, you have defiled her enough already. It is bad enough that your people murdered our daughter, but to treat her body in such a disrespectful manner is shameful. May Wah-kon-tah bring his wrath upon you and your families!"

Although I was startled by his hatred, I remained calm. I did not point out that he and his family had chosen to move to Cahokia and live among 'my people.' Instead, I got to the point: "My name is Walking Stick. The

Sun King sent me to find out who killed your daughter. Where do you live, and when did you last see her?"

Angrily, Red Feather's father replied. "We live just north of here, not far from this road. We sent Red Feather to the market in Deer Toes Lake Town yesterday afternoon. On her way home, she stopped to visit a friend. She never came back."

"Did she go by herself?"

"Yes"

I asked, "Have you heard that people from several other immigrant families were killed south of Deer Toes Lake Town about half a moon cycle ago?" He nodded. "Why did you not send someone with her?"

Her father stated, "It does not matter. My daughter is dead. Her children have lost their mother, and her husband has lost his wife. All I want is for us to mourn her loss and bury her body in a way pleasing to Wah-kon-tah."

I disagree with his statement that what happens in the rest of the world does not affect his family. "What happens in the world is interconnected. If we turn a blind eye to it, we may lose our loved ones too," I said. "If your statement were true, your daughter would still be alive." Moving on, I asked, "Can you take us to the friend's house so we can speak with her, too?"

The old man shook his head vehemently. "No. I will not involve anyone else in your world."

I could understand his pain, but I was becoming exasperated at the lack of cooperation. "Look, I am sorry for your loss, but I am here to find out who killed your daughter and to stop them from killing again. But I need your help to do that. I need to know where Red Feather was going yesterday and who she saw."

"All I want from you is to leave us alone and let me take my daughter home. I do not care about anything else you are doing," Red Hand declared defiantly.

I snapped, "You do not care if we do not find the killers, and someone else's family has to endure what you are going through now?"

He shrugged and replied, "It does not concern us."

I decided to move on to another subject and asked, "Have you seen any Warriors in the area recently?"

Again, he shrugged and said, "We see Warriors occasionally."

I then asked whether they had ever harassed or threatened him, and he replied, "No, they do not bother us."

Unfortunately, I was not getting any helpful information from the family, and I grew frustrated.

Bold Warrior had clearly reached the end of his patience with Red Hand's stubborn silence. He stepped forward, placing himself squarely between the old man and his daughter's body, and spoke directly to him in his own language, without waiting for Gray Crane to translate.

"Listen to me, Red Hand," he said firmly. "Walking Stick is investigating these murders—including the murder of your daughter—on behalf of the Sun King. Whether you care to see her killers found is not the question before us. What matters is that you cooperate, because Walking Stick speaks with the authority of the Sun King, and his work is for the good of all Cahokia."

Bold Warrior gestured toward the surrounding countryside, then back toward the road leading south. "The other victims were taken to the Emerald Acropolis, where the Priests prepared their bodies for burial according to Cahokian custom. That is what will happen to your daughter as well once the Minister of Security learns of her death. The longer you delay, the more likely it becomes that the Sun King's Warriors will come and take her body themselves."

His voice hardened. "If you continue to refuse to help, Walking Stick— or War Captain Spotted Lynx, who stands beside your daughter even now—may decide that you will not take her away at all. And there will be nothing you can do to prevent it. Now listen carefully. Walking Stick will ask you some questions. When he is finished, you may take Red Feather home. If you refuse, we will keep her body and turn it over to the Priests."

Fear rippled through Red Feather's family. Her mother clutched the children close, and several faces went pale, but no one spoke. The threat was clear, and it struck deep.

Through Gray Crane, I addressed Red Hand again, my voice measured but unyielding. "Tell me where your daughter was going yesterday—and who she intended to see."

The old man answered at once, his resistance collapsing. "She went to the market in Deer Toes Lake Town because she speaks Cahokian better than the rest of us. After that, she planned to visit her friend, Soft Willow.

185

She left after the noon meal, while it was still light. She was not meant to be gone long. We expected her back before the evening meal."

His voice broke. "When she did not return, we went to look for her. We found her here. My wife and the children began to scream, and people from nearby came running. More followed after that. We wanted to take her home, but they would not let us. They said this man"—he pointed toward Bold Warrior—"would want to see her. So we waited through the night."

Red Hand's eyes filled with anger and grief. "Then, just after sunrise, you came with your men and began to violate Red Feather."

The accusation hung in the air, heavy and bitter, and I felt the weight of it settle over us all.

"I am sorry for having to handle your daughter's body," I said. "However, it was necessary to determine the cause of her death. During our examination, we found some important evidence. Could you please tell me where Soft Willow's residence is located?" He told me, and I ensured Green Heron heard him so he could lead us there later.

"Do you know anyone who might want to harm your daughter?"

Red Hand's eyes filled with tears. "No, she was a sweet girl. Everyone who knew her loved her, even our Cahokian neighbors."

I asked, "What about you or your family? Do you have enemies?"

"Enemies have surrounded me," he replied. "Ever since I came here as a young boy many cycles of the seasons ago, the Cahokians have persecuted my family and other families from the Oho Valley because of our religion and our different ways."

"Why did you come here? And if you came here to be a part of Cahokia, why did you not adopt the Cahokian ways?"

He was silent for a few heartbeats and then responded, "My father had heard about Cahokia and wanted to be a part of the excitement that people called the miracle of Cahokia. We were among several families who migrated from the Oho country and settled north of the city. Deer Toes Lake Town was a small village then, but as more farmers moved into the area, it grew into the large town it is today. Once we arrived in the Sun King's lands, we discovered that the Cahokian religion differed from ours. We do not worship Morning Star or his more human form, Red Horn. We do not understand First Man or Old-Woman-Who-Never-Dies. We know that Wah-kon-tah is the unexplainable, all-controlling great spirit that created the world and directs our lives. However, most people who migrated with us to Cahokia from the Oho country started to reject Wah-kon-tah and embraced your Cahokian religion."

"Religion is the foundation of Cahokia," I explained. Our belief system has played a crucial role in its growth and power. If Morning Star had not returned, blessed the work of the Sun Family, and showered His favor on the people, Cahokia would have been a large town but not the great city it is today.

"It has been 121 cycles of the seasons since Morning Star returned, and families like yours came here by the thousands from Oho, Waapaahshiiki, the cities on the lower Messipi and Tanasse Rivers, and the Caddoan lands to the south. The miracle of Cahokia lies in our religion. If you haven't accepted our religion despite knowing its significance in our society, why have you chosen to stay? Why haven't you taken your family back to the Oho country?"

He shrugged, his eyes betraying a deep sense of isolation. "I thought we could have a good life here. However, it gets harder every year. We do not want to give up our religion or our language, but more of our people turn to your Cahokian religion every year, and we become more isolated. We feel like we are losing our identity, our community."

I was mystified by his reasoning and stubbornness, but satisfied he was finally answering my questions, so I changed the topic and asked, "Have your neighbors threatened you recently?"

He shook his head and said, "No, they do not bother us; They ignore us. Even families that came with ours from the Oho Valley and later adopted Cahokian ways now treat us like outsiders."

"Tell me again about the Warriors. Have they threatened or harassed you? Have you seen them more lately?" I asked.

"We see them occasionally, but only from a distance. They mostly stay on the main roads and do not come near where we live," said Red Hand.

I had no more questions for him, so I asked Bold Warrior, "Is there anything else you would like to ask him?"

"No," he replied. "He does not know anything. You had better let them go before the Warriors arrive to take her body away."

"Take your daughter and go," I told Red Hand. "Do it quickly before the Sun King's Warriors arrive. Once they get here, we will not be able to stop them from taking her away."

Red Hand did not have to be told twice to remove his daughter. Quickly, he and the dead woman's husband lifted her body and carried her away.

"Well," I said, returning my attention to the others. "Did we learn anything new from my questioning Red Hand?"

No one commented for several heartbeats, and then Gray Crane said, "I feel sorry for them."

"I do not," Green Heron stated. "They chose to come here and then stayed, even though they did not like our ways and refused to adapt. It is their own choice."

Gray Crane said sadly, "That is true, but I still feel sorry for them, living in ignorance and isolation."

"Other than their reason for staying, I do not think we learned anything new," opined Spotted Lynx, joining the conversation. "Their situation is the same as the other victims. No one liked the family, but they had no known enemies. And, it appears the victim was chosen randomly and not singled out for some reason."

"As you said yesterday, she was a target of opportunity. Like the others, she was caught at the wrong place at the wrong time."

"Exactly," Spotted Lynx agreed.

"However, because we were able to examine the body before Muskrat Waits could have it moved, we now have a good idea who the killers are." Bold Warrior asserted. Spotted Lynx bristled but remained silent. "You would probably have learned more from the corpses of the other victims if they had not been moved before anyone had the chance to inspect them. I wonder why Muskrat Waits waited so long to choose someone to investigate the murders, which in turn prevented the person he selected to investigate from examining the bodies where they were found."

I explained, "It is true; it took him several sunrises to select me to investigate the murders. When we first talked, Muskrat Waits explained that he had the bodies removed to prevent panic throughout Cahokia. But you do not believe him?"

"I do not trust him," declared Bold Warrior. "I think he has interests different from what he has told you. It is making your task harder and endangering us all."

"It is also true that he did not have anyone examine the bodies before he moved them. We inspected two of the murder scenes. One had been

188

trampled, and we learned nothing. However, at the other site, we learned that one of the killers was injured in the attack on Bright Eagle. The killers moving the bodies from where the victims were killed and Muskrat Waits then having them taken to the Emerald Acropolis certainly destroyed any clues we might have found. Do you think he had the bodies moved so we would not find any evidence?"

"It is a possibility, but we can discuss all this later. Now we need to question Red Feather's friend, Soft Willow. She was the last person to see her alive, except for the killers, so she is the best chance we have of learning anything else about the murder."

"Do you know that family?"

He replied, "Yes. They are from the Oho country, like Red Hand's family. Questioning them will be almost as difficult as questioning Red Hand; they will be reluctant to talk with strangers. I will come with you to show you the way and act as an interpreter. I can also help if the family resists. It would be best if just the two of us went. They will have already heard about this latest murder, and we do not want to scare them. An old man and a soft merchant do not look too threatening," he joked. I would have been more insulted by his joking about my physical condition, except for the fact that he was right.

"Thank you," I replied, grateful to have his help. "Spotted Lynx, while Bold Warrior and I go to question Soft Willow, I want you to take Gray Crane and Green Heron and question every family that lives near here. There is a chance that they saw something that could help us."

"And Spotted Lynx, do not let the families bully or avoid talking to you. Use your authority as a War Captain of Cahokia. You look menacing enough," Bold Warrior advised. "Green Heron can take you to my house when you are finished. We will probably already be there. My daughter will feed us, and we can discuss what we learned. Is that acceptable, Walking Stick?"

"It is a good plan, thank you," I said. We then split into two groups, Bold Warrior leading the way to Soft Willow's home.

We had walked north on the Great Northern Road for only a few hundred steps before Bold Warrior led us off the main road onto a farm path. We followed the path until I heard wailing in the distance. I tilted my head to hear better, and Bold Warrior said, "That noise is coming from Red Hand's house. The family is conducting a mourning ritual. We should avoid their place." I heartily agreed. We turned onto an even smaller farm path that led away from the grieving family.

It wasn't long before we came to a clearing in the fields of maize, squash, and sunflowers. About a dozen people sat around a fire in the middle of a common surrounded by four houses and storage buildings. The men carried hoes and looked wary. We stepped into the clearing and waited until one of the men noticed us. While the others watched us warily, two men, one of them as old as Bold Warrior, walked over to where we stood.

"Bold Warrior, I thought we might see you today," said the older man. Bold Warrior introduced me to Gray Fox—the father of Soft Willow's husband—and told him about my work for the Sun King.

After the introductions, Bold Warrior said, "You knew I was coming, so you must also know why. Walking Stick needs to speak with Soft Willow."

"Nothing good can come from speaking to her. Your presence here will only bring us trouble." Gray Fox stated.

"I am sorry, Gray Fox," Bold Warrior said in a conciliatory tone. "But people have been murdered—a friend of your family, included. Walking Stick is here to solve the murders. None of us is safe until he finds the killers, including your family. I know you do not like to talk to outsiders, but it will be easier to speak with Walking Stick now than to have a Troupe of Warriors arrive and question your family."

Bold Warrior's threat did not escape Gray Fox. "Come on then," he said, leading us to the common, where the rest of the family waited expectantly. Gray Fox introduced us to Soft Willow, a short, stocky young woman several cycles of the seasons younger than her late friend Red Feather.

Using Bold Warrior to translate, I told the family, "We are going to speak with Soft Willow privately first. However, I would like everyone to stay close by. "This will not take long, and when I finish speaking to Soft Willow, I have some questions for the rest of you." Once the others left, I turned to Soft Willow and asked, "When did you last see your friend Red Feather?"

Soft Willow was understandably nervous, and tears filled her eyes as she began to talk about her friend. "She left here yesterday about the time the sun started to set. She was on her way home from the market. She needed to get home quickly and prepare the evening meal."

"Why had she come to visit?"

"We were working on a dress for my daughter. In six sunrises, she will be four cycles of the seasons old, and we will have her naming ceremony. Red Feather is good at beadwork, so she helped me sew mussel shell beads on Daughter's dress."

"Did she often stop by your house?" I asked. Soft Willow shook her head. "Then why did she stay so late?"

"We were almost done with the dress, so she stayed until it was finished," Soft Willow replied.

I asked, "After she left yesterday, did you hear anything unusual? Were there any noises coming from the direction of her house?"

"No, I did not hear anything," she said.

"Now I have a more personal question," I began. "Do you know if anything was bothering Red Feather? Was someone threatening her? Was she having problems with her husband or anyone else in her family? Was she uncomfortable around anyone in your family? Red Feather was a pretty woman, and I noticed several men in your husband's family. Did any of them pay her unwanted attention?"

She paused for several heartbeats. I found the question somewhat insulting, but it did not seem to upset her. After a few heartbeats, she answered, "I do not think so. She never said anything to me, anyway. Certainly, men looked at her, but not in a way that made her uncomfortable. She wasn't scared or nervous about coming here, and I never heard her say anything about problems with her husband or family. I am sorry."

"There is no need to be sorry," I said reassuringly. "We only want you to tell us the truth. Now, it is not far from your house to Red Feather's house. However, somewhere in between, someone attacked and murdered her as she was walking home. Are you sure you did not hear anything unusual after she left?"

Soft Willow began to cry again. Through her tears, she said, "No, I did not hear anything. I did not know anything was wrong until we heard screaming and shouting toward Deer Toes Lake Town. My husband's brother went to find out who was making the noise and why. When he returned, he told us that Red Feather was dead. We have not left the common since then. My husband's father said that people would come to question us."

191

"I know this is hard, but I have one more question for you," I told her, "Do you see Warriors in the area often? Do they threaten you?"

"We see Warriors occasionally, but they do not threaten us. Usually, we see them on the Great Northern Road going back and forth between Deer Toes Lake Town and North Star Town. I have never talked to a real Warrior. They look scary." They do indeed, I thought.

"I do not have any more questions for her," I told Bold Warrior. "Ask her to bring the rest of the family so I can question them."

The rest of the family returned and gathered around the fire. I let them know I would question them as a group to make them feel more comfortable. They murmured in agreement. I asked them the same questions that I had asked Soft Willow, except for the question about whether she thought Red Feather felt uncomfortable around any men in the family. However, like Soft Willow, no one reported seeing or hearing anything unusual. I had a feeling they would not. I hoped that the men had interacted with the Cahokia Warriors, but they all said the Warriors had ignored them.

I had one final question for Gray Fox. "Is your family going to stay in Cahokia?

He was thoughtful for several heartbeats and then said, "We have talked about leaving, but we have lived here now for many cycles of the seasons. If we return to the Oho country, we will be strangers there, too. All the people here are scared, but we have not decided what to do."

Before leaving, I asked Soft Willow, "Will you show us the trail Red Feather took when she left here last night?" She agreed and led us to the edge of Gray Fox's farmstead clearing, where we found a trail heading south into the fields. I thanked her and wished her well.

Bold Warrior and I followed the trail, which was, in reality, nothing more than a footpath through the farm fields of sunflowers and maize in the direction Red Feather had walked the evening before. After about 500 steps, Bold Warrior stopped and, in a hushed voice, said, "Oh, no."

"Morning Star, save us!" I cried once I noticed where he was looking.

Directly in front of us, on both sides of the road, sunflower and squash plants had been ripped from the ground and trampled. There were footprints everywhere in the soft, alluvial soil. The ground was so torn that it looked like *Wage-rucge*, the man-eating giants, had played a stickball game in the fields. And there was blood everywhere. This was where the Warriors killed Red Feather.

"I wish Spotted Lynx were here now," I commented. "He is an excellent tracker. He could tell us how many men were here and where they went."

Bold Warrior walked off the road to a particularly bloody patch of ground, bent down, and picked up an object. "Creator, save us!" he exclaimed, dropping what he had picked up.

Curious, I trotted over to where he stood and looked at what he had been holding: a severed breast. I withdrew in horror. Bold Warrior had regained his composure and pulled a cloth from his travel bag. He carefully picked up the severed breast along with its companion lying nearby, wrapped them reverently in the fabric, and put them into his bag.

"I will take these to High Priest Blue Wolf at the Temple in Deer Toes Lake Town. He will know how to handle them properly. I think giving them to the family will upset them even more."

I agreed. I did not want any more contact with Red Feather's family.

Bold Warrior scanned the murder site, a pensive look on his face. "Although we have already seen her body, finding the site where she died makes Red Feather's death even more personal. This has got to stop. The people were scared before this murder, but after today, when so many people saw her mutilated body. Word will spread quickly. I would not be surprised if more families leave Cahokia." I did not know the local people like Bold War, but I had to agree with him based on what I had learned over the last several sunrises during my investigation.

We made our way back to the Great Northern Road and headed South towards Deer Toes Lake Town. Shortly after we reached the road, we met Chief Running Deer and three of his Warriors, trotting north toward the murder site. The chief stopped, gasping and panting, when he recognized Bold Warrior. "There was a murder here last night."

"Yes, we know," Bold Warrior replied in a superior tone. He obviously did not fear or like the Chief any more than I did.

"You," said Chief Running Deer, looking at me as if I were a piece of spoiled meat. "You are the coppersmith from Cahokia sent by Muskrat Waits to find the men who murdered those immigrants."

"His name is Walking Stick," Bold Warrior said. "And he is investigating the murders."

Chief Running Deer looked annoyed. "Muskrat Waits also heard about this latest killing. He sent word for me to find the body and have my Warriors take it to the Emerald Acropolis, like the other bodies."

"Her name was Red Feather," Bold Warrior continued to address Running Deer as if he were a dimwitted subordinate. "And the body is gone."

"Gone, what do you mean, gone?"

"The family came and took the body away."

"What family took the body? Where is it now?" Demanded the Chief.

Bold Warrior shrugged. "I do not know where the body is now. It has been some time since Red Feather's family came and carried her corpse away. They have probably already prepared her for burial according to their custom. Even if you found where they had taken the body, it is too late."

"You moved the body," Chief Running Deer said accusingly, pointing at Bold Warrior. "You are constantly interfering in Cahokia's business. This time, you have gone too far. Muskrat Waits wants that body taken to the Emerald Acropolis. When I tell him you have interfered and moved the body, your severed head will top a pole in the plaza at Deer Toes Lake Town as a warning to others not to interfere in the Sun Kings business."

Bold Warrior looked up and observed the sun's position, well past its high point in the sky. I expected him to lash out at the Chief. Instead, a slight smirk appeared on his face. "I think once Muskrat Waits learns how long it took you to react to his orders and that you failed to secure the body before the family took it away, it will not be me who loses a vital body part." He motioned for me to follow, and together, we walked past a gaping Chief Running Deer and his soldiers and continued our journey on the Great Northern Road toward Deer Toes Lake Town.

I marveled at Bold Warrior's nerve, addressing the Chief in such a defiant manner. "Do you really think Chief Running Deer will hang for failing to secure the body?"

Bold Warrior chuckled. "I doubt it. But it was fun scaring that arrogant piece of bear dung. We are almost in sight of the town. He left shortly before we met his party. I will bet he received Muskrat Waits' order some time ago and is just now getting around to carrying it out. If you or I were so incompetent and lazy, he would have us strangled. Only Running Deer's status as a member of the minor nobility protects him."

We soon reached Deer Toes Lake Town and made our way through the crowded village to the home of Bold Warrior's daughter and her husband. The moment I walked into the common next to the house, I smelled something delicious. His daughter, Juniper, stood over a large pot beside a small fire. "That smells wonderful."

Juniper looked up and smiled at me. "It is a stew with fish, green corn, wild onions, and ground sunflower seeds. I also have some maize cakes to soak up the juice. Sit here, and I will get you a bowl." I sat where instructed, and in a few heartbeats, Juniper handed me a steaming bowl of stew and two maize cakes. I had not eaten a good meal since the night before, and I was famished—I was not used to going so long without eating, and I would not say I liked the experience.

Juniper looked on approvingly as I ate. "It is good to see a man with a hearty appetite. It makes a woman feel appreciated."

Bold Warrior frowned at his daughter. "Old people do not eat as much as the young."

I hoped that wouldn't be the case as I got older. In my opinion, eating is one of life's greatest pleasures.

When the rest of my companions returned, I was well into my second bowl of stew and fourth maize cake. Spotted Lynx frowned when he saw me scooping huge bites of stew into my mouth. "I suspected you would beat us to the stew pot."

I almost choked on a piece of fish. Incredulous, I pointed out, "Who seems to show up at my house at mealtime every day?"

"Good point," conceded Spotted Lynx. Everyone laughed. We needed something to break the tension we had all been experiencing and would continue to experience until we found the killers.

Once everyone had finished eating, it was time for each team to tell the other what they had found. First, Bold Warrior and I told the others about our experience questioning Soft Willow and how we discovered the murder scene.

"Did you find any more evidence implicating Cahokia Warriors at the murder scene?" Spotted Lynx asked nervously. I shook my head.

"Tell us what you discovered," I directed.

Spotted Lynx spoke for the group. "We went to all the houses near where the murderers placed the body. No one heard anything or saw anything last night. Some people knew Red Feather, but most of the neighbors claimed they did not know her or her family, even though they lived nearby for many cycles of the seasons. We spoke to a few immigrant families, but most were Cahokian. I even asked if the families had seen any Warriors in their area or if they knew of Warriors threatening anyone." He said begrudgingly. "Although they saw Warriors occasionally, no one had heard of them threatening anyone."

"I was afraid the neighbors would not be much help. However, in fairness, no one lives within sight of where they killed Red Feather or where the murderers placed her body. And even if they did hear something, I doubt if they would tell us for fear of angering the killers, even though no one knows who they are."

"The people are scared," said Green Heron, entering the conversation. "Cahokians and immigrants. Everyone thought the murders had stopped. More of the immigrant families are preparing to leave."

Sundown was quickly approaching by the time we finished talking. We had barely slept the night before, and everyone was exhausted after the walk to Deer Toes Lake Town and our work investigating the latest murder. Bold Warrior kindly offered to let us sleep under his ramada for the evening so we would not have to walk back to Cahokia in the dark, our legs fatigued, an offer I eagerly accepted. I took the sleeping fur Juniper offered and found a place to sleep beside the house. I had barely laid my head down before I was sound asleep.

* * *

Long after the others had fallen asleep, Spotted Lynx sat by the fire, thinking. It had been a hard day for the young Warrior. His companions already suspected the Warriors were involved in the murders. Now, there was more evidence against them. 'It cannot be.' He thought. 'I have spent the last ten cycles of the season as a Warrior, protecting the people. Serving Cahokia. Murdering poor immigrants is not what we do. It is not possible.' But as he sat alone in the darkness, he knew in his heart that it was possible.

Chapter 20

I woke at dawn the day after our Deer Toes Lake Town adventures. My companions were already awake, sitting around the fire and devouring maize cakes as quickly as Bold Warrior's daughter, Juniper, could cook them. I rose and joined them, finding a place beside Bold Warrior. He watched the young men eat with an amused expression.

"These young men are going to eat all our food if you do not find the murderers soon," he remarked.

"They have been eating at my house for many sunrises," I replied. "I am about to go broke feeding them every day. It is amazing. They always seem to appear at mealtimes. It must be an instinct young men have, like waterfowl instinctively knowing when to migrate in the spring and fall."

I asked Bold Warrior whether he had received any reports of injured men, but his agents had found no suspicious individuals. They were still searching. I would have to rely on Muskrat Waits' people to find the wounded killer. I could think of nothing more we could do in Deer Toes Lake Town to aid my investigation, so after we finished eating, we began the long walk back to Cahokia.

On the way home, we once again reviewed the clues we had gathered in Deer Toes Lake Town and compared them with what we already knew. We reached a few grim conclusions. At first, we wondered if it was simply a coincidence that the five victims were immigrants, but now we believe the killers were deliberately selecting immigrants, probably because they had failed to integrate into Cahokian society. That might explain who was being killed, but not why their rejection of Cahokian ways would threaten someone enough to kill them.

Next, despite Spotted Lynx's vehement denials, the rest of us were convinced that Cahokian Warriors were responsible for the killings. Again, however, we could not explain why immigrants would pose such a danger to the Warriors that the soldiers would slaughter them.

A thought occurred to me. "If Warriors are killing immigrants, they are probably not acting on their own. Someone is ordering them to kill."

There was a murmur among the group. Spotted Lynx said, "I do not believe the Warriors committed the murders, but if they did, those orders must have come from a very high-ranking official in the Cahokian government—someone like Muskrat Waits, or even the Sun King."

I shook my head. "You may call me naïve, but I do not believe Muskrat Waits is involved. He did not need to appoint anyone to investigate the murders; he could simply have done nothing and allowed the terror to spread if that was his goal. Instead, he chose me because he did not wish to alarm the immigrant community. Then he assigned you to assist me, Spotted Lynx, knowing you are intelligent and capable. Why would he do that if he did not truly intend to find the killers? And if Muskrat Waits wanted immigrants dead, he could send his own agents, who answer directly to him, rather than Warriors with a military chain of command. It does not make sense."

Spotted Lynx nodded. "I think you are right. But if Muskrat Waits is not involved, then whoever is behind these killings must be very close to the Sun King, or else this is a conspiracy of high officials."

"Or the Sun King himself," Green Heron suggested quietly.

That thought made me sick to my stomach.

We were approaching the North Plaza at the city's edge. Almost home. As we passed, Gray Crane looked up at the North Temple with a troubled expression.

"What are you thinking?" I asked.

He shook his head. "Nothing. I am only wondering."

We crossed Cahokia Creek and reached my house around midday. Whispering Doe and Walks in Water were delighted and relieved to see us return safely. They hurried to serve us a meal.

"We did not know when you were coming home—or even if you were coming home today," Whispering Doe explained. "So we cooked a pot of stew last night and kept it by the fire so it would be ready whenever you arrived."

The woman is a genius. She and Walks in Water had also brewed a batch of maize beer in anticipation of our return. While they ladled stew into bowls, I dipped cups of excellent maize beer from a large pot and passed them to my companions.

As we ate, Whispering Doe asked about our journey. I told her of Red Feather's murder and what we had learned, omitting the worst details. "We keep gathering more information. We think we know who committed the murders and perhaps even a general reason, but it does not make sense. It feels as though one piece of knowledge is missing, and when I find it, everything will become clear. Until then, I do not know if we are any closer to finding the killers. It is not very encouraging. And I am worried about what will happen during the New Maize Celebration—all those people on the roads, traveling to and from Cahokia. Even if they are not immigrants, I believe they may still be in danger."

Whispering Doe laid a hand on my shoulder. "Keep working, my love. You will find him. Muskrat Waits chose you for a reason. You are the cleverest man in Cahokia."

"Usually, when you say that, I think you are being sarcastic."

Whispering Doe laughed. "Usually, I am."

After the meal, I gathered my little band around the fire.

"I am going to see Muskrat Waits," I announced. "I will tell him what we learned in Deer Toes Lake Town and see whether his agents have located a wounded man."

"I am going to the Warrior barracks," declared Spotted Lynx. "I am going to ask my superiors some difficult questions about what our Warriors have been doing north of Cahokia. Even with Muskrat Waits' protection, I hope I do not end up garroted and disemboweled for disrespect. Which reminds me, Walking Stick, I hope Muskrat Waits does not have you strangled on top of the Great Pyramid for moving Red Feather's body before Running Deer and his Warriors could take her to the Emerald Acropolis."

I cringed. That possibility had not occurred to me.

"What about you two?" I asked Gray Crane and Green Heron.

"Unless you need me, I am going to see a girl," Green Heron replied.

Everyone laughed.

The women had been listening. "I would like to meet her," said Walks in Water.

"Bring her to our evening meal," Whispering Doe suggested.

Poor Green Heron flushed crimson. Spotted Lynx snickered.

"And you?" I asked Gray Crane.

He answered thoughtfully, staring at the bloody eagle feather we found under Red Feather's body. "I am going to visit a sick friend, if that is acceptable to you, Walking Stick."

"Of course. I do not suppose I need to tell any of you to be back in time for the evening meal so we can discuss what Spotted Lynx and I learn. You all seem to find your way to Whispering Doe's stew pot at mealtimes without any prompting."

"Be kind to them, Walking Stick," Whispering Doe reproached me from under the ramada where she was mending a skirt. "I like having them here with us."

I wisely swallowed my sarcastic reply and sent my helpers on their way.

Before he left, Spotted Lynx pulled me aside. "I know you do not want to hear this, because you believe the Warriors are involved in the murders, but there is something else you need to consider."

"All right. Go on."

"How did Bold Warrior learn about the latest murder so quickly? He told you that people came to him with the news, but I remain suspicious. He arrived at the scene remarkably fast, and he is always so helpful— sending Green Heron as a guide and interpreter, notifying us quickly after Red Feather's murder. He claims he wants peace and stability in the lands around Deer Toes Lake Town, but is that the truth? What are his real motives? I do not trust him."

I was stunned. I had considered Bold Warrior the one man we could trust. I had never questioned his motives or actions.

"Do you suspect Green Heron as well?" I asked.

"No," Spotted Lynx replied. "I believe Green Heron is doing his best. However, is it not interesting that Bold Warrior sent us a *hiperes* jiną̈k on his very first mission?"

I let Spotted Lynx go and stood in the common, turning his words over in my mind. Could it be that Bold Warrior had his own designs in the Deer Toes Lake region and was using us to further his plans? Green Heron was Bold Warrior's devoted follower; I had assumed he was loyal to me as well. But was he secretly serving another purpose? Or was it Spotted Lynx who could not be trusted? If Cahokian Warriors were involved in the murders, was Spotted Lynx trying to shield them? Was he part of the conspiracy?

Was there no one I could trust?

My thoughts spun wildly. I pushed them aside for the moment.

I was still thinking about Spotted Lynx when I noticed Whispering Doe weeding tobacco plants in her garden. It was time to speak with her about Walks in Water.

"What are we going to do about Spotted Lynx and Walks in Water?" I asked.

"What do you mean?" she replied.

"They are spending a great deal of time together and becoming very close. I do not like it."

Her face darkened. "Walks in Water is sixteen cycles of the seasons. She knows what she is doing. She has never shown interest in any other man. If she does not marry soon, she may never marry."

"So she must marry Spotted Lynx simply because he is the only choice?" I protested.

"You listen to me, Walking Stick," Whispering Doe said firmly. "I am a far better judge of men's character than you are. I know something happened during the investigation that led you to distrust Spotted Lynx. But I told you before, you can trust him. Leave the two of them alone. If it works out between them, so be it. If not, then it is Morning Star's will. We will not interfere."

That was the end of the conversation. It was time to see Muskrat Waits. Usually, I did not look forward to speaking with him, but after my last two visits, I almost found the prospect pleasant by comparison.

* * *

Gray Crane remained seated long after the others had departed from the Black Bear Clan Common. He sat on a log before the hearth, gazing into the ashen remnants of the morning's fire. The pale embers glowed faintly, mirroring the turmoil smoldering within him.

He turned over the events of the last several sunrises, examining each memory with the care of a Priest weighing omens. It now appeared that they possessed proof—real proof—that Cahokia's Warriors were involved in the murders. Walking Stick had suspected the Warriors from the beginning, and the discovery on Red Feather's body seemed to confirm his fears. The broken chert blade. The eagle feather wrapped in red cloth. Such things came only from the Warriors. They were unmistakable.

But that was not entirely true, was it?

Others used those items. Others had access to those symbols. There were rituals, ceremonies, and old practices that blurred the lines between warrior and Priest, between sacred regalia and military badge. It was not impossible.

And yet the alternative was unthinkable. Repulsive. Abhorrent.

The moment the thought had crept into his mind, Gray Crane had driven it out like an evil spirit. But it returned now, stronger, refusing to be ignored. If what he suspected was true—if the trail of evidence pointed not to the Warriors, but to those who served a far darker power—then everything he believed about Cahokia, about its Temples, its divinity, and its order, was in peril.

He felt sick.

And terrified.

But he had to know.

For the sake of Cahokia.

For the sake of his own sanity.

But before he approached Walking Stick with his suspicions, he would find out the truth for himself.

Gray Crane pushed himself to his feet, though his legs trembled beneath him. He drew a slow, steadying breath and turned toward the canoe landing.

There was one person he needed to speak with before he left the safety of the Black Bear Clan Common. One person who might help him steady his resolve.

He went in search of Whispering Doe.

* * *

I followed the now-familiar route from my house to Muskrat Waits' residence on the first terrace of the Great Pyramid. The guards waved me through their checkpoints without question. It felt strange, and not entirely unpleasant, to be treated as someone important. I found Muskrat Waits sitting in his usual place in a padded chair beneath the ramada attached to his house. He was speaking with a man, but when he saw me, he dismissed the fellow with a flick of his hand. The man must have been only a minor clerk.

Instead of a greeting, Muskrat Waits said, "It appears that your sources are better informed than mine, coppersmith." His voice held a tone of begrudging respect. I was relieved that he did not intend to have me strangled that day. I tried not to smirk.

"I had help," I answered.

"That is why it is important to develop sources," Muskrat Waits continued. "You cannot do everything yourself. To be a good investigator, you need eyes and ears everywhere. You are learning. Now, tell me what you discovered in Deer Toes Lake Town before you had the body removed so that idiot Running Deer could not find it."

This time, I did smirk, and Muskrat Waits did not seem to mind.

"Yes, Running Deer is incompetent and lazy," he said. "Unfortunately, his status as a Noble—even a minor Noble—prevents me from having him strangled from the top of this pyramid as an example to the other incompetent and lazy Chiefs in the kingdom. However," he added with a smirk of his own, "there are other, more subtle ways of dealing with Nobles like Running Deer."

I was not surprised when, several moon cycles later, Bold Warrior sent word from Deer Toes Lake Town that Running Deer had died suddenly.

I told Muskrat Waits how we found Red Feather's body, how we located the murder site, and what her family had told us. Then I stretched out my fist and opened my palm, revealing the broken chert knife blade and the feather with bright red cloth wrapped around the quill.

"We found the blade lodged in the wound that killed Red Feather," I said, "and the eagle feather in the dirt beneath her body."

The blood drained from Muskrat Waits' face. He reached out with a trembling hand and took the objects from me. For many heartbeats, he did not speak, and I did not dare break the silence. Whatever doubts I still harbored about his involvement in the killings vanished as I watched his expression.

At last, in a hushed voice, he whispered, "Morning Star, save us."

As Muskrat Waits stared at the blade and the feather, his expression slowly shifted from shock and disbelief to rage and cold determination. He stood, stepped into the afternoon sunlight, and shouted for a *hiperes jinak*.

"Painted Turtle! Come here, now!"

A terrified young man sprinted across the terrace and halted, panting, before the Great Sun's Minister of Security.

Almost screaming, Muskrat Waits commanded, "Go to the Warrior barracks. Find every General and deliver this message: the army will assemble today, just before the evening meal, in the Grand Plaza for inspection. Every Warrior will be there. Everyone. No exceptions. They will wear a full uniform and carry every weapon. I will have any Warrior who misses the inspection garroted from the top of this pyramid. Now go!"

Painted Turtle raced for the ramp as though Underwater Panther himself were chasing him.

After the messenger vanished down the slope, Muskrat Waits turned back to me. "I am going to inspect every soldier in the army, from the Generals to the most junior Warrior. If any of them is missing, or has a broken knife or spear, or lacks a headdress or feather, I will have him tortured by my finest executioners until I learn the truth."

I shuddered involuntarily. Muskrat Waits was not a kind man.

He returned to his seat beneath the ramada, drank from a ceramic water bottle, and, after several heartbeats, asked, "What else do you have for me?"

"Have your agents found any wounded men who might have been injured in the fight with Bright Eagle?" I asked. "We spoke with Bold Warrior in Deer Toes Lake Town, and his people have not found anyone yet."

He shook his head. "No. My agents have identified several injured men, but after questioning them—and I assure you, they were thoroughly questioned—I am certain they could not have been involved. Nevertheless, we are still looking."

I was disappointed. Perhaps that would have been too easy. I still believed that once we identified the man wounded in the fight with Bright Eagle, we would have a direct path to at least one murderer. A thought struck me.

"Did your people inspect the Warriors for an injured man?" I asked.

"No," Muskrat Waits replied, tugging at the copper-covered human head earring in his left ear. "However, tonight's inspection will allow my agents to examine every Warrior. And if a Warrior fails to appear because he is injured, we will find him and examine him. I will ensure every Warrior in Cahokia is inspected. If the Generals are involved in these killings, they will not be able to hide an injured man. I will find him. That is why I ordered the inspection for today, so they will have no time to react or cover their tracks."

I could think of nothing more to ask, so I turned to go.

"Fortunately, you reached the last murder victim before Chief Running Deer and his Warriors," he commented. "They would not have noticed the feather or bothered to look inside the wound."

He did not say "thank you" or "good work," but I was sure that was what he meant.

I left the Great Pyramid and walked to the Black Bear Clan Common.

I found Whispering Doe sitting under the ramada, weaving a pair of shoes. I sat down beside her and told her everything that had happened the day before. She could sense how frustrated I had become.

"Be patient," she advised. "Do not be so hard on yourself. You have learned a great deal, even though the murderers are very clever and have tried to hide any evidence that might reveal who they are."

"While I stumble around, people are dying," I replied. "Others are leaving Cahokia. People are frightened. I am missing something, but I cannot see it."

"Relax," she said. "Let me get you a drink of maize beer, smoke your pipe, and think. You will find the answer when you least expect it. Just keep working, and the answer will come. You are the cleverest man I know, Walking Stick. We are all very proud of you."

I doubted that I was all that clever, but my wife's confidence heartened me.

"Before he left, Gray Crane asked me to give you a message," she said. "He told me to tell you that he is going to the North Temple. He said it might be nothing, but he needs to speak with the Priests there. He promised to explain everything when he returns. He seemed very upset, but he would not tell me why."

"I thought he was going to see a sick friend after the midday meal," I said.

"He is. The injured friend lives at the North Temple. I suggested he take some stew. He waited while it warmed, and we talked for a while. He is a nice boy and very thoughtful. Most men would never think to bring a meal to an injured friend."

A chill ran down my spine. I jumped from my chair and grabbed Whispering Doe by the shoulders.

"Did he say his friend was sick or injured?"

Startled by my reaction, she thought for a moment and answered, "Injured. Yes, I think he said injured."

Click.

Everything fell into place. I remembered my vision at the Emerald Acropolis. I had already understood that the farmers walking out of the Temple represented the immigrants, the burning maize field represented Cahokian agriculture, and the people lining the Sacred Precinct were the people of Cahokia. The burning World Tree represented the collapse of Cahokian civilization. However, I did not understand who or what Underwater Panther represented. Now I did. Underwater Panther represented the Priests of the North Temple—the Temple adorned with an

Underwater Panther mask, where the Priests were curious about my investigation. Where they venerated that ferocious, deceitful being.

Gray Crane knew of an injured Priest at the North Temple. He had already solved the mystery. Why had he not told me? And now he had gone to the Temple alone.

I was nearly hysterical with fear.

Willow Tree came into the common. I shouted at my son, "Willow Tree, come here. Now!"

Startled, he ran to me, trembling at my tone.

"You know where the Warrior barracks are, on the far side of the Sacred Precinct?" He nodded. "Run there now, as fast as you can. Find Spotted Lynx. Tell him I am going to the North Temple. Tell him it is an emergency and I need him there immediately. Tell him to hurry. Run. Now!"

The boy bolted from the common toward the Sacred Way, faster than I had ever seen him run.

Whispering Doe stood beside me. I looked into her eyes and saw terror there—but it was not her own fear; it was my terror reflected back at me. Without a word, I turned from my wife and ran out of the common toward the canoe landing. I jumped into the nearest canoe and paddled furiously across Cahokia Creek, the startled owner shouting after me. I leaped out on the opposite bank and sprinted toward the North Temple.

I reached the ramp and ran up to the summit. When I stepped into the Temple, it was deserted. The only occupants were hideous Underwater Panther masks adorning the walls of the main hall. One mask was missing. The North Plaza below was eerily quiet. No one was nearby.

I walked slowly down the ramp, catching my breath. At the base of the mound, I crossed behind it to the Priest House. It, too, was empty. Where had everyone gone? Where was Gray Crane?

As I stood outside the Priest House, trying to decide where to search next, I heard a noise that sounded like a scuffle coming from a granary on the other side of the deserted plaza. After harvest, dry maize is stored in hundreds of granaries throughout Cahokia. The government distributes grain from these storehouses throughout the seasons and keeps a reserve against famine after a poor harvest. I walked toward the building.

The granary floor stood several steps above the ground to deter rodents. I climbed the ladder to the entrance. The door stood open. I poked my head inside. The maize from this granary had already been issued to the people during the cold seasons before this season's harvest began. The room was empty. It took several heartbeats for my eyes to adjust to the darkness.

When I could finally see, I felt both relief and annoyance. Gray Crane sat against the far wall.

I climbed into the granary and walked toward him. "What are you doing in here?" I demanded.

He did not answer. I thought he was asleep, so I reached down and shook him. His body slumped sideways. With horror, I saw that only a strip of skin at the back of his neck still held his head to his body. His throat had been severed.

I recoiled from the dreadful sight and felt something sticky beneath my shoe that I had not noticed before. Blood. Gray Crane's blood, fresh and wet.

A terrifying thought struck me: the murderer might still be in the granary.

I needed to leave at once, find Spotted Lynx, and notify Muskrat Waits. Those thoughts flashed through my mind in an instant, but before I could move, a blinding light exploded in my skull, followed by the worst pain I had ever known.

I staggered and crashed against the wall. The pain in my head was so intense that I could not open my eyes for several heartbeats. When at last I forced them open, I found myself face-to-face with Underwater Panther.

He loomed over me, snarling. His sharp white teeth gleamed against the bright red blood dripping from his fangs. Deer antlers sprouted from his head, and his face was a grotesque blend of human and feline. Underwater Panther wore a beard, unusual for Cahokian men. Most terrifying of all was the war club clutched in his human-like hand, raised to strike.

As Underwater Panther stepped forward to attack, I believed my life had come to an end. I took some comfort in the thought that I would now journey along the Path of Souls through the stars to the Land of the Dead and join my ancestors.

Before he could bring down the club and end my earthly life, a chert arrowhead appeared in the center of his chest. For a heartbeat, I thought the creature had grown a weapon from his own body. Underwater Panther lurched forward, lunging to impale me—and everything went dark.

Chapter 21

When my awareness returned, darkness surrounded me, and I knew that I had died. I existed in a vast, silent void, without sight or sensation—only thought. Time had no meaning there. It might have been a few sunrises, or it might have been centuries since I had arrived; I could not tell. Then, gradually, sound crept into the emptiness. Voices. Human voices. One of them, I was almost certain, belonged to my wife.

The realization unsettled me. If I were truly dead, I should have been traveling the Path of Souls through the stars to the Land of the Dead. Why, then, was I still here, lingering in the Middle World, close enough to hear the voices of those I loved?

A terrible thought seized me.

What if I had not earned the right to travel the Path of Souls?

What if I were now a wandering spirit, condemned to drift across the earth forever, tormenting the living?

Morning Star, forgive me.

If only I had lived a better life.

Then, as suddenly as fear had seized me, clarity returned. I remembered that our souls do not travel the Path of Souls at all times of the year. The journey begins only on the evening of the summer solstice, when the stars align correctly. Our souls enter through the northern sky and follow the Path of Souls toward the south, enduring the trials of the Giant Hawk, the River of Sorrows, and the Great Serpent. Only those who overcome these challenges reach the Land of the Dead and join their ancestors forever.

I had missed the season by a single moon cycle.

So now I had to wait—patiently or otherwise—until the next solstice before beginning my journey.

As I pondered my uncertain state of existence, the voices around me grew louder. I recognized another voice—Spotted Lynx. Of course, he would be nearby. He was probably at my house, eating from my stew pot and attempting to charm my daughter again. If I truly was doomed to wander as a spirit for almost a whole cycle of the seasons, I decided I would spend some of that time haunting Spotted Lynx. It felt like a productive use of my time while in the spirit world.

The darkness around me thinned. Someone said, "I think he is waking up."

Another voice murmured, "Praise Morning Star."

Something warm touched my hand.

"Walking Stick, wake up, please, my love."

Whispering Doe.

I forced my eyes open—and at once regretted it. Bright light stabbed through my skull, and pain flared so fiercely that I wished myself back into darkness. But Whispering Doe's voice pulled me from the spirit world back into the Middle World and the land of the living.

"Walking Stick, can you hear me?"

It took all the strength I had, but at last I managed a faint, "Yes."

My vision slowly cleared, though the pain in my head did not lessen. Something was wrapped tightly around my skull, and my hair felt stiff and sticky. I turned my head slightly and saw Whispering Doe's anxious face.

"It is a good thing he has such a thick skull, or he would be dead now," Spotted Lynx remarked, in his typical mocking tone.

Other faces became familiar. Muskrat Waits sat near my feet, rigid in his chair. Bear Claws, my daughter's husband, stood behind Whispering Doe, steadying her as she trembled. Another man stood beside Spotted Lynx. I recognized him only when I saw the Sun Family tattoo on his cheek.

Prince Ranging Fox.

My eyes widened, and I attempted to sit up, but the Prince placed a firm hand on my shoulder.

"Stay where you are, old friend. You have taken a savage blow to the head. You are fortunate to be alive."

"Fortunate is right," Whispering Doe snapped. She glared at Muskrat Waits and the Prince with such fury that even those two powerful men recoiled. "Because of you two dragging him into your schemes, he almost died. If not for Spotted Lynx, he would be dead!"

Spotted Lynx?

What had she said about him?

Bear Claws put an arm around her shoulders. "That is enough, Mother. Walking Stick will live. What happened tonight is not their fault. A great evil haunts Cahokia."

"No, she is right," said the Prince heavily. "We should not have brought him into this, but we could think of nothing else to do. Muskrat Waits' agents began the investigation but made no progress. They had no contacts among the immigrant families. They could not even discover the victims' names. That was when we decided to use Walking Stick. It was a mistake."

Spotted Lynx?

Again, her words echoed. What had she said?

I motioned for Spotted Lynx to help me sit up. Whispering Doe gave me a ceramic cup filled with bitter willow-bark tea. I drank deeply, grateful for the slight easing of the pain in my head.

"Gray Crane is dead," I said.

"Yes, we know," Whispering Doe whispered, tears spilling down her cheeks.

"What happened to me?"

Spotted Lynx answered. "Walks in Water and I were leaving the copper workshop when Willow Tree found us. He was frantic. I went to your house first to make sure the family was safe, and Whispering Doe told me she feared that you and Gray Crane were in danger. I still had my weapons from the trip to Deer Toes Lake Town, so I ran to the North Temple. It was empty, but I heard a noise in one of the granaries. When I climbed the ladder and looked inside, I saw a man wearing an Underwater Panther mask standing over you, ready to crush your skull. I put an arrow through his back. He fell on top of you.

"Gray Crane was already dead. But you were still alive, so I carried you to your house, and Bear Claws helped me carry you here. I sent a runner to Muskrat Waits, and he brought a healer and a Priest. They say your skull is cracked, but it will heal."

"What were you doing at the copper workshop?" I asked. "You were supposed to be going to the Warrior barracks."

Spotted Lynx grinned. "Walks in Water asked me if I would like to tour the copper workshop, so I went with her, and then I intended to go to the barracks. I could not refuse her offer."

Spotted Lynx's fascination with my daughter had saved my life. I groaned inwardly.

"Where am I now?"

"At the Deer Clan Shrine House," Spotted Lynx said. "I thought this would be the best place for you to recover."

Silence followed until Spotted Lynx turned to Muskrat Waits and asked, "I must ask—was anyone missing equipment at the inspection tonight? Any Warrior missing a blade or a headdress feather?"

211

I knew the answer to that question was no, but I kept that knowledge to myself for the moment.

Muskrat Waits shook his head. "No. Every Warrior was present. No one was injured. No one was missing anything."

"What about the dead man?" Spotted Lynx pressed. "Did your agents retrieve the body?"

"The body was gone," Muskrat Waits replied grimly. "Someone removed it before my men arrived. Only blood remained. There was no one in the area for us to question. Everyone had gone, even the Priests. I will send my agents to the North Plaza tomorrow to see if the people have returned."

Prince Ranging Fox exhaled heavily. "Now the enemy has struck again—killing Gray Crane and nearly killing Walking Stick. And still we do not know who they are. Until we find someone in the North Plaza community who knows what happened at the granary, we are out of leads."

"That is not true," I said. My voice was steady despite the pain. "I know who killed Gray Crane. And I know who murdered the immigrants."

Every face turned toward me.

"Are you certain, Walking Stick?" Muskrat Waits asked. "You have suffered a terrible injury. Are you sure your mind is not imagining answers?"

"No. I know who is responsible. And I know why. How late is it?"

"The moon has just set," Spotted Lynx replied. "It is past the middle of the night."

"Good. There is still time. Spotted Lynx, assemble your Troupe. Quickly. I have a plan."

I drew a slow breath, steadying my aching skull.

"We are going to end this nightmare at dawn."

Chapter 22

In the pre-dawn darkness, groups of men moved quietly through the sleeping streets of Cahokia, converging on the Black Bear Clan Common. They wore bright red breechcloths and eagle-feather headdresses, with wooden shin guards and quilted coats stuffed with milkweed seeds for protection. Each man carried a spear, knife, and war club, while the archers bore bows and quivers filled with arrows. Their faces were painted half red and half black—the traditional colors of the Cahokia Warriors—making them a grim, intimidating sight in the dim light.

War Captain Spotted Lynx studied his men with a critical eye as they formed into marching ranks. These were 80 seasoned warriors who had fought in many battles, yet this morning they did not know their destination. All they knew was that the Sun King required their service, and that was enough. Spotted Lynx summoned his lieutenants, outlined the plan, and sent them back among the ranks so that every man understood his role in the fight to come.

I did not own any armor, so I pulled on leather leggings and a winter tunic that hung just above my knees. I took my bow and quiver of arrows from their place under a sleeping bench in my house and stepped out into the night to find Spotted Lynx.

Whispering Doe stopped me at the doorway.

"Where are you going?"

To me, the answer was obvious, but I did not say so. "You know I cannot stay here."

"You are still weak from the blow to your head, and you said yourself your vision is still blurry. You are not a young man anymore, my love, and you are not a Warrior."

"I am a Warrior today," I snapped. "I am ready to avenge Gray Crane."

Despite the weakness in my limbs, the nausea in my stomach, the dizziness, and the pounding in my skull, I refused to remain behind while my companions faced danger without me. I blamed myself for Gray Crane's death, and I meant to stand beside the men who would avenge him.

Whispering Doe knew it was useless to argue. "Take care of yourself, you old fool. You always find trouble. Stay close to Spotted Lynx."

I kissed her quickly and walked away.

Before I found the War Captain, I saw Green Heron crossing the common. At first, I did not recognize him. His face was painted solid red— blood red. Like the Warriors, he carried a knife, spear, and war club.

I caught up with the young *hiperes jinąk*. "Where are you going?"

"The same place you are," he said. "I am going to kill them. I am going to kill them all."

A shudder ran through me at the hatred in his eyes. Before I could speak, he trotted off to join the Warriors.

I finally found Spotted Lynx at the head of the column, speaking with Prince Ranging Fox. My old friend was going into battle with us today.

"Green Heron says he is coming with us," I told the War Captain.

"Gray Crane was his friend," Spotted Lynx replied. "You are going. Why should he not?"

I tried the same argument Whispering Doe had used on me. "He is not a Warrior. He is a messenger. He does not belong in a fight. At least I have had some training."

Spotted Lynx only shrugged and walked away.

Ranging Fox smiled at me kindly. "It has been more than twenty cycles of the seasons since old Bowed Willow trained us in martial athletics. Do you still remember?"

"I may be older, fatter, and slower, but I still remember. And I can still use this." I held up my bow so he could see it.

"Yes, I remember," the Prince said. "You were the finest archer among Bowed Willow's students. Let us hope you do not have to use your bow today."

I hoped for the opposite.

Dawn was close. It was time for us to leave.

Just before our departure, Walks in Water ran from the ramada to Spotted Lynx. She leaped into his arms, and he held her tightly. After several heartbeats, he let her go, and she hurried back to the ramada with Whispering Doe. I did not have time to ponder the nature of their relationship, but from what I had just seen, I doubted my opinion would matter anyway.

Spotted Lynx's Warriors were ready to execute the plan. He led the Troupe out of the Black Bear Clan Common toward the canoe landing on Cahokia Creek. More of his men waited there with eight large war canoes already in place. The Warriors boarded their assigned canoes quickly and quietly. With a few powerful strokes of the paddles, we crossed to the north bank and disembarked. The column re-formed, and we moved toward our objective.

We passed the North Plaza, and at Spotted Lynx's signals, squads of Warriors slipped away to their assigned positions, spreading out to surround the North Temple and the Priest House.

Within a few heartbeats, they had thrown a cordon around the entire complex. No one would escape.

Spotted Lynx kept a dozen of his best soldiers at his side and led them to the entrance of the Priest House, preparing to break down the door.

As I watched the precision of the operation, waiting for my chance to act, I saw a lone figure dart from one of the buildings beside the Priest House and run toward the Temple. No one else seemed to notice. I knew who it must be.

Leaving my place, I followed.

I climbed the ramp to the mound's summit and paused to listen. I heard nothing. I slipped into the main hall.

The room was dark. I could not see or hear anyone moving. A faint glow shone from the far end, where the passage led to the Temple's Inner Sanctuary. I moved slowly down the hall toward the light, cautious not to kick anything that might betray my presence. At the end of the hall, I stopped and gathered my courage.

Then I stepped into the Inner Sanctuary and nocked an arrow. I slid to the left of the doorway into a shadow and pressed myself against the wall, making my body as narrow a target as possible. I stood motionless in the shadow for many heartbeats, waiting for my eyes to adjust to the dim light from the small perpetual fire.

The flames cast a shifting glow across the Underwater Panther masks hanging along the walls on either side of the chamber. I was in the right place. Gray Crane had paid with his life to bring me here.

Gradually, as my eyes adjusted to the dim light, a darker shape emerged in the deeper shadows of the far corner. Then a slight movement caught my eye.

Instantly, I drew the bowstring back until the arrow's fletching tickled my cheek. Whoever hid there knew he had been seen—and I knew exactly who he was.

A form lunged toward me from the darkness.

215

I released the arrow.

"No! Walking Stick, no!" Prince Ranging Fox shouted as he rushed into the room and reached toward my bow.

Too late.

My arrow struck High Priest Blue Falcon in the throat. He dropped the war axe he had been holding as the impact drove him back against the far wall of the Inner Sanctuary. For several heartbeats, he stood pressed against the wall, clutching at his neck and trying to tear out the shaft, then he slid down to the floor and lay writhing on his back.

"Walking Stick, what have you done?" demanded Ranging Fox. "We needed him alive. We need to know why his Priests slaughtered those people."

"He is alive," I snapped. "At least for now."

I nocked another arrow and kept it pointed at the figure on the floor as we advanced carefully across the room. A harsh, rasping breath escaped through his ruined throat. Blood and air bubbled from the wound.

"Blue Falcon," I said, staring down at him. "High Priest of the North Temple. The man responsible for the murders of the immigrants. Am I right?"

He nodded. "And you are Walking Stick, the coppersmith."

I nodded in return.

"See? He is alive," I told Ranging Fox. Blue Falcon's eyes were wide open, and there was still an insolent sneer on his face. The arrow had torn his throat nearly in half, but missed the great artery. Speaking must have been agony, yet he seemed eager to talk. He was alive, but not for long.

Ranging Fox studied him for several heartbeats and then asked, "Why?"

Blue Falcon laughed, a harsh, wet gurgle. "To save Cahokia, of course. What else?"

"Save Cahokia?" Ranging Fox sounded sick. "The murders you ordered have nearly destroyed everything we have built."

"No, you are mistaken," Blue Falcon hissed. "You do not understand. During a spirit journey, Underwater Panther came to me and revealed that certain people living among us were upsetting the balance of the cosmos. These blasphemers do not take part in our rituals. They do not venerate the Divine Ones. Our prosperity is bound to the favor of Morning Star and the other Divine Ones. The balance between the Above World and the Below World is delicate. How can we expect to keep their favor and preserve balance in the Middle World if we allow unbelievers to live among us? The Sun King and the Lord High Priest have betrayed Cahokia by refusing to drive the blasphemers from our lands."

Ranging Fox looked ill. "So you killed six innocent people?"

Blue Falcon tried to shake his head, but his muscles were failing, and the gesture was barely visible. "No. Not innocent. Their blasphemy threatened us all."

"You moved the bodies to make it seem the victims lived near Deer Toes Lake Town and not near Cahokia, to draw suspicion away from this Temple," I said. "You did not expect Muskrat Waits to order a serious investigation. You assumed the Sun King would ignore the deaths of a few poor immigrant farmers."

"Yes," he admitted. "That was a mistake."

"And then you tried to make the last murder—her name was Red Feather—appear as if the Warriors had done it," I continued. "Your deception worked. You planted the feather and the broken knife blade cleverly enough that we had to search for them. That way, we would not suspect they were false clues."

"That was easy," Blue Falcon said, clearly pleased with himself. "Gray Crane came to the Temple. He told us everything you knew about the killings—how you suspected the Cahokia Warriors. So we chose a blasphemer from Deer Toes Lake Town and staged the killing to look like the work of Warriors. If you had not brought a Priest who knew the fine chert and eagle feathers we use in ceremonies, you would still be blaming the Warriors."

He paused to drag in another ragged breath.

"That was never meant to be the final sacrifice," he went on. "I intended to continue the cleansing. I chose the day of the New Maize Ceremony. My Priests would have scoured the countryside and killed every blasphemer we could find. Once the people saw what we were doing—and saw that it was right—they would have joined us. Every unbeliever would have been dead or driven from the Creator's lands. It is a pity we cannot fulfill that part of the plan. Perhaps our actions will inspire others to take up the work."

"I doubt it," said Ranging Fox. "You may be dead soon, but when the people see what happens to your followers—how excruciating and humiliating their deaths are—I do not think many will rush to join your cause."

Blue Falcon shrugged as best he could. The suffering of his followers meant nothing to him.

Changing the subject, I said, "And you killed Gray Crane as well."

The dying Priest gave another ugly, wet laugh. "The fool. He came here to visit one of my Priests, Cottonwood Tree—the bungler who allowed a blasphemer to strike him with a hoe. A farmer's hoe. How fitting that a hoe should lead you to us in the end. Such little mistakes. Gray Crane saw Cottonwood Tree on his first visit, when he told us about your investigation. He came back yesterday with the stew your wife made to see how Cottonwood Tree was recovering. I do not know exactly what made him realize we were responsible for the cleansing. He spoke with Cottonwood Tree for some time. Perhaps Cottonwood Tree said something careless. We will never know."

He smiled faintly.

"I killed Cottonwood Tree right after I killed Gray Crane," Blue Falcon continued. "When Gray Crane finally understood that it was my Priests and I who had purged the blasphemers, he confronted me. He told me what we were doing was wrong, that we should reach out to the unbelievers instead. He said we should stop the cleansing and surrender ourselves to the Lord High Priest. How naïve. What did he think would happen? Did he truly believe I would confess and place myself in the Lord High Priest's hands? Did he imagine he could walk into our Temple, accuse us of murder, and then walk out again? Fool. Of course, I killed him. My men dragged him to the granary, and I cut his throat with a ceremonial knife—just like the one we left in the blasphemer's body at Deer Toes Lake Town."

"You also killed my Uncle Rattlesnake," I said quietly. "Why?"

"That was your fault," Blue Falcon replied without remorse. "You asked him to help you find us. He began asking questions. He became a threat. However, we did not intend to kill him at first."

I frowned. "What do you mean?"

"Originally, we planned to kill you and your family," he said.

Bile rose in my throat, and I fought the urge to retch.

"However, when we came to your house in the darkest time of night, we sensed that something was not right. Someone was waiting for us."

"Spotted Lynx," I muttered.

"It was wise of you to keep those young men near your home," Blue Falcon admitted. "If they had not been there, you and your family would now be dead." His tone held a trace of regret, as if he regretted failing to complete a task rather than sparing our lives. "So instead, I chose to silence Rattlesnake, to stop him from asking more questions. Killing him also served to punish you."

As I had suspected, my Uncle Rattlesnake's death was my fault.

"I might not have achieved all of my goals," Blue Falcon said, "but I have served Underwater Panther well. Soon, my souls will travel the Path of Souls through the stars to the Land of the Dead, where I will take my place of honor among my ancestors."

"I am afraid you will never make that journey, Blue Falcon," Ranging Fox said coldly.

"What are you talking about?" the Priest choked.

The Prince smiled, a hard, cruel smile I had never seen on his face before. "Once you are dead, I will have your body taken to the Lord High Priest at the Sacred Mound. His Priests will perform the cursing ceremony on your souls. Then they will sink your body in the dark depths of the Messipi River, where Underwater Panther will devour both your souls. You will spend eternity in the muck and slime of the Below World, tormented by the demons who live there."

"No!" Blue Falcon screamed, his voice torn with terror.

I could not endure another heartbeat of his presence. I decided to hasten his meeting with Underwater Panther. Before Ranging Fox could stop me, I dropped my bow, snatched up the war axe from the floor where it had fallen from Blue Falcon's hand, and brought it down onto his skull, so that the smirking, superior look vanished from his face.

"I suppose you have saved us the trouble of a public execution," Ranging Fox said, still shocked and disapproving.

I did not care. Blue Falcon had been dead the moment I walked into that room.

Spotted Lynx burst into the Inner Sanctuary with an arrow nocked, breathing hard. After a moment, he lowered his bow, glanced at the ruined body with my arrow still in its throat, and asked, "Who is that?"

"That was Blue Falcon," Ranging Fox replied. "Until a few heartbeats ago, he was the High Priest of this Temple and the man most responsible for the murders of the immigrants."

"What happened to him? He looks terrible," Spotted Lynx said dryly.

The Prince gestured toward me. "Walking Stick pinned him to the wall with an arrow through the throat. Then, while I was still questioning him, Walking Stick picked up that war axe he is still holding and smashed the Priest's head."

Spotted Lynx shot me a look full of newfound respect.

"It does not matter," I said testily. "You now know why he butchered the immigrant farmers and why he tried to spread terror among the immigrant families."

Ignoring me for the moment, Ranging Fox turned to the War Captain. "I need a report on the situation outside."

Spotted Lynx drew himself up proudly. "My men rounded up all the Priests. None escaped. We captured eleven alive. Four chose to fight. They discovered it is not as easy to kill a Warrior of Cahokia as it is to butcher an unarmed farmer. Those four are dead. We found three more Priests already dead, but I am not certain who killed them. Someone cut them up, much like they cut their victims."

I thought of Green Heron's cold promise and shivered. He might not have killed them all, but he claimed a share.

"None of my men were injured," Spotted Lynx finished.

"Excellent work, Spotted Lynx," Ranging Fox said. "Thank your men for me and on behalf of the Sun King. In my report to Muskrat Waits, you will receive high praise for your actions in this ugly business. As for the survivors, they will not live long. As soon as it can be arranged, they will be taken to the top of the Great Pyramid. Priests of the High Temple will cut the hearts from their living bodies, while others garrote them. Their bodies will be dismembered, and the pieces carried to the far corners of the Sun King's realm and displayed as a warning to any who might consider tearing at the fabric of our world."

Spotted Lynx looked almost ready to burst with pride.

Then Ranging Fox turned back to me. In a weary, resigned voice, he said, "Well, old friend, we had better go see Muskrat Waits and tell him what we have done, and put an end to this sad affair."

Chapter 23

Spotted Lynx's Warriors carried the bodies of the slain Priests to the Charnel House in the Grand Plaza, where the Priests of the High Temple would curse them and prepare them for burial. Blue Falcon's surviving Priests were marched to the Warrior barracks, where they would be held until the second day of the New Maize Ceremony. On that day, the Priests of the High Temple would execute them on the summit of the Great Pyramid, where all of Cahokia could view their executions.

Muskrat Waits, Prince Ranging Fox, Spotted Lynx, and I sat under the ramada beside the Minister's house and told him how we had solved the mystery of the immigrant murders and destroyed the Priesthood of the North Temple. Unlike my earlier visits, Muskrat Waits was almost cordial. He had servants bring us wooden chairs and ordered cups of maize beer.

"You did not explain to me last night what led you to realize that the North Temple Priests were responsible," Muskrat Waits said to me.

"I am not the one who made the connection first," I replied. "Gray Crane did. On his first visit to the Temple, he noticed that one of the Priests, Cottonwood Tree, had been wounded in the shoulder. At the time, he never imagined that a Priest could be involved. Only later, when we found the eagle feather and the broken blade with Red Feather's body, did he begin to suspect the Temple."

"Why would the blade from a Warrior's knife and a feather from a Warrior's headdress make him suspect the Priests?" Spotted Lynx asked.

"From the beginning, I suspected Warriors were responsible," I said. "We all saw the evidence through that belief and allowed it to confirm what we already thought."

"I did not," Spotted Lynx said indignantly.

"The rest of us believed you rejected the idea because you could not accept that Warriors might do something so monstrous," I admitted. "I am sorry I doubted you, Spotted Lynx.

"Gray Crane, with his gentle and trusting souls, could not imagine that a fellow Priest might harm anyone. Even when we learned that Bright Eagle had injured one of his attackers, I do not think it occurred to him that the wounded Priest he had met at the North Temple could be involved. Only when he saw the blade and the feather did he begin to suspect his own brethren."

"That is twice now you have said the feather and the blade caused him to suspect the Priests," Spotted Lynx grumbled, "but you still have not explained how."

"He suspected that the blade and the feather did not belong to Warriors," I said. "Warriors and nobles are not the only ones who may possess eagle feathers. Warriors are not the only men who use high-quality chert. Gray Crane had seen those very things used by others in his work."

"Of course," Spotted Lynx cried. "Priests use them as well. But if he suspected the Priests of the North Temple, why did he not tell you?"

"I am not sure he truly believed it even then," I answered. "When he left to confront them, he told Whispering Doe it might be nothing. He meant to come back and tell me if he learned that the Priests of the North Temple were involved. It was a mistake that cost him his life. If he had not told Whispering Doe that he was going to visit an injured friend at the North Temple, I would never have known he had solved the mystery. Poor, trusting Gray Crane. He never imagined they would harm him."

I paused a moment, then continued.

"I had a vision at the Emerald Acropolis," I said. "I understood parts of it—the farmers represented the immigrants, the burning maize field represented Cahokian agriculture, the people lining the Sacred Precinct were the people of Cahokia, and the burning World Tree Pole represented the collapse of Cahokian civilization. But I did not understand what Underwater Panther represented. Everything became clear when I realized that Gray Crane suspected the North Temple Priests. In my vision, Underwater Panther was the spirit that seduced them, and the Temple I saw was not a symbol at all but the North Temple itself. If I had shared that vision with all of you sooner, Gray Crane might have made the connection earlier."

"You could not have shared your vision," stated Prince Ranging Fox. "That is not how visions work."

"Then why did you run off to the North Temple once you knew those Priests might be responsible?" Prince Ranging Fox asked. "That was not wise. You almost died."

"I had to try to save him," I said quietly. "It was my fault. If I had understood sooner, Gray Crane would still be alive."

I turned to Muskrat Waits. "Have your people found any connections to other Temples?" I asked. "Did the Lord High Priest know what was happening at the North Temple?"

Until that moment, Muskrat Waits had listened calmly, but at the mention of the Lord High Priest, his face darkened with anger.

"My agents have only begun their inquiries," he said, "but so far, it appears the heresy was confined to the Priests of the North Temple. No, the Lord High Priest and the Priests of the High Temple were not involved. That does not mean the Lord High Priest is blameless. He failed to notice an entire Temple of deviant Priests almost within arm's reach of his own mound. Unfortunately, he is of the Sun Family. The Sun King will decide his fate. If it were my decision, I would have him garroted on the top of his own Temple Mound and his body thrown down the ramp."

"The Sun Family Council has already met," Prince Ranging Fox said, giving Muskrat Waits a disapproving glance. "We do not garrote senior members of the Sun Family. However, very soon, the Lord High Priest will decide it is time he gave up his position because of his advanced age. He will move to a smaller Temple, far from Cahokia."

That was good news to me. I had never liked the haughty old man. Still, I suspected his replacement would be another Sun Family member just as arrogant.

"What about Blue Falcon?" I asked. "Before he died, he told us that Underwater Panther came to him during a spirit journey and ordered him to restore balance to the cosmos by killing immigrant blasphemers. Does anyone believe that?"

Muskrat Waits nodded slowly. "Yes," he said. "I believe Underwater Panther seduced him. Underwater Panther is a deceitful creature. He found in Blue Falcon a man who wanted to believe such things. From what you have told me, Blue Falcon already hated the unbelievers in our lands and was looking for a reason to persecute them. Underwater Panther gave him that excuse.

"Underwater Panther has no interest in balance," he continued. "He thrives on hatred and disorder. Seven deaths were enough to drive some people from Cahokia and fill many others with fear. Imagine what would have happened if you had not destroyed that Temple and his Priests had slaughtered hundreds during the New Maize celebration. Underwater Panther would have spread terror through all of Cahokia."

There was nothing more to say. We rose to leave.

"Walking Stick, I would have a word with you before you go," Muskrat Waits said.

Ranging Fox and Spotted Lynx withdrew, leaving me alone with the Minister of Security. Muskrat Waits sat in silence for several heartbeats, then spoke.

"You have done well, coppersmith," he said. "The people of Cahokia owe you a great debt. When I gave you this task, I had doubts. But you learned quickly and found clues that even my agents might have overlooked. You have proved yourself a clever man. I will not forget what you have done for Cahokia and for me."

Praise from such a man startled and pleased me. Muskrat Waits was not generous with compliments. Nevertheless, I could not claim the credit for myself.

"I did very little," I protested. "The young men who helped me made most of the discoveries. Gray Crane solved the mystery. Without them, I would have learned nothing."

"Perhaps," Muskrat Waits replied, "but whether you recognize it or not, you are a natural leader, Walking Stick. Someone must give directions, offer guidance, and make decisions. You gathered a band of bright young men—perhaps by chance—but you recognized their talents and used them to solve the mystery. Now, tell me about Spotted Lynx."

"He saved my life," I said. "He is intelligent and a good leader. He was the most valuable member of the team, including me. He is also disrespectful, conniving, argumentative, and generally a nuisance."

Muskrat Waits smiled faintly. "That sounds suspiciously like someone else I know."

If he expected me to admit that Spotted Lynx and I were alike, he was mad. I kept silent.

"When we first met, I told you I had assigned Spotted Lynx to protect you," Muskrat Waits continued. "That was only partly true. I also sent him to support you. I knew you could not manage the task alone. Few men could, even experienced agents. I knew Spotted Lynx would help. I have plans for that young man. That should please you, since I hear he will soon be a member of your family."

"He has not spoken to me about that yet," I said sourly.

"Do not begrudge the young their choices," Muskrat Waits replied. "He is a fine young man. You will be fortunate to have him in your family and in your house."

I must have looked startled, for he added, in a reasonable tone, "I expect he will follow Cahokian custom and move in with his wife's parents."

I had only just begun to accept the idea that Spotted Lynx might marry Walks in Water. I had not truly considered that he would then live in my house. Of course, that was the Cahokian way. When I married Whispering Doe, I moved into the Black Bear Clan Common, and our children became Black Bear Clan. So it would be with Walks in Water and Spotted Lynx. Their children would be Black Bear Clan as well. I quickly changed the subject.

"When my head feels better, I am going to North Star Town to tell Gray Crane's parents what happened to their son," I said.

"Yes, I know," Muskrat Waits replied. "Spotted Lynx told me. He asked whether he could remain on special assignment as your protector until you return. I permitted him. How would it look if I let the Guardian of Cahokia travel to North Star Town alone, and you were killed on the road? You do have a talent for finding trouble."

"The Guardian of Cahokia?" I repeated.

"That is what Spotted Lynx calls you," Muskrat Waits said. "He is a very clever young man."

He reached behind his chair, lifted a leather bag, and handed it to me. "I want you to take this to Gray Crane's parents," he said. "Tell them the Sun King regrets the loss of their son, and that he was a fine young man."

I peeked inside and caught my breath. The bag held a small fortune in shells from the Southern Sea, used in trade as I used copper. Gray Crane's family would never want for anything again. The gesture surprised me. I had not thought Muskrat Waits was capable of such generosity.

He gestured that I was dismissed, but I decided to press my luck.

"Perhaps I might see the Sun King today," I said lightly, "and thank him personally for the honor of choosing me to investigate the murders?"

Muskrat Waits stared at me. I thought I saw the faintest hint of a smirk at the corner of his mouth.

"No, I suppose not," I said. "Well, perhaps next time."

"Perhaps," Muskrat Waits replied. "Next time."

I turned back in surprise. I had expected him to be joking, but his face was grave. Muskrat Waits never joked.

Chapter 24

The sky was low and gray with the promise of rain as Spotted Lynx, Green Heron, and I gathered our traveling gear and prepared for the day-long walk to North Star Town. I packed a sleeping fur, a cloak sewn from deer bladders to shed the rain, an extra pair of shoes in case mine grew wet, a ceramic water bottle, and a neat stack of maize cakes arranged with Whispering Doe's usual care. I wore my best breechcloth, shoes woven from rattlesnake master fibers, and a soft doeskin tunic with a beaded Deer Clan symbol stitched on the chest.

Spotted Lynx wore his full uniform: a bright red breechcloth trimmed in gold, a matching cape trimmed in gold, and his brilliant War Captain's eagle feather headdress. On this journey, he wanted every person we passed to see that he was a War Captain of Cahokia. Green Heron proudly wore a new breechcloth I had given him, woven from rattlesnake master fiber and dyed a vivid green.

Our bellies were full of a rich stew of deer marrow, hominy, little barley, and wild onions. It was a long walk, and there was no reason to linger. There were no tearful farewells this time. The danger had passed, and everyone knew we would return in a few sunrises—everyone except Green Heron, who would go back to his home near Deer Toes Lake Town after we visited Gray Crane's family. The women held Green Heron a little longer when they embraced him, and then we set out.

We followed the now-familiar route we had taken so many times in the past moon cycle, crossing Cahokia Creek and walking through the North Plaza. I tried not to glance toward the granary where Gray Crane died or the Temple where I had killed Blue Falcon. My skull still ached at times from the blow I had taken in that granary on the day I found Gray Crane's body.

Soon, we left the city behind and walked through the rich farmland that surrounded Cahokia. Harvest time had begun, and the fields were full of farm families harvesting their crops. Many of the maize plants had already turned brown and brittle, their multicolored kernels plump and hard, ready to be ground into flour or boiled into hominy. Fat squash lay in orderly piles along the road, waiting to be stored for the winter behind their tough rinds. It promised to be a good harvest, and the people of Cahokia would eat well in the coming cold season.

We reached Deer Toes Lake Town shortly before high sun but stopped only long enough to eat a simple meal of maize cakes. Then we set out again. Just north of town, we passed the place where the North Temple Priests had laid Red Feather's body, hoping to deceive us into believing the murderers lived in that region. If only Gray Crane had told us his suspicions before we returned to Cahokia, events might have unfolded very differently. No matter how I wished it, I could not change what had already happened.

By the time we reached the outskirts of North Star Town, the sun was slipping toward the western horizon. North Star Town was the largest city and the seat of the Cahokian government in the North. Aside from Cahokia city, Traders Town, and River Bluff Town, it was one of the largest communities in the kingdom. At its center rose fourteen mounds arranged around a broad plaza. The Temple and the chief's house stood upon the two greatest mounds. A member of the powerful Beaver Clan ruled this city.

We were tired and hungry, and the ceremonial heart of North Star Town did not interest us that evening. Instead, we stopped on the edge of town at the Warrior barracks. In principle, only Warriors could lodge there, but when Spotted Lynx showed the local War Captain Muskrat Waits' seal, the officer's manner changed at once. He quickly led us to the guest quarters, usually reserved for important visitors.

We joined the Warriors in their great hall for the evening meal. When they learned that their barracks housed the Guardian of Cahokia and the now-famous War Captain Spotted Lynx, they demanded a story. I asked Green Heron to oblige them. The young *hiperes jinak* happily complied, giving them a highly edited—and even more highly embellished—account of how we had solved the immigrant murders. The Warriors of North Star Town ate well, and, after two heaping plates of food, I went straight to our sleeping room and fell into my furs, asleep almost before I could close my eyes.

The Warriors rose before dawn, earlier than I cared to wake, but we had another long day ahead of us. I forced myself up from my furs and joined my companions and the soldiers in the hall for the morning meal. When we had eaten, we set off to find Gray Crane's family, accompanied by the shouted blessings and well-wishes of our new friends in the barracks.

In the sunrises following the assault on the North Temple and the public executions of its Priests during the New Maize celebration, our roles—Spotted Lynx's and mine—in the affair became common knowledge throughout Cahokia. We were now celebrities. As Mad Owl, the Black Bear Clan Patriarch, had predicted, my involvement in the investigation brought honor to my Deer Clan and to Whispering Doe's Black Bear Clan. I pretended to be modest, but the truth is I secretly enjoyed the attention.

Yet Gray Crane's part in the story went largely unmentioned. Only those directly involved in the investigation knew that he, not Spotted Lynx or I, had solved the mystery. Gray Crane was dead now, and few people even knew his name. Whenever I tried to discuss his role, most listeners quickly lost interest. I feared that his family might not have heard anything at all about his fate, and that they would be learning about their son's murder from me. I had never told anyone that their child was dead. The thought left me restless and uneasy.

Green Heron had been closest to Gray Crane, so he knew roughly where our friend's family lived. From the barracks, we walked south along the Great Northern Road for a time and then turned east into the farmland surrounding North Star Town. At several farmsteads, we stopped and asked whether anyone knew where Gray Crane's family lived. After a few false leads, Green Heron found a man who could give clear directions, and soon we were standing in the common of the farmstead where Gray Crane had grown up.

The farmstead consisted of three small houses and a storage building arranged around a shared open space. As we approached, a man of about thirty cycles of the seasons stepped out to meet us. He was tall and slender, with familiar features and mannerisms. I knew at once that he was Gray Crane's brother.

I spoke in Cahokian while Green Heron translated into Oho. "Greetings. My name is Walking Stick, and I come on behalf of the Sun King. My companions are Spotted Lynx of the Cahokia Warriors and *hiperes jinąk* Green Heron."

The man called something in Oho, and an older woman emerged from one of the houses to stand beside him. "My name is Big Rock," he said in careful Cahokian. "This is my mother, Blue Crane. Our father died two moon cycles ago. She does not speak Cahokian well. Will your *hiperes jinąk* continue to translate for her?"

"Of course," I said.

Big Rock studied me with calm, sad eyes. "Your visit concerns my brother, Gray Crane, does it not?"

I nodded.

"I cannot think of any other reason for representatives of the Sun King to visit a poor family like ours," he said quietly. "Tell me. Is he dead?"

"Yes," I answered.

Blue Crane began to weep at once. Big Rock stood rigid and expressionless. "Please," he said. "Tell us what happened."

I told them how we had first met Gray Crane at the Emerald Acropolis, and how Shining Mountain had assigned him to serve as our interpreter among the immigrants of Deer Toes Lake Town who spoke only Oho, and as our liaison to the Temples. I described our investigation and Gray Crane's role in it. Finally, I told them that he had been the one who uncovered the truth about the killers and how he had died near the North Plaza in Cahokia.

"Gray Crane is the hero of this story," I said. "When we speak of the immigrant murders, we tell people that he was the one who solved the mystery. Gray Crane saved hundreds of lives and kept Cahokia from sliding into chaos. You will feel his loss deeply, but know this: he did not die in vain, and for as long as we live to tell the tale, the people of Cahokia will remember his name."

"This is our fault," Blue Crane said through her tears. "If we had not been so poor, we would not have sent Gray Crane to the Priests, and he would still be alive."

"Perhaps you did send him to the Temple because of poverty," I said gently, "but you did him a great kindness. He loved being a Priest and worked hard to become a good one. He was happy. His death is not your fault. The Priests of the North Temple and the evil stirred up by Underwater Panther are to blame. Gray Crane was one of the kindest men I have ever known. You should be proud of the son you raised. No one deserves more than he to walk the Path of Souls through the stars to the Land of the Dead and live among his ancestors."

At Big Rock's direction, one of the children who had been watching us from a distance ran into the fields to summon the rest of the family. I soon learned that more than twenty people lived in that small farmstead. When everyone had assembled, Big Rock asked me to tell the story of the immigrant murders and Gray Crane's role from the beginning.

I turned to Green Heron. "You should tell it," I said. "You knew him best."

He agreed, though it was not easy for him. As he spoke, his voice sometimes cracked with emotion, especially when he described the last sunrises of his friend's life. The family listened in silence.

While Green Heron was speaking, Big Rock drew me aside. "I know the story you told was meant to comfort my mother," he said. "Please tell me the details of Gray Crane's death. I wish to hear the truth."

"Are you certain?" I asked. "The truth is unpleasant."

He nodded once.

"Very well," I said. "After we discovered the knife blade and eagle feather with the last victim, Gray Crane began to suspect that the Priests of the North Temple might be responsible. He went to confront them. He believed that if they were indeed guilty, he could reason with them and persuade them to surrender to the Lord High Priest in Cahokia. Poor Gray Crane. His souls were gentle and trusting. He did not believe Priests could be seduced into such evil. He never imagined they would harm him. Once he confronted Blue Falcon, the High Priest, they dragged him to a granary near the North Temple and slit his throat. That is where I found him. If Spotted Lynx had not arrived when he did, they would have killed me as well.

"I already told you how we attacked the North Temple at dawn and captured the renegade Priests," I continued. "What I left out is that four of the Priests died in the fighting. Spotted Lynx's men killed them. Green Heron killed three more. The Sun King had the survivors executed at the top of the Great Pyramid on the second day of the New Maize celebration. As for Blue Falcon, the High Priest—the man who murdered your brother and who was seduced by Underwater Panther—I killed him myself."

"How did he die?" Big Rock asked.

"I put an arrow in his throat," I said. "Later, when I grew tired of his arrogant boasting, I took a war axe and smashed his skull. He died painfully."

Big Rock nodded once, firmly. "Thank you," he said.

"I am glad Green Heron has this chance to speak to your family," I added. "He and Gray Crane were close, and he is taking his friend's death very hard."

We remained at Blue Crane's home past high sun when Blue Crane served us a simple meal, sharing stories with the family about the young Priest they had lost. When it was nearly time to leave, I said, "High Priest Shining Mountain will probably send a messenger to inform you of Gray Crane's death, but we felt it was important that you hear the full story from those who knew him best in Cahokia."

Blue Crane began to sob again. I handed Big Rock the bag of shells that Muskrat Waits had given me. "This will not bring your brother back," I said, "but the Sun King wishes you to know that the people of Cahokia honor Gray Crane's sacrifice. Your family need never want for anything again."

Big Rock opened the bag, saw the wealth inside, and could not speak. He did not need to.

Before we left, Green Heron addressed the family. "When I have a son," he said, "I will name him Gray Crane. In that way, my friend will live on."

After many embraces and expressions of thanks, we took our leave and turned our steps toward Deer Toes Lake Town. Green Heron asked whether we might spend the night at his parents' house rather than in town, and I agreed. We had stayed longer with Gray Crane's family than I had planned, and it was well after the sun had passed beyond the western horizon when we finally reached the farmstead where Green Heron's parents lived in the countryside near Deer Toes Lake Town.

His parents were delighted to see their son and surprised to find him in the company of a Cahokia Warrior and a merchant. Nevertheless, his mother immediately began preparing a meal for her son and his guests. After we had eaten, we sat around the fire and told them about the immigrant murders and their son's role in the investigation until weariness overcame them and they went to sleep. The three of us stayed up almost until moon set, speaking of Gray Crane and of things we hoped never to see again.

* * *

In the morning, Green Heron's mother had a hearty meal waiting for us. After we had eaten, Green Heron walked with us as far as the Great Northern Road. "I am going to spend a few sunrises with my parents to help with the harvest," he said, "and then I will return to Bold Warrior and see what he has planned for me. I doubt anything will ever be as interesting as working with you, Walking Stick."

He put his hand on my shoulder. "Remember," he added, "if you ever need me, send a message to Bold Warrior. I will come."

We parted there. Spotted Lynx and I set our faces south while Green Heron stood in the road and watched us until we passed from sight.

"They were fine young men," I said at last.

"They are fine young men," Spotted Lynx corrected me.

"And now it is just the two of us again," I said, "as it was in the beginning."

"It feels as if a lifetime has passed since we first set out," he replied.

"Who could have guessed, when we left for the Emerald Acropolis more than half a moon cycle ago, how much would happen, and how many people would enter our lives whom we had never known before?"

Spotted Lynx fell silent for a while, and then I said quietly, "Thank you."

"For what?" he asked.

"For saving my life," I replied. "Everything moved so quickly after I awoke in the Deer Clan Shrine House that I never had the chance to thank you."

The familiar mischievous glint returned to his eyes. "You are welcome," he said.

"So now you will owe me," he added.

"Ugh. Yes, I suppose I do."

Spotted Lynx laughed.

We walked in silence for a time, then left the Great Northern Road and followed a familiar farm path.

"One more stop," I said.

"Yes," Spotted Lynx agreed. "One last stop."

We passed men and women in the fields harvesting maize, squash, sunflowers, and goosefoot. Before long, we saw a familiar figure. I walked up to the man and said, "Beaver Swims, do you remember me—Walking Stick?"

"How could I forget?" he replied. "You brought word of Bright Eagle's death. Did you discover who killed my sister's son?"

"Yes," I said. "Have you heard about the Priests of the North Temple who were seduced by Underwater Panther and killed six immigrants?"

His family lived less than half a sunrise's travel from Cahokia, but their isolation kept them from hearing much news from the wider world. So I told him the story from the beginning.

"I want your family to know that your sister's son did not die in vain," I said. "When the Priests attacked him, Bright Eagle fought back and wounded one of them. We were able to identify the murderers because of the injured Priest. By fighting back, Bright Eagle helped save many lives, perhaps even your family's. The Priests planned to strike again during the New Maize celebration and kill every immigrant they could reach. We are grateful for his courage."

Beaver Swims bowed his head. "Thank you for coming," he said. "We have mourned his death for many sunrises. Now we will also be able to honor his bravery."

"I owed it to your family to tell you why Bright Eagle died," I said.

I had nothing more to add, so I handed him a bag of copper pieces and left him with his grief and pride and turned back to the path.

I was in a melancholy mood as we left Bright Eagle's family behind and set off on the last leg of our journey. The weather matched my thoughts. The rain had held off for several sunrises, but now, across the flat floodplain, I saw heavy, dark clouds piling up over the bluffs on the western bank of the Messipi. It would be a race to see whether we reached home before the rain caught up with us.

As we regained the Great Northern Road and walked south toward Cahokia, I thought about all that had happened and the part I had played. I had completed the task Muskrat Waits had given me. I had led the band that solved the mystery of the immigrant murders, brought the killers to justice, and prevented many more deaths. Muskrat Waits' gratitude assured that the copper concession and my family were safe. By all measures, I should have been pleased.

But the memories would not leave me. So much blood. So many dead. Poor immigrant families, already struggling, were left even poorer by the loss of a son, a daughter, a husband, or a wife. My own uncle's life had been taken because of my involvement. And Gray Crane, whose gentle souls had been torn from the Middle World in such a cruel way and far too soon. Their deaths were bound to my choices, and I would carry that burden for the rest of my life.

"This is the worst work I have ever done," I said at last. "So many people have died because of me. I do not think I will ever put this behind me."

Spotted Lynx stopped and placed a firm hand on my shoulder. "The deaths were not your fault, Walking Stick. The murders of your Uncle Rattlesnake and Gray Crane were not your doing. You carried out your task as best you could, and you saved far more people than you lost. The ones responsible for this bloodshed are Blue Falcon and his North Temple Priests—and the deceit of Underwater Panther himself. It is difficult to fight a deity, but you fought him well, and you defeated his design."

He grew quiet, his gaze fixed somewhere far beyond the fields.

"I understand how you feel," he said. "I have led my Troupe into battle many times over the past cycles of the seasons. Men I trained—men who trusted me—have died under my command. Good men. The first time it happened, I was broken with guilt. I blamed myself for every breath they would never take again. I am not saying it becomes easy, but over time, the sharp edge of grief dulls. You learn to live with it. You must, or you cannot live."

"This will be the last time people die because of my decisions," I muttered. "I have done Muskrat Waits' bidding. I have protected the copper concession. I am finished with his intrigues."

I looked at Spotted Lynx and shook my head. "It is strange. At different moments during the investigation, I distrusted almost everyone. I believed Bold Warrior had his own designs, and that Green Heron had been sent to advance them. I never trusted Muskrat Waits, and more than once I suspected you of serving his interests—or the ambitions of the Warriors. In the end, every man I doubted proved to be exactly what he claimed: an ally. Except for Gray Crane. I never suspected him of disloyalty."

I hesitated. "I am sorry that I mistrusted you, Spotted Lynx. Whispering Doe told me more than once that you could be trusted. She is a far better judge of character than I am."

I expected a sharp reply, but he only said, "You were right to question everyone. This was a dangerous and confusing path. What matters is that, when the moment came, you chose to trust us."

We resumed walking, heading south at a strong pace. My anger simmered the longer I thought about the Cahokian elite and how they had pulled me into their schemes. Finally, disgust overwhelmed me.

"I will tell you something, Spotted Lynx. If that dried-up piece of bear dung Muskrat Waits ever asks me to take on a task like this again, I swear I will grab my bow, put an arrow straight through his chest, and pin his shriveled old body to the wall of his house."

Spotted Lynx considered this gravely. "After seeing what you did to Blue Falcon," he said, "I believe you would."

We both laughed.

The farther south we walked, the lighter my spirits grew. It appeared that we would reach home before the rain. Soon I would be back with my family, eating a hot meal, then curling into my sleeping furs beside Whispering Doe. The next morning, I meant to sleep late before returning to the copper workshop. I am a simple man. I wanted my simple life back.

After a while, the Great Pyramid rose into view above the dry, rustling maize stalks swaying in the late summer breeze. We were nearly home. Spotted Lynx, however, grew more restless the closer we came to Cahokia. Before we reached the canoe landing, he halted and turned to me.

"Father Walking Stick," he said, his voice suddenly serious, "there is something I must ask you before we get to your house."

Resigned, I sighed. "Yes," I said. "I suppose there is."